For Amber

Slumber

Beauty Never Dies Book 1

J.L. WEIL

www.jlweil.com

ISBN: 1545158576
ISBN-13: 978-1545158579

xoxo

J.L. Weil

D1466840

Dedicated to Becks and Mimi. You guys are rock stars in my book. The best sister and niece a girl could have. Love ya.

BEAUTY NEVER DIES CHRONICLES

DIES CHRONICLES

BOOK 1

"One day you'll awaken to love's first kiss. Till then, Sleeping Beauty, sleep on."

---- Sleeping Beauty Song, Sleeping Beauty

Prologue

Dash

Lights flickered down the long, dull gray corridor, flashing annoyingly in the back of my eyes. They were the kind of lights that left an imprint even after you'd escaped their sputtering. It thumped behind my lids, pulsating even when I slammed my eyes shut. Nothing helped. There was a staleness to the air, damp and mossy, suffocating me with its pungent scent. The vile smell burned in my nose, smelling of hopelessness, despair, and fatality. God, I despised the decomposing holding pods, filled with all the nameless, lifeless bodies caught in the frozen slumber—utterly and wholly clueless.

I snorted. The sound echoed off the concrete walls, and it was the only sound of life, aside from the beeping of machines. It was more like a holding cell—a prison.

The world had gone to shit.

Well, as far as I was concerned, it had.

How many of these *holding pods*, as they'd been commonly termed, had I been to in the last year? Ten? Twenty? Fifty? Hell, at this point, who was counting? The number didn't matter, not when the results were always the same: disappointment, anguish, bitterness.

At seventeen, I'd woken to find myself in a replica of a building just like this, lying on cold steel, shivering, sick, and dizzy. Since that day, my life had been in a constant state of tormented perdition. And I wasn't speaking figuratively. There hadn't been a moment of peace since I'd opened my eyes to the horror of the dominion that used to be Earth, now called Starling Heights.

Who made up these names?

There was nothing promising about the world as it was now. In a way, I envied the sleeping bodies, blissfully ignorant of what awaited them. Some days, I wished I'd never woken in that cold-ass, dreary room, that I was still one of those peaceful, oblivious forms, drugged out of my mind. Reflecting wouldn't do me any good now. What was done was done. Wishing wouldn't change the past.

My long steps clattered on the hard slabs of gritty concrete as I headed for the exit. The sound was a constant reminder I was alone, and I hadn't found what I'd come for.

Only the usual—frustration and heartbreak.

Why did I subject myself to these raw emotions over and over again? Because I vowed to find them, I reminded myself. Because I couldn't give up; to give in would be letting *them* win. And I wasn't a quitter. I might be many things: a killer, a fugitive, a survivor, but I wouldn't stop until I found what I was looking for.

The farther I traveled down the corridor, the faster my steps became, as if I couldn't stand to be shut inside another second. But what waited outside the locked doors of the holding house was no freaking walk in the park. A quick glance at the dial on my wrist reminded me time was of the essence. The little hand clicked faster and faster. I'd lingered too long as it was. If I didn't get out of here, there would be another kind of trouble to find me. And soon. I'd rather take my chances out in the savage, unpredictable world.

Quickening my pace, I made a beeline toward the exit, until a flash of gold caught my eye, breaking my hurried strides. The ornate keyhole popped against the wood. I didn't have time for a distraction, but something pulled me toward the door.

Flattening my hands on the warped wood, I pushed and was surprised the door gave. The old hinges squeaked as I pressed. From somewhere in the small room, water dripped, plopping onto a steel drain in a steady rhythm. Caution was second nature as I stepped into the tiny, solitary box, eyes scanning the shadowy parts of the room. Best to leave no corner unturned. *How had I missed this in my search?* It was a secret alcove tucked away from all the others.

Moving deeper into the room, I reached behind for the dagger tucked under my shirt. Precautionary, of course, but I was no fool. My body tensed for the unknown. There was nothing alarming in the room, nothing but a girl just like the gazillion others. Except this one was—

The air stopped in my lungs. She was breathtaking. Stunning.

A thousand adjectives came to mind, yet none of them did her justice. My heart jumped in my chest as I approached. She stood out against the boring room like flame to a fire. Dark red hair outlined her delicate face in soft waves. Such vibrant color was unusual in a place stuffed with nothing but dirty white walls and dreary gray floors. Her hair glinted in the waning light and immediately caught my eye. It was the kind of color that was hard to miss in a room colder than the arctic. Bold and silky against her pure and porcelain skin, untouched by any damages of the sun, she was like a beacon of light on a foggy night—the brightest star.

My eyes roamed over her face, completely captivated by her. She looked like a dream come true, a princess—Sleeping Beauty. Cliché, but it wasn't any less true. My heart sped, thumping wildly, as I stood above her. She drew me like no one had, calling me. I abandoned the training that had been beaten senseless into me, as the world and the dangers in it ceased to exist—time forgotten.

Full, spiky lashes fanned her closed eyes. Briefly, I wondered what color laid behind those thick lashes. If only I could see them. Then reality slammed into me with cruel force. I would never see those eyes, never know her name, and a sudden sadness seeped into my heart. The frozen slumber didn't care about feelings, didn't care about wants or needs. It didn't answer to anyone, doing as it pleased, when it pleased. No one knew why some awakened and others carried on, dead to the altered world around them. Ageless. Lifeless. Lost.

With a heavy heart, my gaze roamed over her face, etching every feature into my memory. I didn't know why it mattered—why she mattered—or why I wanted to remember her. I just did. Maybe so I could remember beauty still existed in such a cruel world.

On a quick intake of breath, my inquisitive eyes landed on her cherry lips, lush and magnetic, the kind that begged for attention. A mouth like hers shouldn't be neglected. In all honesty, it was better for her, better for us both, if she stayed peacefully asleep. This world would only destroy her natural beauty, and even though I knew nothing of her, I didn't want anything to mar her milky skin. Beauty like hers belonged in the castles of old Ireland, in the misty hills of Wales, or between the pages of a fairytale.

Who the heck knew why I did it. I couldn't say. I only knew I had to. Once. Just once. After all, she was the first beautiful thing I'd seen in a year.

Maybe ever.

The mist had ruined everything.

Lately, all I'd seen was death, destruction, and misery. I was way overdue for some good in my life, something lovely, succulent, and irresistible.

Leaning in close, I breathed the same air as her. She smelled like fresh-cut roses, removing any trace of the staleness that lingered, tempting like the forbidden fruit. Closing my eyes, I inhaled and was engulfed, transported to another place and time. Her soft even breaths whisked the hard lines of my face. I could no longer restrain the need bubbling inside of me, no longer deny what I longed for the moment I walked into the hidden room. Today was the first day I'd felt hope.

And then I pressed my lips to hers.

Dizziness swarmed over me, a shudder racking my body. The glass slab trembled, cracking down the center, and the quake traveled under my feet in a wave of thunder. *What the—*

Chapter One

Charlotte

My eyes fluttered open.

Slowly at first, adjusting to the light in the room. It was bright; it was as if my eyes had been deprived for so long that they stung initially. Blinking rapidly, I waited for them to adjust. When the fog cleared, my eyes were enraptured by sparkling silver. It was spellbinding, like a shooting star on winter's first glistening frost. The longer I stared, the more mesmerized I became. Gradually, the shining silver took shape, transforming into a pair of glittering eyes, and the face belonging to those eyes shifted into focus. The wild beating of my heart filled the quiet room. Hair so black it almost looked streaked with blue trickled over smoky eyes.

This must be a dream.

One of those fairytale dreams I had as a little girl, where the princess was swept away by her prince charming, because surely a face like his could only belong to a knight in shining armor. Dark hair slashed over his forehead to one side, outlined by chiseled cheeks. I wanted to reach up, trace the lines of his jaw, but my entire body felt heavy.

Neither of us said anything, our eyes wide and unblinking in those few seconds as we stared at each other. He seemed stuck on my face, unable to pull away from my eyes. I couldn't help but wonder what he saw when he looked at me.

The rattle of keys shot through the silence like gunfire, breaking the spell, and I got my first glimpse of my surroundings. It hadn't occurred to me before to question where I was, but confusion settled in, along with a swift dose of panic. How did I get here? Where was here? Was I lying on a glass table? This was nothing like my room in St. Louis; it was in desperate need of an interior decorator. I could feel my sense of style being sucked right out of me.

"Shit." The mysterious prince swore under his breath, bringing my attention back to him. The scowl that pulled at his lips told me the fantasy was about to end. With reluctance, he pulled his gaze upward, looking over his shoulder at the hallway beyond the large wooden door that was ajar.

From that point, my life was thrown into disarray. I didn't know just how life altering it would be.

"Crap. This is bad, very bad," he mumbled, eyes sharpening.

The tone in his voice made the hairs on the back of my neck stand up. Something was wrong, more wrong than waking up in an unfamiliar room, and it had this stranger on edge. The distinctive sound of a lock turned in the distance and alarm jumped into his silvery eyes. They darted to the doorway, and his muscles stiffened. I wasn't certain what the immediate danger was, but his body language was loud and clear—trouble.

I didn't mind a bit of trouble. But I hated danger.

At the all-girl prep school I attended, I'd been in my fair share of fights, but the thought of spending a Saturday in detention gave me hives. I was hardly a Goody Two-shoes, but I made sure never to get caught.

Using my arms, I pushed myself clumsily into a sitting position. The feeling slowly began to return to my legs, making my movements sloppy and bringing his gaze back to me. I might have moved a tad too fast. The room began to spin in dizzy circles, and my head pounded like it was going to explode. I gasped, automatically lifting a hand to my temple. If the pain hadn't been so intense, I would have been embarrassed at my awkwardness.

When the room stopped whirling, the eyes I had found so hypnotic had gone to flints of steel. I blinked, uncertain he was the same person.

This was no prince or knight as before.

His body was hard and unyielding. Danger oozed from his pores. The change had been swift, nothing more than a second, and now that I could see the whole package, I thought he was more of a warrior than a prince. Too much battle and bloodshed showed in his eyes. There was nothing pampered or entitled about him. He looked lethal, prepared to strike, to take on even the biggest of challenges.

An air of urgency cloaked him. "Can you walk?" he asked in a whispered rush. His dark voice sent a string of warm fuzzies zooming through my belly.

Nodding, I swung my legs over the side of the glass slab and swayed onto my feet. His arms shot out to steady me. The weak limbs were unexpected, and I leaned my body heavily on his as color stained my cheeks. I wasn't used to being feeble. The muscles of his arms strained through his shirt, holding onto me. "I think so," I replied. "I don't understand. Why am I here? What's going on?"

He shook his head, a frown pulling at his lips. "I should have known your voice would be musical," he mumbled, more to himself than out loud.

"What does that matter?" I demanded, feeling the first inklings of annoyance.

His lips twitched ever so slightly. "Just an observation. Don't get your panties in a wad. We got bigger problems, Freckles."

"What problems?" He was confusing my already muddled brain.

"The clock has struck midnight, and we're out of time. If we don't move now, there is no telling whether we will get out alive. We're cutting it damn close."

"What are you talking about? I'm not going anywhere with you. I don't know you." There were actually a whole slew of "I don't knows."

He shrugged, taking a step toward the door. "Suit yourself. Stay here. The Night's Guard will *love* you. Either way, I don't care."

Asshole.

"Who are the Night's Guard?" I whispered, pressing him for answers. It was true I didn't want to stay in this room, but could I trust him?

"Your worst nightmare," he muttered. And then his eyes clashed with mine.

Confusion and fear refracted inside me. I was beginning to think I'd awoken to a living nightmare. I wanted to go home, not off with this stranger.

He let out another curse. "There's no time to explain," he said in a rushed voice, emphasizing haste. "In less than a minute, this place is going to be swarming with guards. You can stay here where they will find you, or you can come with me, but you must decide now. Every second we linger is a moment closer to our capture. I don't know about you, but I am no one's prisoner."

Wow. No pressure. All this talk of guards and prisoners made my head pound like a subwoofer. To make matters worse, I had no idea where I was or who he was. Why should I trust him? But as I stared wide-eyed into his steely eyes, the urge to take my chances with the dark prince was nagging at me. Plus, I didn't like the sound of *being captured*. Raising my chin a notch, I made a decision. "What are we waiting for?"

He snorted, holding out his hand. "Waiting on you, sleeping beauty. We'll be lucky if we make it out."

On cue, the jingling of keys jamming into the metal door chimed down the hallways. I could only assume by the darkening of his eyes that the so-called Night's Guard were headed our way.

He wasted not a second more. Weaving his fingers with mine, I clutched him tightly and tried to ignore the tingle that spread throughout my body. It had to be fear. What else could it be? But I held it together, knowing if we truly were in a precarious situation, I needed to keep my head.

We slipped into the hall as soundless as we could, careful of where we stepped. "Stay close," he warned, just above a whisper.

I tried not to think about his warm hand enclosed over mine, dwarfing my tiny one. It held strength. Instead, I concentrated on my feet, moving them one in front of the other, a task that was harder than it should have been. The last thing I wanted was to trip and wipe out, not only making a fool of myself, but also drawing unwanted attention our way.

Iron scraping against concrete shrilled as the doors opened and in shuffled the Night's Guard. My mysterious rescuer paused, listening to the sounds of feet scuffing against the cement floor. He counted them off, lips moving silently. Three. Four. Maybe five. He snorted. I guessed he was unimpressed by the number.

I didn't have the foggiest idea what was going on or who these men were chasing after us. It could be they wanted the guy with the silver eyes and would let me go home. All I could hope was that I wasn't making the biggest mistake of my life by trusting this guy. I didn't even know his name.

This was off-the-wall nuts.

As soon as I got out of here, I wanted answers. Pronto.

We hugged the hard wall, silently moving through the corridors. The swishing of my dress on the floor was unavoidable. No matter what I did, short of tearing it off, I couldn't quiet the sound. Not too far in front of us was movement. The silver-eyed prince stopped abruptly, and I bumped right into his solid form.

Sweet baby Jesus.

I might only be seventeen, but I knew what the heat was that rushed through me. What was it about this guy? Was it the heightened sense of danger that made me ultra-aware of each accidental touch? The length of his body, pressed to mine, was impossible to ignore.

I bit my lip. He was ripped in all the right places.

Looking over his shoulder, he glared silently at me.

I smiled sweetly. "You said to stay close," I whispered.

"Not that close," he muttered. "I need room to breathe."

Tell me about it. I was finding it increasingly hard to do either with him so close to me. My gaze roamed to his lips. They were pleasant lips, kissable even.

It was the heavy steps of a guard that snapped me from making a mistake. *What the hell was wrong with me?*

The guard came closer to the corner, and my hand squeezed the dark prince's. It was probably too much to hope the guard would turn around. Four more steps and he would come face to face with us. Each second my heart rate jacked up. I didn't want to be anyone's prisoner, and the thought filled me with trepidation, but I didn't see how we were going to get out of this.

Prince Trouble stiffened, slowly unwinding our fingers and just in time. A guard came into view, dressed in full, dark blue combat gear with a white crest on his left breast in the shape of a star. "What the he—"

With no warning, my companion moved to strike before the guard could alert the others. I stifled a gasp as the poor sap hit the ground with a *thump*. The prince's black T-shirt had lifted with his precise movements, giving me a glimpse of his tantalizing abs. My gaze dropped to his waistline where a silver dagger was tucked in his shirt.

My eyes bulged. *What is he doing with a knife? Had I made a mistake?*

What if he hurts me? Kidnaps me? Or worse!

A gazillion horror movie scenarios ran through my head. Was it too late to change my mind? But as I stared down at the unmoving Night's Guard, I liked what I saw even less. There were guns or Tasers strapped to either side of his waist. The guard was a fairly large guy, at least twice the size of Prince Trouble.

The prince with ninja reflexes snuck a glance at me, a glint of curiosity reflecting in his face. Impressed? No doubt he had expected me to squeal like a girl.

I kept my expression blank and arched a brow.

Thank God I hadn't fainted or screamed. I wouldn't want to give him the satisfaction of being right.

Who the hell is this guy?

One thing was certain. ... I wasn't in Missouri anymore. So where was I?

Chapter Two

His dark head shook at me before he started to crawl again cautiously down the corridor. Impatience vibrated off him. He didn't like being inside these concrete walls, and who could blame him?

There was nothing pleasant or comforting about this place. It gave me the willies, and I was just as ready to get the heck out of here.

As he peeked around the bend, a sigh of relief exhaled from his chest. The metal door I assumed held our freedom was slightly ajar. His sharp gaze scanned the hall to our right and once behind us. There was a cold, calculating gleam in his eyes, only increasing my curiosity. He wasn't someone to make rash decisions.

With a quick jerk of his head, he indicated we needed to move. It was weird; few words were needed between us. I was in tune with his movements, except, of course, for our little collision earlier. We had barely spoken, and yet, it was like I could read his mind.

Too bad the rest of my body wasn't as keen. On shaky legs, I slinked against the wall. The cold of the concrete began to worm itself over my skin as I waited on his next move. He was such a striking mystery to me, and I couldn't help but be intrigued. Taking down a man with one hit was no easy feat (I didn't care who you were).

Biting down on my lip, I tried to keep my teeth from chattering, not wanting to be the reason we were detected, even if I didn't fully understand who we were running from. All I did know was there was a sixth sense inside me, telling me to trust this stranger—to trust the guy with the unbelievable, starry eyes.

I had only just met him, and he already had my belly doing loop the loops.

Mimicking his stealthy movements as best as I could, I followed him to the massive iron door. It looked as if it could withstand the force of a battering ram. The old door creaked as he put his shoulder to it, pushing just far enough for us to squeeze through. I was almost to the other side, with one foot balanced inside and the other outside, when a voice rang out.

"Hey!" a Night's Guard yelled from behind, shooting a blast of yellow light straight toward me.

My head spun around, and I squeezed my eyes shut, bracing to be incinerated by plasma matter, but the blast never came. Prince Trouble yanked me through the door without hesitation, and I tumbled outside, his arms keeping me upright.

Thank God one of us was quick on his feet.

I inhaled greedily as I got my first taste of freedom, fresh air filling my lungs. I couldn't remember the air ever smelling so sweet. How long had it been since I was outside? A day? A month? A year? A decade? I couldn't say, but it was the earthiest scent—damp and luscious.

While I basked in the twilight, Prince Trouble put his weight against the door, shoving it shut. The sound vibrated over the trees that hid the building. "Run!" he hollered, grabbing my hand.

I barely had time to process what he had said before I found myself being dragged through dense woods. Tangled brush and overgrown thorns thrashed at my feet and ankles, snagging my gown at every step. It would be shredded to pieces before we got to wherever we were going.

But more than anything, I couldn't wait to shower and change into something more practical. *Why the hell am I in a formal dress, anyway?*

I winced as a pine needle jabbed me for the hundredth time, going through the sole of my slipper, but I didn't slow my pace. He didn't give me much choice. If we hadn't been running for our lives, I would have dug my feet in and given him a verbal thrashing that would have made his ears bleed. I wasn't a ragdoll to be pulled about.

A light drizzle fell from the dark sky, soothing the fire blazing on the bottoms of my feet and the scratches bleeding on my legs. I cursed him to hell and back. Moving through the shadows, he pulled us under a mossy cypress, pressing a finger to his lips. I watched his face as he looked to see if we were being followed. He was focused on the sounds of the night.

Under moonlight, his features were softer, but no less drool-worthy. He had a street thug quality—rough around the edges. *Who are you?*

As minutes passed, nothing but the chirping and singing of wildlife and the occasional rustle of leaves sounded through the forest. He relaxed his shoulders. "Come on. Let's go," he instructed. "Before those idiots grow a brain."

I tugged my hand from his, turning my blazing eyes on him. "I. Am. Not. Running. Anymore," I panted, still trying to catch my breath. I was winded for a number of reasons.

His features bordered on annoyed. "Listen, Freckles, what you want is not my concern. Right now, all I care about is finding shelter and somewhere to rest my head. It's been a helluva night. I've been traveling for days to get to that holding cell, and now, I want to sleep. If you have other plans, have at it."

I wrinkled my nose. "My name's not Freckles."

His lips twisted as if he knew something he wasn't telling me. "Oh yeah, what is it?"

I wracked my brain, trying to pluck the answer that should have come naturally. Why couldn't I remember my name? It was right there on the tip of my memory, but something was blocking it. My brows drew together in concentration.

"Don't hurt yourself," he mumbled.

That does it. The anger gave me the extra push, and *bam*, the memory slammed into me. "Charlotte! My name is Charlotte Winston," I said smugly.

"Is it really?" he challenged, folding his arms across his broad chest.

I was curious about his age. Nineteen, maybe? "Why would I lie about my name?"

"For starters, most people don't remember who they are after waking, not right away."

Okay, that didn't really mean a whole lot to me. "You didn't tell me your name," I prompted.

"It's Dash," he replied, walking out from under the tree branches, leaving me no choice but to follow or be left stranded in the wilderness with no food, no sense of direction, and defenseless in a foreign place.

Uh, no, thank you.

I forced my legs to move. "Tell me where we are going."

A corner of his lips lifted. "See for yourself, *Freckles*. We're here," he stated and proceeded to walk a few feet in front of the weeping tree and into the mouth of a very dark, dingy cave.

Umm, he had another thing coming if he thought I was going to climb in there. It looked like a family of monstrous spiders had already set up camp. Webs covered the top of the rocky cave, extending to the tree branches across from it. Scary, big-ass webs.

These weren't the weavings of a normal daddy-long-legs. Hell, no. These looked like they could capture small children.

Drops of rain glistened off the sheer webs, reflecting in the moonlight. Dash poked his head out of the cave entrance. "What are you waiting for? An invitation?"

Mocking him under my breath, I muttered and cursed as I made my way to the entry, all the while trying to avoid touching the spun silk. "I'm waiting for someone to tell me this is a joke."

This place gave me the willies. Nothing good ever lived in the dark.

I shivered as I entered the mouth of the cave, unable to shake that heebie-jeebies feeling, the kind where it feels as if there are invisible spiders crawling over my skin. I fought the urge to swat at my arms and shake my hair.

Inside, I could see absolutely nothing. A small beam of twilight streamed in behind me, shining on the rocky floor and offering only a minimal amount of light. In front of me was utter darkness.

"Don't you have a flashlight or something?" I grumbled. My hand fumbled along the wall, afraid to move any farther. Who knew, I could fall down a giant hole for Pete's sake! Okay, so I was a tad dramatic, but still. …

Dash chuckled in the dark, and the sound was like sex on a hot summer's night. "Freckles, you're in for the shock of your life. Give me just another minute and. …" There was a bunch of noises—scraping, snapping, and chafing—followed by a flicker of firelight. It caught and illuminated the dark cavern. He gave me a crooked grin. "There. Happy now?"

Leaning against the wall, I rubbed my arms, feeling the damp chill in the air. "Not really." I moved farther into the cave and sat in front of the roaring fire.

Now that there was light, I let my eyes wander the room. The walls were jagged, jutting and carving out the cavern. I pulled the lengthy material of my white dress around me like a blanket and turned my gaze to Dash. He looked awfully comfortable in the cave. "You're just a regular Boy Scout. How did you know how to do that?" I asked, inquiring about the fire.

He shrugged his broad shoulders. "You learn all kinds of things to survive. We should be safe here for the evening. The Night's Guard don't know about this little gem."

"We're actually spending the night here?" I asked, my eyes surfing over the cavern. I'd been glamping before, but this brought a whole new meaning to roughing it. What I wouldn't give for some silk sheets and a down pillow.

"It's either that or you can brace yourself for the harsh elements out there. I don't know about you, but I'll take my chances in here. But hey, it's up to you. No one is going to force you to do anything, least of all me."

God, he was so infuriating. Why did he have to turn and twist everything I said? My eyes drifted to the bedroll spread out on the other side of the fire and a backpack of sorts leaned up against the wall. Someone had definitely been here before. Had it really been him? "How do I know I can trust you?" I asked in a small voice.

He eyed me with a watchful gaze, measuring me. "You don't. It would be wise if you didn't trust anyone, especially me."

My shoulders heaved and sagged with a long breath. "Great," I mumbled. My hands outstretched toward the flames, and I closed my eyes for a moment, letting the warmth seep into my chilled bones.

I felt his eyes on me.

"Take a picture. It will last longer," I snapped, letting my lashes flutter open. The events of the day were catching up to me, making me crabby.

He snorted, leaning his head back against the cave wall. "You're in for a rude awakening. Cameras don't exist anymore. Pretty much everything you remember is gone."

If he was trying to frighten me, he'd already done a bang-up job. I could only handle so much before I reached my breaking point, and the tears I'd been keeping at bay threatened to break free. "What does that mean? Why were those guys after you?"

I could see the weariness in his face, and I thought for a moment he wouldn't explain. He sighed, placing his hands behind his head, and stared into the fire. "I bet you're just brimming with questions. I'll give you the gist, as I am too tired to answer them all right now. What do you remember from before? What's your last memory?"

I pulled my legs to my chest, resting my chin on my knees. "I was shopping with some friends at the mall."

He made a noise in the back of his throat.

I glared at him. I could see in his eyes he'd already made his mind up about me. Rich, pampered brat. Honestly, he wasn't that far off, but I would be damned if I told him so. "I got a call from my father. And. …" Black wall. There was nothing after that.

His eyes softened, understanding gathering. "You can't recall, can you?"

My heart lurched. "No." Apprehension galloped through my veins. What the hell? Was I suffering from amnesia?

"Don't panic. It's normal to have memory loss after coming out of the slumber. It's the aftereffects of the drug and the mist, assuming you were exposed."

If that was supposed to make me feel better, he failed … by epic proportions. Bleak thoughts rampaged through my head. "Mist? Drugs? What are you talking about?"

His chin dipped, and the soft, yellow glow of the fire glanced off his defined cheekbones. "In the year 2016, a toxic mist was released into the air. It spread from state to state, country to country, sweeping over the country at alarming rates. A state of emergency was issued, and everyone went ape-shit bananas."

Nice analogy. If I hadn't been so bewildered, I would have found the statement humorous, but there was nothing funny about Earth being destroyed. I could imagine the absolute terror that must have ensued. And then I realized, it wasn't my imagination. I could remember it. The frantic faces screaming in horror, pushing and shoving. My dad's voice instructing me to get to his office immediately. It all came rushing back in tumultuous waves. Fear clawed at my insides as I relived those dreadful moments.

My breath quickened, and my stomach contracted into a tight ball.

"Hey, are you okay?" Dash was crouched down in front of me, watching me with concerned eyes.

Tears stuck to my lashes. "I remember."

He raked his fingers through his dark hair, taking a seat beside me. "Well, I'll be damned."

"We were ushered into safe houses." I continued down memory lane. It wasn't a delightful trip.

"You were one of the lucky ones."

I blinked up at him. "I don't know about that. I almost didn't make it. My friends and I wanted to make one more stop, for shoes." *What outfit isn't complete without the perfect pair of shoes?* "My phone rang. It was my father. He was so pissed at me, yelling and screaming for me to get to his office. I never made it."

Dash's lips turned down, probably thinking the same thing my father had at the time. Shoes weren't going to save my life. How stupid I'd been. "Let me guess, you stuck it to the old man."

My lips twisted into a sad smile. "He was always on my case, harping on me to be the best: get the best grades, be the model student, grow up to be incredibly smart like him, change the world. It didn't matter what I wanted." None of that was important now. I would give anything to see him right now. It was hard to even drum up his image from my memory, but there was one thing that came through, clear as day. "The ... mist." I got a bit choked up before I could continue. "It burned, everywhere. My nose, my skin—I could barely breathe."

Dash nodded, awareness reflecting in his face. "That explains the eyes."

My forehead wrinkled. "What's wrong with my eyes?"

He stared at me. "Nothing."

"Bullshit," I argued. "Something happened to me, didn't it, because I've been exposed?" I beseeched him with my expression. I wanted the truth, no matter how desolate.

He shrugged, scooting back over to his side of the fire, and stoked the dwindling flames. "I can't be certain, but I'm going out on a limb and assuming you didn't have rainbow-colored eyes before."

Uh, what? "My eyes are green," I protested.

"Hate to break it to you, Freckles, but you now have a striking blend of violet, blue, green, and pink running through your irises. They aren't eyes anyone is likely to forget."

I didn't want to believe him. "Any chance you're packing a mirror?"

He chuckled. "Afraid you're shit out of luck."

"Is it permanent?"

"I don't know, probably. It could mean that you're one of the gifted ... or cursed, as I like to say."

"Gifted how?" I asked, leery.

He sighed, realizing he'd opened up a whole another can of worms. "It varies. And like I said, I don't know. It could be that the drugs had an unusual effect on you."

"How will I know?"

A muscle drummed along his jaw and a moment later stilled. "If your cells have been mutated, it will make itself known eventually. It always does in some way, shape, or form."

"Did the mist change you?"

For a moment, his eyes were bright and wild, like a feral mutt, but then he blinked and was normal again. That brief glimpse of fury told me what I needed to know; Dash had been affected by the mist. "What's with the fifty questions? Here," he tossed a rolled up blanket at me, completely ignoring the question. "I wasn't expecting company, but it should do for the night."

I got the answer loud and clear. Anything personal about his life was off limits … for now. I wrapped the dark blue material around my shoulders, trying not to wish it were softer. "How long has it been since the attack?"

He poked a twig in the fire. "A hundred years."

It hit me with the force of an unbridled tornado, my eyes bulging. "I've been asleep for over a hundred years?"

He leaned back, crossing his arms. "It's a real ball kicker, isn't it? The ceraspan was designed to keep our bodies frozen in time for a hundred years, giving the world time to rid itself of the deadly mist and restore life. Joke was on us. The mist might not be present, but its consequences are everywhere."

"Do you have any good news about this world?"

"No. Tonight was just a taste of the disappointments to come. Get used to it, Freckles. You haven't seen anything yet."

My face flamed. "Are you always so pleasant to be around?"

He flashed a dazzling smile, and all I could do was stare, stupefied, like a moron. "You caught me on a good day."

"Oh, goodie." He was trying my patience. I thought I was handling everything pretty damn well, so why did he insist on being such a d-bag? If I hadn't felt like a fish out of water, I would have strolled right out of this cave and left Dash eating my dust. As much as it burned my butt, I needed him. How else was I going to find my family? Or survive? I had no idea what I was dealing with out there.

"I'm going to Hurst in the morning—a settlement north of here. Unless you have other plans, you can tag along." He stretched out on the cold, stony surface, yawning. It was clear he was a walking zombie. "Right now, I need to sleep before I drop dead. Then you'll really be screwed." His silver eyes were half closed. Shifting on the ground, he propped his head under his arms. "You'll be safe," he mumbled almost inaudibly.

An unsettled feeling formed in the pit of my stomach. The thing was, I couldn't shake the feeling I'd never be safe again, and this was just the beginning of something big.

Chapter Three

—❖—

I tried to ignore the way his shirt strained across his chest. "I can't sleep," I said, fidgeting on the hard, bumpy surface. A tinge of guilt wove through me as he yawned.

"It will pass ... in time." He spoke with experience.

I wanted to ask him about his first night—how he had awoken—but something held me back; something in his eyes told me not to unlock those memories, not just yet. We barely knew each other, but he had secrets. There was more to Dash than meets the eye. "I don't want to close my eyes," I more or less pouted.

His half-lidded gaze filled with empathy. "Everyone is afraid to sleep those first few days, weeks even. Eventually, your body and mind will betray you. You're going to need your strength."

"Do you live in Hurst?"

"No, but the quarters are much more ... accommodating," he added, eyeing the rocky cave walls.

He made me sound like an ungrateful snob. I might have been at one time, like decades ago, but I was beginning to see things differently. "A settlement? What is this, the 1800s?"

"You have no idea." His eyes drifted shut, voice trailing off as he dropped into the world of dreams, leaving me utterly alone.

My mouth dropped open. I couldn't believe he was going to sleep—the gall. The last thing I wanted to do was sleep. I'd just woken up from a hundred year slumber, and the questions buzzing around in my head were getting louder. The silence gave me a moment to think ... actually, overthink was more like it.

What was I going to do?

I had no home, no place to go. I didn't know if my family was alive. Or awake.

The fire crackled as I stared into the low flames. Tomorrow was a long ways away; what did he expect me to do for the next seven hours? Twiddle my thumbs?

Looking over my shoulder, I cut a glance to the mouth of the cave. I could always do a bit of exploring, not far of course. See if the world had really changed that much. It sounded like a very bad idea, especially when I caught a flash of two glowing eyes the size of buttons staring back at me. Holy crap. Whatever was watching me was as big as a raccoon, but instead of scampering, it slithered. Hell-to-the-no. I covered my mouth, stifling a yelp. The shelter of the cave was beginning to look quite appealing.

Giving the entrance my back, I wrapped my arms around my legs and studied the mysterious Dash. I unabashedly took my fill, admiring how sleep softened his features highlighted by the dancing of firelight. He might make me want to bang my head against a brick wall, but at least he was smokin' hot.

A small giggle escaped.

Had I really just thought that? It didn't make it any less true. A piece of dark hair fell over the side of his face. There was something about him, something unusual that I couldn't put my finger on, but one thing was for certain: I was insanely attracted to him.

I'd rather die than ever admit it to him, though.

Holy smokes! A thought just occurred to me: I hadn't kissed a boy in over a hundred years, and I was still a virgin. That had to be a world record.

As entertaining as it was, staring at him like a total creeper, I eventually got bored, but not before I had a few interesting fantasies. And Dash had the starring role.

"Dash," I whispered. Nothing. "Dash," I called a tad louder, contemplating poking him with a stick, and then sighed. "You can't just leave me alone like this," I muttered. Didn't he understand there was no way in seven kingdoms I could sleep?

I laid my head on my hands, observing him, waiting for morning. It was like watching corn grow. I wasn't known for my patience, apparently that hadn't changed after a hundred years.

Wow. That was insane to think about. This was going to be the longest, loneliest night of my life.

The next time I blinked, the sun was rising at my back, streaming beams of light across the floor. That had been a wild dream—a frozen slumber, sleeping in a cave, the guy with the silver eyes. Too bad he wasn't real; he'd been totally datable.

I stretched, thinking about breakfast, and my stomach grumbled like I hadn't eaten in a month. The material covering me scratched at my arms, itching in uncomfortable places. On a normal day, I pulled the covers back over my head and hit the snooze button for at least another thirty minutes. But as I rolled over to check the clock on the nightstand, I wanted to cry.

What in the holy hell?

Staring up at the stalactite ceiling, a scream bubbled up in my throat. It hadn't been a horrible dream. Everything seemed surreal and foggy, as if I'd imagined the whole encounter.

The icicle-shaped formations glittered in the beams of sunlight like amethyst crystals. I must have dozed for a few moments. Shaking off the weird sensation of being in a strange place, I drew in a breath, steeling myself for what was to come next. Less than twelve hours ago, I'd been fast asleep, unaware of what had happened to the world around me. It was understandable that I was a wee bit paranoid.

I inhaled the scent of charred wood, a damp musk, and something masculine. Sitting up, I hugged my legs, eyes zeroing in on a black and red spot. It crawled over the cave walls—big, hairy, with eight red beady eyes.

Son of a lipstick.

There was a demonic spider eyeballing me.

Squealing like a little girl, I scooted across the rocky floor, moving closer to Dash and as far as I could from the tarantula thingamabob scuttling alongside the edge of the wall. I don't know how it entirely happened, but I ended up in Dash's lap.

Impossibly full lips curved into a slow grin, revealing deep dimples on either side of his cheeks. Dash had dimples. "Well, hello, sunshine," he greeted, his voice husky from sleep. He had his hands on my hips to catch me, as I had pretty much jumped on top of him.

A strange edginess moved into the air as we stared at each other. An almost electric feeling coursed through me. He was all male and hard in the places I was soft. Being this close to him was startling, causing all sorts of sensations. I wiggled, making a move to untangle myself from this intimate, yet awkward situation, when I felt something. I blushed; my cheeks matched my hair, making me look like my whole head was on fire, and my blood was pumping way too fast.

Had I really felt what I thought? I got more than I bargained for this morning. Quickly, I jumped off his lap. Oh God, I was going to die of embarrassment. "Sorry, I didn't mean to wake you."

His lips twitched, and he cast me a long look, brushing the disheveled hair out of his eyes.

I dropped my head into my hands. Shoot me now. "That, ah, came out wrong."

The smug smile was plastered all over his face. "They're harmless, you know. It's one of the few things in these woods that is."

"Good to know." I still didn't want to be within ten feet of one. "What was it?"

"A laider."

I shuddered. "Gross."

"Are you hungry?" he asked, rumbling through his pack.

I'd forgotten about my hunger, but now that he mentioned food, I was dying for a Big Mac and a supersized fry. Screw a salad; I needed something with substance, but I was guessing there wasn't a drive-through around the corner. "I could eat." And eating was way better than thinking about being in his lap.

He tossed me a cloth-wrapped bar.

"What's this?" I asked, inspecting the contents. It looked similar to a granola bar—dried fruit of some sort embedded in a crunching coating.

"Food."

"Thanks, Captain Obvious. What's in it?"

He bit off a huge chuck of his. "Who knows? But it won't poison you. Just close your eyes and pretend it's blueberry pancakes and bacon."

Why did he have to mention bacon?

Apparently, I wasn't the only one with foodie cravings. Taking a nip out of the bar, I chewed. It wasn't half bad, but it wasn't amazing. It would curb my appetite for a while.

And then what?

"We'll have to grab something to eat midday, but this should hold us over until we can find something to kill."

"Kill?" I echoed, the granola going stale in my mouth.

"Survival of the fittest." Dash had already managed to scarf down his breakfast and was snuffing out any lingering sparks of the fire with his boot. "We need to head out; put as much distance between us and the holding house as possible. It's going to take most of the day to get to Hurst."

"I'm assuming you don't have a car?" I asked, pushing to my feet. I stretched out my achy muscles.

Turned out that sleeping sitting up on a cave floor was hard on the body.

He chuckled, holding out a canister of what I assumed was water. "Cars are a thing of the past, Freckles."

Of course they were. That would have been too convenient. I took a swig, not wanting to be overly greedy with his rations. But I could have drank a river my throat was so dry.

Together we quickly gathered up his measly supplies, and Dash tossed the bag over his shoulders. At the mouth of the cave, he surveyed the area. "Look, I travel alone. After I get you to Hurst, you're on your own. I don't have time to babysit, so make sure you keep up or get left behind. Got it?"

Sheesh, he wasn't winning any nice guy awards. Was he giving me a choice? Because it didn't sound like it; it sounded as if he couldn't wait to get rid of me. Whatever. I didn't need him. I tilted my chin up just slightly. "Fine," I agreed. "On one condition."

He arched a brow.

I crossed my arms, firming my stance. "You get me there in one piece, unharmed." Momma didn't raise no fool. Traveling alone with a stranger, I needed to keep my guard up, regardless of how dreamy he looked.

His grin spread, and those dimples decided to play peek-a-boo. "Promise."

Oh, boy. That smirk was going to get me into trouble. I could tell.

Dash had told me not to trust him, and damn if that mischievous grin didn't tell me he wasn't exactly a man of honor. I had a feeling this journey was going to be anything but uneventful. Yet what choice did I have? I had to trust him.

Some of the impishness slipped out of his eyes. "Here's the deal. We're in the middle of the Dying Labyrinth. If you want to survive the maze, don't wander. Watch your step wherever you go. Too many nasties lurking. We wouldn't want you to get snatched up by a kelstag or fall down a rabous hole. Don't eat anything in the woods. *Nothing*," he emphasized, holding my gaze.

"Got it." I took a step and winced. A jagged rock had sliced into my sole. I steadied myself with one hand on the cavern wall, removing the sharp pebble from my slipper. How was I going to hike through the woods in ballet slippers? I wouldn't last an hour.

Dash took notice of my discomfort. "You should have said something last night," he scowled, sounding angry.

What did he have to be pissy about? I was the one in agony. "We were sort of busy."

He shook his head, like I was the one at fault.

"It's fine," I assured him. "I'll survive."

"The day isn't over yet," he said, before jumping down off the rock.

I waited a moment or two to see if he was going to lend me a hand. My mistake. I huffed, lifting my skirt and took the plunge. Jerk. I guess chivalry had died with the mist.

I began to follow behind when I was struck with the uncomfortable urge to pee. It was starting to hurt. "Wait," I called.

Dash paused and turned around to face me, arching a brow.

Short of doing a pee-pee dance, I squeezed my legs together. "Um, I kind of need to use the bathroom."

"Pick a tree … except for the ones with yellow tipped leaves. Once those suckers get their vines on you, you're pretty much toast. I'll keep watch."

Watch for what? I didn't ask. Guess I was doing this old school, like really, really old school, peeing in the woods. I glanced between the trees and settled on the big one we hid under last night with its weeping branches. Wiggling the material of my dress up, I judged how long I could hold it. Considering I hadn't gone in a hundred years, one sneeze or cough and I'd lose all bladder control. Ugh.

I could hear Dash whistling as he waited. Hiking up my dress, I did my business, pushing aside any embarrassment. It was a human action. Everyone had to go.

Feeling like I could breathe again, I shoved the long, sweeping branches out of my way as I exited the coverage of the tree. Dash was lounging against the side of a trunk, looking bored. "Everything go okay?" he asked as I approached.

"Did you want details?"

Dash didn't respond. A confused, almost curious look crossed his face. He shook his head and we started our journey.

I followed like a lost puppy, leaving behind the safety of the cave. We traveled with the sun to our left, picking up a narrow path buried deep in the thicket. I didn't know how he found it or how he knew which direction to go, but he hadn't been kidding about the woods being a maze, so I was overjoyed to see the little trail. The last thing I wanted was to get lost in this eerie yet beautiful place. It was as if it couldn't make up its mind whether to scare the bejeezus out of me or lure me with its decadent wares.

And there were plenty: shining red apples, deep plums, trees strung with cherries, and bushes nestled with a variety of berries, but Dash had been very strict on the no eating policy. My stomach was protesting.

Just as we reached the path, my ridiculous skirt caught on a bristle, shortly taking my mind off my hunger. I yanked, but the bush was stubborn, like it had its claws in me. Squatting down, I cursed, fighting to pull the material free, but the harder I wrenched, the more snarled I found myself. A section of my skirt was now weaved with vines.

Huh?

A shadow fell over me. "If this is how our morning is going to go, we're never going to get there before nightfall."

I glared at his boots, contemplating stomping on them. "Oh, so it's my fault I'm wearing a ball gown."

"Why are you wearing one?"

I swallowed a laugh as mad as the hatter. "Because I have nothing else."

His brows drew together. "No, that's not what I meant. Most people after the ceraspan were issued prison-like jumpsuits."

"How would I know?" I snarled. "You're the one with all the answers."

"It doesn't matter. What *does* matter is you being able to move, quickly if necessary. Here. ..." The next thing I knew, he was pulling out a blade from inside his boot and hacking at the bush. I swore the thing gave a high-pitched yelp before the lacerated vine wiggled wildly and shriveled up.

Oookay.

Dash didn't bat an eye. He crouched before me. "This thing has got to go." Then he proceeded to put his hand up my skirt.

Uh, that was unexpected.

I tried to ignore the tingles rushing through my body as his hand brushed my inner thigh. Even at seventeen, I knew what the ache was between my legs. The flash in his eyes told me I wasn't the only one who felt the sudden shift in the air.

"What are you doing?" My tone was huskier than intended.

"Hold onto my shoulders and steady yourself," he said gruffly.

I wanted to argue for the sake of arguing. He was bossy, and it rubbed me the wrong way, but I did as he instructed, trying to ignore the very provocative position this put us in. I bit my lip. What was wrong with me? Did I wake up a sex-craved stripper?

He snatched the slip attached to the dress with his hand and yanked.

Riiiiip.

The material separated, lightening the weight of my attire.

There goes my dress.

"Good thing it wasn't sentimental," I muttered.

Throwing the white silk aside, he took his blade and cut the remaining material to just above my knee, giving me more mobility and showing more skin. "Nothing out in the Heights cares about value, lesson number one." He bunched up the fabric, stuffing it into his backpack.

Unable to suppress the smartass inside me, I said, "Actually, I think that's lesson number three." If we were counting, he'd already told me not to wander and to watch my step.

"Take notes," he replied, stretching to his full height, a good nine inches over my five foot one frame. "There are enough lessons to fill a book, and I learned the hard way."

"Are you trying to scare me?" I pulled out a loose strand of thread tickling my leg, suddenly becoming self-conscious of my appearance. It had been a century since I'd seen my reflection in a mirror. I could only imagine what a hot mess I was. Smoothing my flyaways with my hand, I tried to maintain control of my hair.

It was a losing battle.

He watched me with an intense glare. "If you were smart, you'd be terrified."

I was curious about how he had survived. "If that's true, how are you still alive?"

"Because I learned how." His voice went soft and dangerous.

Goosebumps crawled over my arms. Another touchy topic. There seemed to be nothing that didn't make him pucker.

We walked in silence, me trailing behind. There was no way I was going near him. Not even if he dangled a double chocolate chip muffin in his hand.

Taking my eyes and mind off Dash, I was curious about the world and how different it had become. The sun was warm, the breeze balmy. I lifted my face up to the moist wind, the faintest taste of rain in the air. I would love to feel the drops of water wash over my face. At first glance, the woods appeared magical, but as I took a closer look, I swore there were eyes everywhere, watching us from under the brush, up in the treetops, buried in the ground. It was eerie, and the fear I told myself I wasn't going to feel came sneaking inside me.

Five minutes had gone by, and the quiet was killing me. "You're a real joy to talk to."

He said nothing.

My point exactly.

We came across a down tree laying in our path. Dash hurdled over the thing before turning around and offering me a hand.

I stared at his fingers. Was it wise to touch him? The fact that I questioned it was my answer. As I lifted my hand in the air, a feeling I didn't expect appeared: anticipation. What would it be like to have my tiny hand encompassed by his? I got my answer.

The moment our skin connected, static passed between us. If he felt it, he did a good job of hiding it. His face stayed neutral, which bugged the crap out of me.

"Is your name really Dash?" I asked, trying again to make conversation as I jumped down off the log. I regretted prodding the second the hurt flickered in his eyes, before he quickly defused and froze it behind an impenetrable shield of iron. The longer I was around Dash, the more of a mystery he became.

"It is now. This is a new world. You can be whoever you want to be." His long legs carried him easily over the uneven terrain.

Trotting beside him, I increased my speed to keep us at the same pace. "Is that what you did? Changed your name? Became someone different?"

"I had to." He shrugged off the ominous tone that had crept into his voice. "Most everyone who has woken from the slumber has."

I stuck out my lower lip. "I don't want to be someone different."

He angled his head to look at me. "This place changes you, whether you want it to or not."

"How are you different?"

"Do you always ask so many questions?"

"Do you always dodge them?"

He snorted. "I was trouble. I stole, cheated, and lied."

A curious look crossed my face. "And now?"

"Pretty much the same, only I'm more cynical and deadly."

I shook my head. "I don't buy it."

"Then you're a fool."

I kicked a pebble with the tip of my slippers and scowled. "Maybe. Or you don't know who you really are."

"Whatever. You'll find out soon enough, Freckles." His tone rolled over the endearment like it was battery acid.

"Why do you insist on calling me that?" I fired back. "I have a name."

His lips curled. "Right, Charlie."

"Charlotte," I interjected.

His starlit eyes twinkled, and he flicked the end of my nose. "Freckles suits you better."

I resisted the urge to flip him off.

The curse of being a natural redhead. The pesky brown dots covered the bridge of my nose and down over the tops of my cheeks. They were light, only a dusting, but without the coverage of foundation, they were visible.

I groaned internally as the realization hit me—no more makeup. Not that it would have made much of a difference today. In this heat, I would have sweated my face off and ended up drenched in mascara and eyeliner. It was God-awful humid.

"How did it suddenly get so hot?" I plucked a jumbo leaf from a passing tree and fanned myself. I'd sell my left butt cheek for a shower. It was all I could think about, other than donuts. I felt as if I was drowning in my own funk. It was only a matter of time before this heat was going to fry brain cells.

Dash wiped the back of his hand over his forehead. "We're near the border of the Plains of Despair."

"That sounds pleasant," I mumbled.

"Oh, it is," he said in a way that implied it was hell. "Give it a few more minutes, and it's going to feel like you've been sitting in a sauna all day. The heat in the Badlands is unforgiving and merciless."

Worry lines wrinkled my forehead. I would be burnt to a toast in two minutes flat. "Badlands?"

"You'll find that the mist not only changed the organisms inhabiting Earth, but Earth itself. The shape and biomes are no longer the same. We just left the Dying Labyrinth."

It was becoming evident I had much to learn, and Dash had been right: However much that grated my pride to admit, I was way out of my element.

He abruptly stopped and dropped his pack with a thump. "We'll take a break here. I'm going to see if I can find us something to eat and drink. Don't move," he warned with a stern look.

I made a mocking face to his back as he walked off and, for shits and giggles, flipped him off. I'd been dying to do that all afternoon.

Spinning in a circle, I took in my surroundings. We'd stopped in a small clearing, and as I listened to the rustling of the woods, it was accompanied by the lapping of water. It didn't sound far, and my curiosity was piqued. There was a small ledge to my left only a few feet away.

He had said to stay put, but really, five feet? It wasn't like I was going to get lost. Padding toward the edge, a picturesque view came into sight, and I gasped.

Water like I'd never seen shimmered in a color of liquid glass. The sun melted over the northern horizon, spilling oranges and pinks into the sky and shining upon the water. Except for the buzzing of pesky insects, the air was quiet. On the other side of the lake, dragonfly-like creatures danced and twirled above the surface. Their wings shimmered in fuchsias, blues, and purples. If a dragon had decided to fly by, dipping its feet in the water, I wouldn't have been surprised. It was kind of expected.

I felt transported to another time and place—a magical realm.

Deciding I deserved a moment's rest and some tranquility, I removed my slippers and dangled my toes over the water. I sighed. My feet were aching and my legs were burning. If I stretched just a bit, I could dip my toes into the water, but Dash's constant warnings echoed in my head, and I was no longer tempted to test the waters. Instead, I peered down at my own reflection floating on the mirror-like surface.

Holy mackerel. My hands roamed over my face as I turned it from left to right. I looked like me, or the me I remembered, except for the eyes. And the eyes made all the difference. Regardless of the fact that Dash had commented about the uniqueness of them, it was hard to believe without seeing, and now that I did, I wasn't sure how it made me feel.

Strange for sure. The blend of pink, blue, green, and violet, each color split up into a slice on my irises.

As flabbergasted as I was over the change in my eyes, I noticed something in the water. I blinked, focusing beyond my reflection and into the water. Something was definitely there. A glowing neon green light glided through the water, moving closer to the surface. I squinted, bending down to get a better look deeper into the liquid gold. A bubble of air floated to the water's surface, startling me. I wasn't alone. A dark shape began to take form. It had a long body, covered in bumpy scales like the largest snake I'd ever seen, but its head was triangular, similar to a crocodile, equipped with multiple rows of fangs.

WTF.

It was moving quick and coming straight for me. Panic rose up inside me like black tar. I scrambled to back away from the edge as its head came barreling out of the water, jaws snapping. My hands grappled on the slippery slope, clawing the ground frantically for traction, for my life.

I screamed, teetering on the brim of a grassy cliff, straight toward that thing and its razorblade snappers.

Chapter Four

Oh God, I'm going to die. I'm going to die. I'm definitely going to die.

My arms flailed in the air, and if I didn't by some miracle get my bearings, that thing was going to have me as a midday snack. I didn't want to end up a gory mess floating downstream. My heart was in my throat, my death imminent, and I squeezed my eyes shut, expecting to plunge to my demise.

A strong arm encircled my waist. "Don't move," Dash whispered near my ear.

I stilled my failed attempts at scrabbling and went lax in his arms, exhaling. Relief swarmed inside me. We might not have known each other long, but he wouldn't let that monster munch me up into little pieces.

Dash's grip tightened on my midsection, and with his other hand, he secured his blade. The next time that thing reared its ugly head out of the water, he drove the knife straight into its brain. The sound was sickening. I turned my head away and into Dash's shoulder, shielding my face from the splatter of brain matter. The beast gave a high-pitched, tortuous yowl that rang over the lake, sending the dragonflies scattering.

Dash backed away from the edge, taking me with him. His entire body was taut from the attack. My heart was pounding so fast, I wondered if I was going to have a heart attack. God, wouldn't that be embarrassing? I could see the headline: Girl survives a vicious monster attack only to die minutes later from coronary heart failure.

With my hands flattened on his chest, I dragged in several deep breaths and glanced up. Our eyes met. A wavy lock fell across his forehead, and the specks of his silver eyes shifted in small degrees over my face.

Neither of us spoke.

My chest rose and fell as his hand curved from the small of my back to my waist. Wow, the warmth that flooded my cheeks could have melted ice. I wanted to beg him not to let go of me, at least until I stopped shaking. The only time I had been safe in this godforsaken place was in his arms. I bet he was a phenomenal kisser, with lips that weren't wet or gross, but the kind that curled your toes.

I needed to stop staring at him in general. Too bad my mind and body weren't on the same page.

Seconds ticked by as his gaze lingered on my face, and I waited for him to make a move. Disappointment ate at my belly as he released my waist, taking a step back. I had to bite my lip to keep from leaning toward him, concentrating on the pain.

He cleared his throat. "Are you okay?"

Physically? Yes. Mentally? Hell, no. "What was that thing?" I breathed, horrified. What I really wanted to ask was: Why didn't you kiss me, you fool?

Dash sheathed the blade, returning it to inside his boot. His shoulders rose, and our eyes met. Shadows crept into them, dulling the gray hue. "A snyker."

"Gesundheit," I replied.

His lips twitched. It was obvious he didn't want to be amused by me but couldn't help it. "Cute, but you wouldn't be laughing if its jaws had wrapped around your pretty little neck." He backed up, putting some distance between us.

"You think I'm pretty?" The words popped out of my mouth before I thought about it, but it didn't stop me from wanting the answer. Did he find me attractive? If so, he had a funny way of showing it.

"I thought I told you not to move." His voice was thick, but it didn't cover the underlying anger there.

"You never mentioned there were monsters living in the water," I blasted back. I couldn't believe that moments ago I had wanted to kiss him!

He raked his fingers through his hair. "I thought it was pretty clear when I told you to stay put. Next time, I'll be more specific. Freckles, there are monsters, not just in the water, but everywhere."

I shot him a peeved look, because if I didn't let the irritation consume me, I was going to cry. "You don't have to be such a jerk about it."

"Are you trying to get yourself killed?" he barked.

No longer in danger, I wanted to wring his neck. My chin jutted in the air. "Maybe you should think about being a detective, because you've got me all figured out, don't you?"

"I should have let it bite you," he mumbled and turned on his heel, walking back toward the path.

I stood where I was, fuming, little billows of smoke streaming from my ears. Argh. I'd never met anyone who was so infuriating. Glancing over my left shoulder—the opposite direction Dash had gone—I contemplated tackling the woods on my own. I didn't need the know-it-all, holier-than-Buddha Dash.

As I was working myself up, convincing myself I didn't need anyone, a twig cracked, followed by the rustling of leaves. I squeaked and took off toward where Dash had disappeared.

Screw that.

I'd rather deal with the asshat than another snkyer thing.

Dash glanced up as I, looking frazzled, bolted through the bushes. He was propped up against a tree with a smug brow arched, chomping on a fruit that resembled a dreary cherry. "You made it past sixty seconds. That's forty more than I expected."

My hand fisted at my side, and a buzzing noise sounded in my ears. I didn't know what had happened, but it was like Dash had just flipped my bitch switch.

Static rushed over my skin, crackling like Pop Rocks on my tongue. The tiny hairs on the back of my neck rose. Something was happening. The air pressure had changed, thickening with an invisible force. Eyes huge, I sought out Dash, silently asking him what was going on. I didn't expect to see the same look of confusion.

The ground shook and groaned under my feet, and I froze. There was a loud crack.

A bolt of lightning thundered from the ground at Dash's feet, lighting up the air between us. Little sparks of energy fizzled on the dirt before eventually extinguishing. Brisk wind blew over my warm cheeks.

We both stood, shell-shocked. Utter surprise rippled through me, my eyes as big as alien saucers.

Dash was gaping at me. "Holy shit, Freckles. Did you just try to electrocute me?"

My mouth hit the ground. He thought I had done that? Was he insane? "Yeah, it was totally me. What next? Are you going to accuse me of witchcraft?" I said dryly.

He rubbed the back of his neck, eyeing me with suspicion. "It's not unheard of. The Earth wasn't the only thing that suffered the chemical assault of the mist. I told you it altered human cells as well."

"T-that's impossible." But even as I said the words, the tips of my fingers were tingling and radiating a shimmery lavender smoke, like glitter. "It wasn't me, okay," I reiterated with sharpness. "It's ludicrous to think I would try to kill you. We both know I need you. How else am I going to survive?"

"Your eyes," he stated, staring intensely at me.

I shot him a dark glare. "Are you determined to insult me? We've already established they're different." The eyes were a touchy subject for me at the moment, having just seen them for myself.

He rubbed the stubble under his chin. "Maybe, but they flashed purple, a solid, glowing purple for a moment ... I think."

"You think?" I echoed, like a crazy person. "Can we just forget this happened and get out of here?" The sooner we got to Hurst, the sooner I could ditch Dash and find my parents.

Then why did the thought of leaving him suddenly fill me with a flash of panic?

Ugh.

"Whatever you want," he said, frowning.

My shoulders went slack. Thank God. I wrapped an arm around myself and chewed on my nails. I hated the tension between us. I'd never been good at holding a grudge or staying mad. It took too much energy, and I found it wasteful.

Dash bent to the base of the tree and picked up something white. "Here, you need to eat, before you don't have any fingers left." He held out a triangle-shaped folded cloth.

I hesitated before taking the small package. It was lighter than expected. "Did you have to kill it?" I asked.

The corners of his lips twitched. "Not this time."

Peeling back the corners, there was a batch of fruit nestled inside—the same ones I'd seen him snacking on. A lackluster berry of sorts, it was the color of a plum, but the size of a grape. I picked up a piece and turned it around, testing the squishiness.

"It's not poison," he informed, plucking one from my hand and tossing it into his mouth. He glanced up through thick lashes as he swallowed. "See? They're not bad."

My stomach growled. "How do you know what's safe and what isn't?" I asked, popping one in my mouth, unsure what to expect. This place had left nothing but a bitter taste in my mouth, so when I bit down and the sweet juice filled my mouth, I was surprised.

"If it looks tempting and shiny, don't even touch it. There are plants out here that touching their rind alone can cause your organs to shut down in under a minute."

I swallowed. "Wonderful."

We continued our journey as I attacked the berries with a vigorous hunger. My only complaint was that they were gone before my appetite was curbed. I didn't know how much longer I could run on such little nourishment. Already, I could feel my body burning through the little boost of energy the berries packed. If we didn't get to Hurst soon, I had a feeling I would be swaying on my feet, eyes going loopy. I'd never been one of those girls who starved themselves. This girl cleared the dinner table. Leftovers weren't a thing in my house, yet I still managed to be as thin as a beanpole. I blamed genetics. What I wouldn't give for a little baby-got-back. My mom had been blessed with va-va-voom curves and shared those blessed curves with my little sister. I took after my dad's side of the family. Where I lacked in the hourglass figure, I made up for in personality.

"How much farther until we get to Hurst?" I asked, sounding like a five year old in the backseat of the minivan.

"Not soon enough," he mumbled, sidestepping around an overgrown brush.

I chose to ignore his moodiness and bombarded him with questions. "What's it like in Hurst?" I wanted to prepare myself. Were we talking about Chicago or Galena? Big city or country bumpkin? I didn't know what to expect from this settlement.

"Hurst is what is considered an enclave, a group of people who the Institute discarded as unimportant."

"The Institute? What's that?"

"You remember those guys we ran from in the holding house?"

I nodded. "Hard to forget."

"The Night's Guard are part of a link in the chain of command known as the Institute—the so-called government here," he explained.

"I take it you don't share their political beliefs." Politics had never been one of my strong suits; the calculating maneuvers and strategic measures were not my thing.

An icy hardness leapt into his eyes and set his jaw. "The Institute's biggest concern is assembling a military of gifted and using them to take control."

"Is that why you were running from them? You don't want to be a part of their army?"

I couldn't help but notice how the light streaming through the trees glistened over his tan skin. "Something like that," he muttered.

Was there any subject that didn't make him shut down and become close-lipped? There was one thing for certain: Dash had secrets.

"Are there more of those … snykers out here?" I asked, eyes darting over the forest floor. If I kept him talking, then I wouldn't be thinking about my angry belly.

"Only in the waters outside the maze. As long as you don't take a swim or dangle yourself along the water's edge, they won't bother you. But get close enough to tempt them, and they will try to take a bite. They have a tendency to be snippy. Kind of like you."

"Ha. Ha. Ha."

He smiled sideways, revealing a dimple.

All I could do was gawk at him. That smile was heart stopping.

It seemed unfair that he should be so devastatingly good looking but have such a prickly personality.

Dash stopped, his gaze snapping to me. For a moment, he stood there, blinking, and then his eyes narrowed. He flashed right next to me, grabbing my wrist.

Chapter Five

"You better have a good reason for manhandling me," I spat.

"The guards have picked up on our scent," he said, tugging me forward. "They are coming for us."

"What?" I shrieked, confused.

"If you don't want your first day in Starling Heights to be your last, then move your ass."

The rustling behind us grew louder, and that was all the encouragement I needed to get my feet going.

We tore through the forest, branches and leaves slapping at my face. Dash's fingers were weaved through mine, and I could feel the muscles in his arm tense and roll. I did the best I could to keep up with him and not slow us down. Behind us, voices echoed, twigs cracked, and the grunts grew closer.

A lance whizzed through the air, sinking into the dirt at my heels. I yelped.

Oh, my God! They were shooting at us.

There was a clearing to our right, and I thought for sure that was the way we were going. But no—Dash cut left, straight for a patch of tangled brush with large yellow leaves that were encased in thorns. My feet slowed, thinking he was nuts. If we went that way, we'd be sliced to pieces, but Dash only pulled on my arm harder.

"This way!" he urged, darting into the patch of wicked thistles.

Shit. This was going to hurt.

I briefly closed my eyes as we entered, never feeling so out of my element and lost. At every turn, something in this world wanted to do me harm. I'd be lucky if I survived another night—a week maybe—with Dash's help.

But what would happen after we get to Hurst and he leaves? What then?

To my great relief, as we approached the thistles, the leaves turned inward, rolling themselves into little cocoons, revealing a narrow dirt path winding through the trees. I snuck a quick peek over my shoulder to see if we were being followed, but the thistles had unfurled and were once again a patch of poisonous thorns.

"You hanging in there?" he asked, letting up just a tad on his grueling pace.

It was a good thing I'd been an athletic chick in high school. Between fencing classes and cheerleading, I managed to stay fit and quick on my feet. As I opened my mouth, another lance zipped over my head.

"Dammit," Dash swore. "Unrelenting bastards."

Once again I found myself being pulled along over the woodsy terrain with Dash's insistent strides. I followed behind, or risked getting my arm yanked out of the socket. My ragged breaths echoed in time with my pounding heart.

I stumbled out of the woods, not expecting the ground to abruptly drop. My feet skidded to a screeching halt, tearing my fingers from Dash's grasp.

He whipped around, already teetering over the side. "Hurry," he ordered, holding out his hand.

I hesitated. He wanted me to scale down a small mountain? What next?

Biting my lip, I stared into his eyes. He was fearless. His courage and my terror gave me renewed strength. I placed my hand in his again and said a silent prayer.

Geronimo.

Together, we staggered down the side of the bank, rocks tumbling alongside us. The blood drained from my face, and my legs burned with exhaustion as I struggled to keep my balance. The alternative was using the foothill as a Slip 'N Slide, and I didn't think my butt could handle it. Without Dash's strength, things would have been painful.

I exhaled a sigh of relief when my feet touched the bottom, but we wasted no time dashing for the cover of trees at the base of the bank. This time we managed to shake them off our trail, but who knew for how long.

We walked for hours, or at least it felt that way. Dash kept a steady, grueling pace, wanting to put as much distance between us and the Night's Guard as possible. Fast. I had to, more or less, speed walk to keep up with him, or get left behind. The trail often split off into different directions, but Dash chose each path without hesitation.

My feet were aching, my stomach was rumbling, and my legs felt like I was on a treadmill from hell with no off switch. Just as I thought I would drop from exhaustion, we came upon a huge tree with a gnarly trunk. The bark of the tree was knotty and rough, making it appear as if there were faces embedded in the trunk. Eyes trailing up, my breath caught. Heart-shaped leaves dangled from the branches in colors that reminded me of a summer sunset. Against the waning light and the sparkling stars above, the canopy of leaves set the tree afire.

Beyond the magnificent tree, the flickering of an orange firelight glowed in the distance.

Civilization.

Halle-freakin'-lujah.

I was starving. This place better have a restaurant. I wasn't asking for a five-star, but real food and not berries and twigs. I'd kill for a chocolate croissant and a tall glass of milk.

"A-are they … friendly?" We were only a few steps away, and the nerves had set in.

Dash's eyes softened at the anxiety in my voice. I wouldn't admit it, but I was scared shitless. Nothing of this world had shown me any kindness. A girl like me, in a universe this harsh and foreign, didn't stand a chance.

Once we crossed over into Hurst, my time with Dash would come to an end. He had promised to see me to safety, and he had, though it was debatable how safe our travels had been. I hadn't signed up for nearly getting killed at every turn.

"Depends on your definition of friendly."

I glanced sideways at him. "Okay, how about this: Are they nicer than you?"

"Definitely." He grinned.

Damn, those dimples again. What was he trying to do to me?

I sighed.

"You'll be safe here," he assured, "until you decide what you want to do. If your family is out there, then the people of Hurst can help. It is the largest settlement north of Diamond Towers and filled with trackers."

Trackers, I'd learned, were rebels who searched for the missing or those in slumber, but usually at a price. I didn't have anything to offer, except for a ratty dress, a slim ring, and the silver charm around my neck. It had been a gift from my little sister. I doubted either would fetch me a fair price for a tracker.

Dash suggested the option of working off the debt—a job. I'd never had one a day in my life.

"Are you going to stay the night?" I asked. There was comfort in a friendly face, even one as devilishly handsome as Dash's.

His voice was soft when he spoke, devoid of his usual sarcasm. "I'm not leaving just yet."

Hurst was like something out of a movie, something not quite real. There was an eight-foot fence surrounding the perimeter with only one way in and one way out. As soon as you walked through the gates, vendors lined the rocky road—a farmer's market of sorts, selling a variety of wares from produce to linens and furs to handcrafted jewelry. My eyes took in everything, absorbing the drastic change in life.

Dash stopped at one of the vendors to speak to a man who had an eye as milky as cream. He was rail thin and smelled like a fourth of July grill out. I tried not to stare, but it was the most unusual sight. "I'm sorry, Rubian, I found nothing," Dash said regrettably to the fragile man.

Rubian gave a sad nod. "Thank you for looking."

He laid a sturdy hand on the man's shoulder. "Do not give up hope," Dash murmured, surprising me with his conviction.

I glanced sideways at him, studying the guy who remained a mystery to me. There was another side to Dash he rarely showed to people, and it made me wonder why. What had made him so cynical and guarded?

"Here, for your trouble." Rubian swung around to the grill sizzling behind him, plucking two skewers of meat, and handed them to Dash. "For you and your lady friend. I am sure after your travels, you are famished. It's the least I can do."

Dash nodded, taking the payment of sorts. My guess: Rubian had asked Dash to look for someone, possibly at the holding house where he had found me.

"Eat," Dash instructed, holding out a stick as we continued to weave down the market through the crowd.

I rolled my eyes, but took the skewer, my stomach growling.

As Dash walked through the dirt streets of Hurst, people turned their heads, whispering or offering the occasional nod. There was a general wariness in their eyes. I wanted to ask him why the people of Hurst were afraid of him, but a burly form suddenly blocked our path, his large shadow looming down on us.

Swallowing the last bite of smoked meat, I glanced up. An intimidating man stood with his arms crossed, a gruff auburn beard covering most of his face, reminding me of a mountain man—burly, hairy, and boorish. Blue eyes twinkled behind all that hair. I wanted to offer him a hair tie or a scrunchie.

When he spoke, he had a deep tone that made me think of roaring rapids and unrestrained storms. "Dash," he greeted, putting a large hand on Dash's shoulder. "We didn't expect you until the next full moon."

"Plans changed." His eyes shifted sideways to me, a frown pulling at his lips.

I scuffed my slipper into the ground, offering a friendly smile.

"I see." The mountain man's eyes rotated from Dash to me. "You're too pretty for the Institute to throw away." He watched me under scrutinizing eyes. "So did you finally take my advice and find yourself a wife?"

I scrunched my face.

Dash was quick to set the record straight. "You couldn't be more wrong, Cyan."

Cyan chuckled deep in his belly, a booming sound. "I'm not so sure about that." He crossed his arms over his expansive chest. "A runner then," he concluded.

Dash snorted, and the absurdity behind it made me want to smack him on the back of the head. "Wrong again, though she definitely has spunk."

Intrigue lifted Cyan's bushy brows.

"I got to her before the Night's Guard did, just as she awoke," Dash said, filling in the mystery of my presence.

Cyan didn't say anything for a moment. I got the feeling he thought there was more to the story. "Interesting. It's not like you to rescue the damsel in distress."

Dash rubbed the back of his neck. "Yeah well, I've done a lot of things lately I never thought possible. Any chance you got room for two stragglers?"

Cyan's eyes lit with humor. "You're in luck my friend. We always reserve a place for you, but we only have one hut available. That won't be a problem?"

Dash's jaw clenched. "I won't be staying long, but Charlotte will need somewhere to stay while she figures things out."

"Of course. Join me for a drink tonight after you've washed the stink off you both. I want to hear about your journey. And I'm sure the lady is starving." Cyan winked before carrying his big frame down the market.

My nose wrinkled. I felt rank and was dying for a shower and clean clothes. Cyan's suggestion made me realize how awful I must look.

Dash blew out a breath, shifting his weight. "Come on. You look like you're about two seconds away from passing out."

"I do not," I protested as I swayed on my feet.

A lopsided grin appeared on his lips. "Uh-huh."

We moved along past the vendors and through a narrow alley that opened up into a valley housing small structures made up of a mixture of mismatched materials: steel, wood, brick, anything that was of use to construct a small home and keep out the elements.

Ivy climbed up the sides of the little huts, coiling around the buildings like a snake, penetrating every crevice. I was gawking, but I couldn't help it. Instead of being thrown a hundred years in the future, it was as if I'd been transported back in time, before electricity, before MacBooks, before plumbing. All modern luxuries no longer existed.

A horrifying notion blossomed in the bottom of my belly.

"Yep, running water is a thing of the past," Dash said, seeing my mouth hit the ground.

I stood gaping at the row of wooden stalls situated in front of a flowing brook. Water sped over the rocks, twisting and turning downstream. There was a contraption humming in the water, tubes running to the showers, a filtration system. The showers weren't completely enclosed, but covered all the important bits, leaving a small space at the bottom open for drainage and the top exposed. They were at least over seven feet tall, but if there was a giant around, he could peek over and get a free show.

Dash handed me a folded fabric square I assumed was a towel. "Not what you expected, huh? Hope you're not shy?"

I was a seventeen-year-old girl with body issues. Of course I was reluctant to shower in a less than private setting, but modesty aside, I would have bathed in a lake. The desire to get the grime off outweighed any timidity.

"Just make sure you check the shower for critters," Dash advised, smirking.

I squished my face at Dash before stepping in and locking the door. He better have been kidding. I wasn't normally a squeamish girl, spiders being the exception. Something about all those beady eyes, hairy bodies, and quick legs gave me the willies.

Stepping out of the tattered dress, I hung it over the top ledge alongside the towel. I cranked the water, half-expecting it to be cold, but was pleasantly surprised when the water ran warm. The moment the spray hit my skin, I let out a sound of pure bliss. A hundred years was a long time to go without bathing. I swore Dash let out a similar sigh of heaven.

I cleaned my hair twice and scrubbed my skin until it was as smooth as a newborn's butt. As I stood under the pounding spray, the events of the last twenty-four hours replayed through my head. Had I made the right choice going with Dash? Was the Institute as bad as they were portrayed? There was still so much I didn't know. How was I going to find my family?

And that was my top priority. I needed to find Dad, Mom, and Monroe. If they were out there, I would do everything I could to locate them. What else was I supposed to do on my own? Did they have schools here? Where did they get their clothes?

My mind was going off into a hundred different tangents when the shower automatically shut off, and I groaned. Apparently, there was a time limit, and fifteen minutes hadn't been nearly enough.

I sighed, staring at the once-white, now-shredded dress that had once been fit for a princess. The last thing I wanted was to put it back on, but the alternative was my birthday suit. I was feeling pretty good right about now, but not enough to go streaking.

Toweling off quickly, I yanked the dress over my head and stepped out of the shower, shaking out my wet hair with the balmy evening breeze. I peered over my shoulder, and there leaned Dash, shirtless with a lopsided grin. "Did you die and go to heaven?"

That was one way of putting it.

My mouth watered. The rich tone of his tan skin gleamed with beads of water, dark hair glistening. He had a towel in his hand, and a thrill danced in my belly, seeing the line of curls disappear into his pants. My gaze traveled upward, following a scar that ran over his chest in a diagonal from the left side of his torso to his right pectoral. It appeared to be an old wound, and I was curious how he had achieved such a warrior mark.

My curiosity overtook propriety, and I twisted, my hand reaching out toward him. With a light touch, I traced the tips of my fingers along the scar. "What happened?"

"It's nothing." His voice was rough, the sinister grin slipping from his lips.

Realizing I was touching his skin, I snatched my hand away and met his gaze. "It doesn't look like nothing. It looks like something tried to gut you."

He gave a nonchalant, one-shoulder shrug. "Close enough."

I searched for a quip or something flirty to say, but the intensity in his eyes scattered any coherent thought. He leaned down, and his fingers lifted my chin toward him.

My lips parted slightly. *Was he about to kiss me?*

Confusion flashed in his eyes as his thumb traced circles along my jaw. "I can't figure out what it is about you," he said, barely above a whisper.

My heart fluttered, anticipation welling up inside me. This was insane, but then again, so was everything that had happened to me so far. Kissing a hot guy just might be the sanest thing.

Lightning cracked in the sky, striking close enough to feel the energy on my skin. It was followed by the booming snap of thunder roaring overhead. Dash jerked back, breaking the trance that held us both. I sucked in a sharp hiss. My body was still tingling and missing the warmth of his. Disappointment churned in my stomach.

Dash's eyes moved over to my battered dress. "Let's get you something to wear. I don't know how much longer that dress is going to hold up."

I swallowed, his implication making my cheeks flush. "We're not going to the mall, are we?"

A soft chuckle shook his shoulders. "Hardly, Freckles. Knowing Cyan, he would have had someone drop off something for you to wear. Call it a care package."

He was right.

It was only one room but with two small areas designated for sleeping. The *beds* were piles of fur layered onto each other, and on the far left one laid a pair of pants, a shirt, and boots. It felt like Christmas morning.

Dash was watching me. "Might not look like much, but it will keep you warm and there are no snykers hiding in the corners."

"It beats the hell out of sleeping in a cave," I replied, already inspecting the clothes.

His lips twitched. "Sure does."

I spotted a divider at the back of the cabin. Gathering up the clothes, I went into the tiny bathroom, just big enough for a mirror and a pot that resembled an old-fashioned toilet. I changed into the fresh pair of tight black pants—I barely managed to squeeze my butt in—and a T-shirt that was a tad loose on me, falling off the shoulder on one side. The best part wasn't even the clean clothes; it was the socks. My feet sighed in relief as the soft material covered them, before I slipped them into the boots.

Running my fingers through my hair, I twisted it into a messy bun and secured it with a strip of fabric from the dress. A girl had to get creative in apocalyptic times. Satisfied I was almost human, I stared at myself in the mirror.

No way am I ever going to get used to this.

My eyes were so ... freaky? I didn't know how else to explain them. The center of my irises was divided up into each color, one blending into the next, from violet to pink to blue to green. As I studied my new look, a pit knotted in my stomach.

If what I'd learned about the mist was true—that the exposure altered your DNA—I wouldn't be able to ignore the fact that these eyes meant I was different. The knowledge of who I might be, or what I might be capable of, was nerve rattling.

With a deep sigh, I opened the door, telling myself I was prepared to take on this new world and the trials it brought my way.

But it was a lie.

Nothing could have prepared me.

The scent of stale beer and grease smacked me in the face. Yuck. Trying not to inhale too deeply, I moved behind Dash, sticking as close to him as possible without tripping him. My stomach was having a fit, both in hunger and revolt, unable to make up its mind.

The Odd Hill was like the mess hall, lined with old wooden tables and chairs. It was the only place to get a decent meal, and by only, Dash meant the one and only.

We moved around the edge of a group at a table and headed toward the bar. Most of the patrons were dressed like Robin Hood—leather pants, flimsy material buttoned loosely at the neck, each with a weapon of some kind strapped to their hip. I recognized Cyan from the few guys already situated on the stools. His overall robust stature gave him away. Dash pulled out an empty seat, leaving me the one sandwiched between him and Cyan.

I scooted my butt onto the stool, folding my hands on the tabletop. Cyan dwarfed the seat beside me, and I was afraid the poor stool wouldn't hold him.

"Gunner," Cyan summoned the guy behind the bar. "A round of drinks and two house specials for Dash and his lady."

"She's not my lady," Dash muttered, scowling. I swore he wore a frown like a permanent fixture.

My eyes narrowed at how quickly he had shut down the idea. I didn't want to be his anything.

Cyan only grinned.

Gunner winked at me. "Good thing." He was on the shorter side with pale skin and neon-blue lips that curled sardonically at the edges. It was obvious he'd been touched by the mist. His eyes looked over me for two full seconds before dropping to my chest.

Typical.

Some things never change, not even after a hundred years, like the ability for a guy to see a girl for who she is instead of what size is filling her bra. The loose top wasn't helping matters. I shoved it back up my shoulder for it only to slip down again. Sighing, I gave up.

Dash cleared his throat, and Gunner gave me a cheeky grin before turning to get our drinks.

I'd been so distracted with the bartender and his wandering gaze, I hadn't noticed Dash had company. We'd only been here a few minutes, but it had been long enough for Dash to catch another girl's eye. She had long chestnut hair tied in braids that swept up on her head in an intricate design, accenting high cheekbones. Her skin was the color of mocha, creamy and flawless. Big, blue, sultry eyes purred at him behind enviously long lashes.

He said something that made her throw her head back and laugh. She took the opportunity to touch his arm and move closer to him so that her perfect breasts were touching him.

Ugh, that was so not on my list of things I wanted to see tonight—some floozy flirting with Dash.

What do you care? I berated myself. The only thing I cared about was food and finding my family. So what if not that long ago he was almost kissing me? It's not like I wanted him or anything. He was free to do whatever he wanted with whomever he wanted.

I didn't know what was worse: her overpowering "I'm desperate" perfume or the rancid stink of the spilled, stale beer.

On a huff, I turned my back to them as Gunner placed a frosty mug in front of me. I didn't even ask what was in it, just downed the cool drink at brain freeze speed.

"That's my daughter, Harper, making a fool of herself," Cyan informed, his head nodding the direction of the two-bit floozy.

I quickly lightened my frown and plastered a smile on my lips, trying not to gag on my drink, which was darn addicting. There was definitely a kick of something alcoholic. I took it there wasn't a drinking age anymore.

Cyan wrapped a brawny hand around a glass bottle. "She has a thing for the slayer, as many of the girls do," he said, with a hint of fondness in his deep timbre.

It took me a second to realize he was talking about Dash. It was of no shock that Dash didn't lack for female attention, but Cyan had referred to him as *the slayer*, and I could see it. There was a dark precision to his keen eyes and an aura about him that warned others to back off.

I drummed my fingers on the side of my glass, wondering what secrets Dash was hiding. Maybe I could pump Cyan for details. "Dash is a slayer?" I prompted, fishing for information. I wasn't sure what that meant here, but it didn't sound nice.

Cyan tilted his head to the side and frowned. "It's a nickname he earned. There isn't a single guy or girl for that matter who would be dumb enough to challenge Dash Darhk. Not unless they were looking to commit suicide."

Were we talking about the same Dash? Yes, he could be rough around the edges, but since I'd opened my eyes, Dash had done nothing but make me feel safe. "He kills people?" I asked, astonished.

Dash? A hit man?

I wasn't buying it, but there was no denying the caution in the eyes of everyone in the bar, avoiding Dash like he was the big bad wolf.

"Not for fun." Cyan wasn't a world of help on the gossip front. "You were touched by the mist," he commented, staring into my eyes. They weren't hard to miss.

I blinked. "I guess so." It was an awkward topic for me. I didn't know what to say about the rainbow eyes.

His voice softened—well, softer for him. "You'll find that most everyone in Hurst is a misfit cast away by the Institute."

He was trying to make me feel at ease, and I appreciated it, but I wasn't sure I would ever get used to this world. However, I started to take notice of little things I'd been too preoccupied to see about the people of Hurst. Gunner's neon lips. Cyan's bear-size form. The guy in the market with his milky eyes. The mist had altered us all in some way or shape.

The Institute was still a foreign entity for me. I didn't fully understand the inner workings of their role in this world. "Are they gathering an army?" I asked, half-joking.

"You're pretty quick for someone who just recovered from the slumber. You would be wise to keep off the Institute's radar, stay off the grid. Those eyes of yours aren't just pretty to look at. I have a hunch the Institute would love to get their handcuffs on you. Have you figured out how this mist mutated your cells?" Cyan asked, taking a swig from his bottle.

To my left, Harper threw back her head and let out a husky laugh, disrupting my train of thought. I wanted to shove a sock in her mouth, but only shook my head at Cyan's question. "No, I have no clue." And it was fine by me if I never did.

The dim yellow light cast shadows over Cyan's hairy face. "Well, you'll find out sooner or later. We always do. It's best Dash found you instead of the Night's Guard."

"Why is that?"

"There's nobody in Starling Heights more capable of outmaneuvering the Institute than Dash. The things they put him through. ..." A shudder rolled through Cyan as if he had firsthand experience with the Institute.

I wanted more deets. How had Dash escaped the clutches of the Institute? Was he a misfit, thrown away like the others in Hurst? But that didn't make sense. Why were the Night's Guard hunting him? What had the Institute done to him? It was bad, of that much I was sure. I thought about the scar on his chest. Was that from his time with the Institute?

A twinge of sympathy squeezed my heart. "They experiment on people?"

Cyan's eyes hardened to glass. "Experimenting is too bland of a word to describe what they do in the cages."

WTF.

I was tempted to give Dash a kiss on the cheek for saving me from such a fate, but then I remembered Harper. I didn't want to be accused of cramping his style.

Leaning my head on my hand, I attempted to block them from my eyesight. I suddenly felt utterly alone, and my chest panged with a longing to see my mom. "Did you and your daughter wake at the same time?"

Cyan lifted a finger, letting Gunner know he was ready for another drink. "No, it took me six months to find her, and if it wasn't for Dash, I'd probably still be looking."

"Are you a tracker?" I asked, thinking maybe I could enlist his services. He looked the part and appeared more than capable.

Cyan's eyes sparkled, and his busy mustache bobbed as he chuckled. "I only oversee the settlement—keep things running smoothly and in order, make sure the Institute doesn't bust down our doors. It's a demanding job. If you're set on finding your family, you already know the best tracker in the Heights. No one knows this land better than the slayer."

Dash?

I traced the water drip patterns on my mug with my fingertip and chuckled. He was exactly what I was looking for, but not once had he offered to help me find them, only to bring me here and to go our separate ways.

Gah. If Dash was my best bet at finding my family, then I was going to have to make him help me. Lifting my glass to my lips, I downed half my drink.

Speaking of the devil, his arm brushed against mine as he leaned toward me at the bar, silver eyes finding mine. "Whoa, slow down, slugger. That stuff can hit you pretty hard if you're not careful."

I swallowed a huge slurp, and my cheeks flushed from the potent drink. Or so I told myself it was the drink. "What is this stuff?" I asked, my limbs feeling relaxed and light. My eyes shifted over Dash's shoulder. Harper was nowhere to be found. Couldn't say I was disappointed.

Dash leaned back, a hand on the bottle of his drink. "You ever have a margarita before?"

"I've drank alcohol," I retorted dryly, like I was a pro. Truth was, I'd snuck a few wine coolers with my friends and had a few sips of champagne on New Year's Eve, which had made me pucker, but other than that, I was a booze virgin.

"Uh-huh," Dash replied, like he knew I was embellishing.

Damn him.

Just to prove him wrong, I held my glass up to Gunner. "I think I need a refill."

Gunner grinned, happy to oblige.

Dash shook his head. "Suit yourself, but I'm not holding your hair when you start puking up your intestines."

I scrunched my face. "I wouldn't let you touch me, not even drunk."

He arched a challenging brow that said he could prove me wrong. Leaning his face close to mine, he whispered, "Should I prove you're a liar, Freckles?"

The warmth of his breath tickled my reeling senses, causing a series of cartwheels in my belly. Oh wow. I needed to slow down on the booze. Things were happening inside me that I couldn't control. My teeth caught my bottom lip. I was such a liar. If he pressed his mouth to mine right this second, I would gladly sink into him. I swear, I could almost feel the smooth texture of his lips as they glided over mine, as if we'd kissed before.

His eyes darted to my lips and darkened. Tiny shooting stars glowed in his irises. The tavern faded into the background, leaving only Dash, his dimples, and his totally kissable lips.

I think I might have leaned forward. Our noses might have even brushed, but I was so lost in the humming of my body, I wasn't sure of anything.

Cyan cleared his throat, laughing.

And Dash rocked back, a victorious smirk on his lips.

Asshat!

I couldn't believe I almost fell for it. Only moments ago he'd been flirty with another girl, and here I was drooling over him. I shoved at his shoulder. "You're such a jerkwad."

His smirk turned downright wicked. "Everyone has to excel at something."

I rolled my eyes, relieved that the food had showed up. If I was stuffing my face, I wouldn't say something I'd regret and risk Dash not helping me. Turned out, I hadn't needed to worry. Harper appeared, weaseling her way between Dash and me.

"You're the new girl everyone is buzzing about. Rainbow Brite." There was a sneer under the sweet girl charm.

She wasn't fooling me. This girl was trying my patience, and I had never been very good at keeping my cool. My first reaction was to reach over and grab her by her long, dark locks. The hair pull had been my signature move in high school. Something about her rubbed me the wrong way. "Charlotte. My. Name. Is. Charlotte."

She let out one of those annoying high-pitched giggles, followed by a twist of her hair around a finger. "Cute."

I pasted a smile as fake as her boobs on my lips. "Do you work here?" I asked, returning the sweet-as-apple-pie tone.

Her body language was clear. She didn't want me moving in on her territory. Her pink lips curved. "Cute and funny. Don't worry. It won't last long."

My cute factor or my sense of humor? Or Dash's interest in me? Not that I cared either way. I'd dealt with girls like her in high school—the top bitch on a power trip who thought she ran the place. "Kind of like your phony personality." The drink was making my tongue a bit looser than normal.

"Watch out. Or you might find yourself eaten up by this place. Nice meeting you, Rainbow Brite." An evil gleam lit her expression before she flipped her braid in my face and strolled off without looking backward.

I watched her go, wondering what kind of chaos I'd walked into. Drama was nothing new to me, and it seemed to have followed me into the next century. Flipping fabulous.

Chugging the frozen drink, I winced as the icicle sensation faded, but in its place was a blissful fuzziness. It didn't last long. The more I sucked down, the less *great* I felt. The longer I sat listening to Harper and Dash, the more I drank. It was a vicious cycle I would regret tomorrow.

I was drunk.

I couldn't handle the flirting between Harper and dickwad a second longer, especially with the room starting to spin. Not a good sign.

Boosting myself off the stool, I looked left and then right, trying to recall which way the door was. I took a gamble and stumbled as gracefully as I could to the right, running a hand along the tables as I went. It also helped me walk in a straight line.

I thought Dash called my name as I pushed the heavy oak door open, but it was hard to hear over the buzzing in my ears. A brisk gust of wind blew over my face as I stepped outside. I lifted my chin, enjoying the cool sensation on my flushed cheeks.

It was hard to judge what time it was, but from the complete darkness outside, I guessed it to be almost midnight. I didn't think about walking alone in a strange place by myself, thanks to the aftereffects of indulging in too much of Gunner's concoction.

I have no idea how I remembered the way back, and as I walked into the one-room lodge, the bed looked super appealing. Praying I wasn't imposing on someone else's bed, I plopped down fully clothed, expecting instant relief, but as I lay on the makeshift bed of fur, the room started to twirl.

Fan-freaking-tastic.

I was going to puke all over the wooden floor.

Damn Dash to hell.

I wasn't sure what dragged me from sleep, but I woke up with a ball of icy terror low in my stomach and pulled the blankets up around me. It did nothing to chase the chill in my blood or the nightmare. This one had been a doozy. I'd been frozen in a perpetual sleep, only to wake up and find that my entire family had been killed by a toxic mist that had wiped out over two-thirds of the planet. The kicker: While I'd been fast asleep, I could hear my little sister screaming my name, over and over again. It had been a bloodcurdling sound, as if the mist had been eating away at her skin.

I'd suddenly been thrust out of the dream and into the real world, with my heart in my throat and her scream ringing in my ears.

My eyes popped open as the haze of sleep wore off. On impulse, I bit the inside of my cheek. The sharp pain was followed by the taste of blood, telling me this was real indeed and not a drunken stupor or a dream.

I really was sleeping on a bed of furs, the mist had been very real, and the world truly had gone down the crapper.

What next?

Staring at the wooden roof, a trickle of fear moved through my veins, forming a knot of unease in my chest. Would there ever be a time when I woke up without forgetting where I was? I took long breaths, but it didn't lessen the feeling.

The start of day two was already challenging my courage and inner strength. Loneliness and hopelessness followed me from the dream, weighing heavy on my soul. I needed to find my family but knew virtually nothing of this world or where to start. Without someone's help, I was doomed. The only other alternative was to stay put and hope they find me … assuming they were looking.

I rolled onto my side, expecting to see Dash's sleeping body across the room, snoring and wrapped in a cocoon of fur. My stomach sank. The bed was unoccupied and looked untouched, as if he hadn't even slept in it.

A fresh bout of panic seized my chest.

He left.

The bastard left me here. Alone. Without saying good-bye. He just took off in the middle of the night like a thief, never giving me the chance to ask him for help.

My doom-don just moved straight into catastrophic.

Chapter Seven

I lay there in shock, staring at the empty bed, unable to will my muscles to move. Okay, Charlotte. Calm down. There could very well be a reasonable explanation for him not being here. Like he spent the night with Harper.

Barf.

That explanation did nothing to calm my tattered nerves, and the longer I lay there letting my mind sprint off into tangents, the deeper my worry rooted. I had a tendency to be a worrywart, among other things. I was far from perfect. I knew my flaws, and Dash had been right about one thing: I had been pampered. I grew up with a doting family and parents who had always been there for me. I grew up wanting for nothing—never hungry, never without clothing, a home, or love. I'd never truly ever been out on my own.

It was a scary thing.

And as much as I wanted to curl into the fetal position and pull the covers over my head, I forced myself out of bed, and the door squeaked opened. My eyes flew to the figure darkening the doorway. I didn't pay much attention to the warmth skipping down my neck, acting on instinct, and opened my mouth to scream.

The intruder was quick, reaching me before I let my lungs sing and wrapping a hand around my waist, the other over my mouth. "Freckles, it's me," Dash growled in my ear.

I turned in his arms and more or less attacked him. My fists beat on his chest. "How could you do that to me!" I yelled.

Dash scowled, grabbing ahold of my wrists and tucking them against his chest. "Bring you breakfast?"

Tugging on my hands, I tried to remove myself from his clutches, but he stayed firm. "No, you, douchecanoe. Leave me."

Confusion splashed across his striking features. "Are you still drunk?"

"Argh," I groaned, throwing my head back.

"I was only gone for five minutes," he reasoned, staring at me funny and releasing my wrists.

My hands fell to my sides. "I thought you left," I whispered.

His eyes softened. "Not yet, Freckles, but I am leaving … soon."

My temper slipped away like a melting snowflake. "How soon?"

"Tonight," he informed me. "It's easier to avoid the Night's Guard at night." He handed me something wrapped in a napkin.

I took the package, sinking down onto the edge of the bed. The sweet scent of sugar hit my senses, and I felt myself turn green. There was no way I could eat. I set the sweet roll aside on the bed and looked up. "Where are you going?" I asked, ignoring the thumping that had begun to pulse behind my eyes.

"Not hungry?" Dash responded, an all-knowing glint twinkling in his expression. He knew I was suffering.

Stupid drink.

I pressed a hand to my head. "If what I'm feeling is a hangover, I never want to touch that stuff again."

He chuckled, leaning a shoulder against the wooden support beam in the middle of the room. "I warned you."

That he did. "You never told me where you're going," or what he was searching for. I assumed it was a someone.

"To the Plains of Despair."

Oooh. Sounded like buckets of fun. "You're going to another holding house like where I was?"

He nodded.

"I want to go with you."

"No," he stated flatly, eyes crystalizing with no hesitation. Just like that, he didn't even consider it.

No wasn't the answer I wanted. "Why not?" I demanded, pushing myself to my feet.

He shoved off the beam, a wavy lock falling across his forehead and into his eyes. "Because I travel alone."

"Fine, then I want to hire you." I folded my hands across my chest, ignoring the this-isn't-up-for-debate vibe radiating off of him.

He angled his head. "And just what do you think I do?"

"Cyan told me you're a tracker. I want you to help me find my family."

"I'm not your guy."

I don't know how it happened, but we stood toe-to-toe. "Is this about money? Because I swear I will find a way to pay you."

"I don't need your money, Charlotte. Like I said, I work alone."

He said my name in the way my dad used to when he meant business—stern and serious. "Then what is it you want? I'll do anything." I chewed on my lip as I waited. I'd never begged for anything in my life, but I was willing to do just that if it got Dash to help me. Finding my family was my only priority.

Dash took a step back, and his eyes flipped to mine before traveling over my body and then flicking back up. "Anything, huh?"

The drop in his voice did weird things to my belly, and I swallowed. It shamed me to admit the idea of giving him what he implied didn't gross me out. Nope. I was tempted to challenge him and see if he would follow through, or if he was just trying to scare me.

My guess was the latter.

Several moments passed, and when I didn't immediately balk at the idea, he shook his head. "This world is going to eat you alive, Freckles. You're safer here, away from the danger."

And that danger included him. We were still close. Close enough I could feel the heat from his body. "Okay, if you won't help me, at least take me with you. You're going out there, looking for people; I want to come."

"No."

"What bug crawled up your butt?"

"Where should I begin?" Dash stepped to the side.

"I need to find my family," I insisted. "I won't be any trouble, I swear."

He stopped in his tracks and spun around, brows raised. "Trouble? You? Are you forgetting our trip here? If that is your idea of no trouble, then let me rephrase it: Hell, no."

I flipped him off. "Does this hand gesture still mean something?"

Dash tipped back his chin and laughed.

I'd take that as a yes.

How could someone be so nerve-wracking and stimulating at the same time?

The little room was suddenly too small for the both of us. No matter where I moved, it felt as if Dash and I would constantly be brushing elbows. "I've spent twenty-four hours with you, and I can't count how many times I've almost been killed. What does that say about you?"

"You made it here, didn't you? That's all that counts," he barked.

He made me so mad, I wanted to scream or kick him in the gonads. The second might be more satisfying. Clenching my jaw, I blew out a hiss between my teeth.

"Trust me, Freckles, you're better off on your own or finding someone else to help you. I'm doing us both a favor by leaving." Then the coward stormed out the door he came in.

Ten seconds went by, and that was all I could stand before I ran out after him. No way was I letting Dash get off the hook that easily. He was the only person I knew here, and I understood he had his reasons for not wanting me tagging along like his little sister—not that there was a moment I thought of him as brotherly—but I was determined. That had to count for something.

Whipping the door open, my eyes searched the multiple paths. "Dash!" I called, jogging to catch up to him.

His steps faltered before pausing, but he kept his back to me. "Don't ask again," he said with a compressed jaw.

It was at that moment I knew I was weakening his resolve. He might want everyone to think he was the big bad wolf, but I was starting to think that no one really knew Dash. If they did, they might not think he was so callous.

I placed my hand on his forearm and looked up into his silver eyes, pleading with him. "Please." My voice quivered. "I have to find them. I can't stay here. You're the only one who can help me." Tears stung my eyes. I didn't know a guy who could resist a weeping, helpless girl. Yep. I had resorted to the oldest trick in the female book.

He stared at my trembling bottom lip, and his shoulders dropped. "Fine," he agreed, sounding anything but happy about it.

I started to grin, but he stopped me with his next words.

"But I'll just track them on my own. You stay here and out of the way. That's the deal."

Well, that backfired. He wasn't supposed to offer to help but still leave me behind. "No deal." The tears dried up.

"Look, I can't be responsible for you."

"Who is asking you to?" I argued. "I can take care of myself." Truth or not, I was too heated to care.

He snorted.

Gah. That was it. I'd been pushed to the limit. He didn't want to help; well, I didn't need him. I would find them on my own. Starting right now.

Without another word, I spun around, flipping my hair in his face, and took off in the direction I was pretty sure was the exit. I didn't have a single thing to my name, and unless Dash stopped me, I would be doing some bartering in the market before he left. It was a gamble—leaving—but it was one I was willing to take. If I was wrong about Dash, he would just let me go. But if I was right. ...

"Charlotte," he called, but I ignored him. "Charlotte, where do you think you're going?"

I made my feet keep going, regardless of the fact that my pulse skipped. There was a guy with a heart in there after all.

"Goddammit," he grumbled.

His feet hit the ground behind me, and I picked up the pace, but I didn't get very far. A pair of strong arms swept around my waist, lifting me off my feet. I squealed as Dash hauled me over his shoulder, dragging me back into the cabin kicking and screaming. No one bothered to check out the commotion.

"Stay put," he growled, dropping me down. "And stop being a pain in my ass."

Like hell I would. Shoving my hair out of my face, I glared. "I'll just leave again as soon as you're gone."

A frown pulled at his lips. "Then I'll hogtie you to a tree."

"Why do you care what happens to me anyway?"

"What makes you think I care?"

"God, you're such a tool," I snapped. "Leave, then. I don't need you. I don't need anyone." The words just flew from my mouth like verbal diarrhea, even though I didn't mean them. The last thing I wanted was for him to go.

My eyes stung again as he turned to leave, and before I knew it, the tears were streaming down my cheeks once again. There was nothing I could do to change his mind, but I needed to say good-bye. "Dash," I called out with a big sniffle.

He surprised me by stopping.

I walked up to him and placed my lips on his stubbly cheek. He smelled like autumn mornings, crisp and warm. I told myself not to get carried away about him or the tingling of my lips. It was probably best for both of us if he left before my heart became entangled, because looking up into his face, there was more than one reason I didn't want him to leave. "Thank you for saving my life ... more than once," I whispered.

Bright silver eyes bore down on me. There was a sound at the base of his throat—part growl, part moan. "I knew you were going to be a problem the moment I set eyes on you. You're carrying your own shit."

Stunned, I blinked, and then my heart swelled to the point of bursting. I smiled broadly at him, and before I thought about what I was doing, I wrapped my arms around his neck. "Thank you," I whispered against the space between his shoulder and nape.

A shiver rippled through his body, and he stiffened. Dash placed his hands on either side of my hips, pulling me away. "Don't thank me yet, Freckles. I can't guarantee we'll find them."

Color brightened my cheeks. I couldn't believe I'd just thrown myself at him. What was wrong with me? "I know. It's enough that you're helping me."

"Be ready to leave at sundown." He sighed.

I grinned.

Our journey was only beginning. Certainly, it would be eventful, but something told me we'd be lucky to come out with a pulse. Who knew? Dash and I might kill each other before either of us found what we were looking for.

Packing for vacation was something I knew how to do. Preparing to backpack through a world where nothing made sense and everything was a new experience—simpler for sure, considering I owned nothing, technically, not even the clothes on my back.

I spent the rest of the day perusing the dirt streets of the market. My eyes took in all the sights and colors, listening to the busy chatter. There were handwoven rugs, fresh produce, and clothing. Vendors called out with enticing words or sales of the day. I weaved in and around the crowd, unable to believe I hadn't stepped back in time, instead of being propelled into the future.

It boggled my mind how a mist could do so much damage, but even as the thought flittered through my mind, I remembered vividly the crippling pain of the mist when it attacked my lungs, a horror I'd prefer to forget. What I needed to do was keep my mind focused.

There was a stand selling a variety of swords, daggers, and knives that caught my eye. It was the gleam of metal reflecting off the sunlight. Now that's a necessity. I thought back to the snyker and how helpless I'd been without a weapon to defend myself. Or what if we ran into more Night's Guard? It was apparent the world was wild and abandoned, and everyone here was packing.

I ran a light touch over the hilt of an intricately laced sword with decorative vines etched down the blade. With my fencing experience, a sword would have been ideal if it weren't for the weight. I could barely lift one. What I needed was something small, light, and deadly. As I was admiring the range of daggers, an older woman with long, stringy gray hair stepped out of the shadows. Her back was slightly hunched as she walked, but her light blue eyes were sharp and filled with keenness. The cloak that she wore dragged over the ground, kicking up dust in her wake.

"You're Dash Darhk's girl. The one he saved," she croaked, eyeing me with interest.

I wasn't precisely his girl, but he had saved me. I nodded. What harm was it in letting this little old lady think what she wanted? "Charlotte."

A crooked smile lined her pale pink lips. "You're very pretty, but the pretty ones always seem to be drawn to darkness."

I didn't know what to say, partially because I had no clue what she was talking about.

"Come." She waved with her hand, beckoning me forward with nails pointy enough to draw blood. "You see something you like, yes?"

"They're all beautiful," I said, smiling. "But I'm just looking."

She clucked her tongue. "Nonsense. I insist. Pick one that speaks to you. Surely there is one that sings to your heart."

I tried to keep the are-you-crazy off my face and humor her. There was a specific dagger my eyes kept going back to. I picked up the slim silver blade—the one with the single crystal encrusted in the hilt. My eyes narrowed as the metal hummed in my grasp.

Astonishing. I didn't expect to feel anything, let alone the buzzing under my fingertips. "I've never held anything like this," I murmured.

"It's yours," she said.

I lifted my eyes and shook my head. "I can't do that. I-I don't have anything to pay you with." Not to mention, I didn't even know if money existed in this new world. Regret pierced inside me as I went to put the blade back on the table. There was no denying I wanted the dagger.

She closed her hand around mine, tightening my grip on the blade. Her touch swept a chill through my bones. "It's yours. A perfect fit. The stone mirrors the colors of your eyes."

It did feel amazing in my hand—lightweight and impeccable. "I don't know what to say. Thank you."

Her eyes pierced into mine but at the same time looked right through me. "You have a destiny, Charlotte. It whispers in the winds, calling your name and Dash's, for your paths were meant to cross. Change is coming, and you're at the heart. Endings. Beginnings. Fate. It is waiting for you."

Um. Okay. My eyes shifted from left to right, checking to see if anyone else thought this was as weird as I did. "A-are you a seer?" I stammered. Hey, anything was possible.

"In a way. The mist changed my sight. I see things, but only flashes, and not always clear. The Institute wanted someone with more clarity ... and younger," she added, smiling.

"I'm sorry," I replied, unsure what else to say. I could tell that she had been through a traumatic experience.

"Don't worry for the old woman. You, my dear, have been given something rare. Don't let them break you."

I assumed them was the Institute. "What did you see?" I whispered. If she knew something about me, I wanted to know.

Her frail hand tightened over mine, showing a strength that surprised me. "Death. Love. Sorrow. Tragedy. Betrayal. The road ahead is paved with trials and tribulations, but it won't be without rewards, given the choices you make."

"What choices?" My voice had taken on an air of panic.

She released my hand, amber eyes growing sad with regret. "Not many know the true heart of Dash Darhk. But you see through the darkness. I owe him my life, and if I had the answers, I would give them to you, but I don't know."

"It's okay. You've done enough," I said, holding up the dagger.

"You'll need this as well." She handed me a holster to strap on the weapon—much more convenient then trying to stuff it down the back of my pants or in my boot.

"Thank you ... I never got your name," I prompted, realizing she knew mine without asking.

"It's Mira."

"Thank you, Mira. I won't forget your kindness." Or your warning.

This had turned out to be an eventful day. I had never put much stock into fortune tellers, but there had been something sincere and heartfelt in her eyes. Everything I knew and trusted didn't apply here. I had to open my mind to possibilities I never considered.

Like people seeing the future. Or crossbred creatures with unusual abilities. I'm sure the list went on, and I was bound to be shocked at every turn.

Tucking the blade safely in its sheath, I made my way back into the crowd, heading toward the sleeping quarters. Dash was nowhere to be found when I opened the door to the little cabin. With only the sun to tell time, I figured there was still another hour or two of light left. Just enough time to indulge in another shower before hitting the road. It could be days or weeks until I saw shampoo again.

I took my dagger with me.

Relieved that the showers were empty, I made quick use of discarding my clothes. The soap smelled lightly of honeysuckle and vanilla. It was refreshing and made me feel girly.

Afterward, I squeezed back into my tight pants and slipped my hands through a form-fitted shirt I had managed to barter from a ruthless woman with one gold tooth. The cost had been a silver ring I received for a birthday gift and somehow still had on when I woke. I had no use for such items, and it felt glorious to ditch the dress and slippers for a kickass outfit and a knife attached to my thigh.

Oh, yeah. I was ready to take on the world.

Maybe.

I exited the shower with a smile of purpose when a shadow fell across my path, blocking me from walking any farther. My eyes glanced up, and I bit back a sharp curse when I saw Harper.

Her lips were turned down, and she stood, tapping her boot on the ground, dark sapphire eyes spitting flames. She had her long, chestnut hair twisted up into another one of those complex braids.

Hmm. This didn't appear to be a friendly bon voyage. I couldn't help but feel like I was the girl being cornered by the school bully in the bathroom.

"Just so we're clear: If you touch him, I'll break your fingers. One by one."

Wow, can we say "crazy bitch"?

I arched a brow. "That's so unoriginal."

Two shades of red bloomed on her cheeks. "You must be stupid. Do you know what I could do to you?"

I might not know the ins and outs of this world yet, but when it came to girl fights, I was no dummy. "The last girl that threatened me ended up with a bloody nose and missing hair extensions. You remember what those are? Or have you been out in the jungle too long?" I angled my head and delivered my threat in the most condescending voice I could muster.

"I knew you were a bitch," she hissed.

"Takes one to know one," I said, shrugging. My fingers glided down the side of my thigh, touching the tip of the blade. So many words rose to my tongue, but I was going to be the bigger person and walk away, like an adult. And I was going to be pretty dang proud of myself if I pulled this off.

Harper had other ideas about being an adult. She slid to the side again as I moved to walk around her. "Dash would never fall for someone like you."

Screw being the bigger person. I was never good at it anyway. Stepping forward, our glares connected, and we both knew I was seconds away from bitch-slapping her. My hand twitched, but then her expression lost its hostility.

A familiar aggravated voice filled the air. "Everything okay, Freckles?"

All the muscles in my body tensed. Dash was behind me. "Just peachy," I said, adding necessary warmth to my bitter tone.

Harper's expression completely transformed. Gone were the lines of malice and the glare of death. Her locked jaw loosened into a sickeningly sweet grin. "I was just wishing Charlotte safe travels."

I choked.

Harper brushed past me, just barely nicking my shoulder in the process. I spun around, my patience dangling by a thread. She cozied up to Dash's side.

Bright silver eyes met mine, and his lips thinned in a straight line. "Is that what you are wearing?" Dash asked outraged, ignoring an extremely put-out Harper.

I grinned inside, but the satisfaction didn't last long, and it was Harper who was now smirking like the Cheshire cat.

Dash's eyes swept over the length of me, giving me the warm fuzzies, a feeling I wasn't too happy about. Damn, I hated it when he did that. My chin rose. "You got a problem with it?" Seriously, what did he care what I wore?

"Hell, yes, I have a problem with it. We don't need to draw any unwanted attention. Distractions get you killed."

When it came to Dash, I had no idea what to begin to think. I smiled sweetly. "Are you saying I'm going to distract you?"

He grumbled, shoving a blade in his boot. "Just keep up, and try not to attract every creature within a hundred mile radius."

Harper shot me a smug, I-told-you-so look.

My lips turned down, as I was hardly able to keep the wince off my face. I bypassed both Dash and

Harper, heading back to the cabin to gather my things. The sun had set, and the thin crescent moon offered little light. Dash better have flashlights.

He was on my heels, leaving Harper in our dust. We had said our good-byes and good riddances.

Well, this was starting off on a good foot. How many days until we reached the next settlement? Far too many alone in Dash's prickly company. It would be a miracle if we got there without killing each other. Or there was another option, but I refused to let myself think of Dash as something sexy and yummy. He was a means to an end. I needed to find my family. He knew the land better than anyone and was supposed to be the best tracker. Who better than Dash Darhk?

Holy banana boat.

His name even gave me the warm fuzzies.

Shit. I was in so much trouble. The warm fuzzies were going to be a problem. His damn dimples were going to be a problem. Dash was going to be a problem.

Chapter Eight

Once upon a time I had longed for a boyfriend. Nothing about Dash fit that girlish fantasy. He proved it almost every time he opened his mouth. Yet, I had feelings for him. What those feelings were, exactly, was still to be determined.

"Where did you get that?" he snapped, interrupting my rambling thoughts as his finger grazed over the dagger strapped to my upper thigh.

Stop thinking about his hand, I berated myself. I should be grateful I wasn't thinking about his fantastic butt.

Drats.

Now I was definitely thinking about his ass. Why did he have to be so good looking? Was it too much to ask for a tracker with a face that wasn't cut like he could be in a punk rock boy band?

I shook the haze of hormones from my head and replied, "From the little old lady in the market, Mira. And before you jump to conclusions, I didn't steal it. She gave it to me as a gift."

"Her son is one of the Night's Guard," Dash informed, brows drawn together.

Surprised, I cut him a look. "She said you saved her life."

He snorted, grabbing his gear from the ground outside the cabin. "I did. From her son killing her."

My mouth hit the ground. "Why would he do that?" I get being pissed off at your parents, but killing them...

"The Institute," he answered without hesitation. "They have a way of making people do things they would normally never consider. Like killing."

The more I learned about the Institute, the more I understood the reason to fear them. It was evident the people here held great contempt for the Institute. "They're looking for you?"

He stood in the shower of moonlight. "Are you reconsidering this ridiculous idea of you coming with me? Because you should."

I glanced out into the distance, feeling a sense of foreboding, but there was no avoiding it. I had to trust that Dash lived up to the reputation everyone gave him. "No." I tightened my hand around the strap of my bag and prepared to walk off into the sunset with him. "I have to find them."

Overhead, the moon winked in and out of the clouds, the stars glimmering. The night became our defense, shielding us from the eyes of the Night's Guard. Dash moved through the darkness with stealth and resolve. We hardly spoke as we put distance between us and Hurst, leaving the settlement fires at our backs and traveling east.

Although I was feeling better than this morning, the dull ache at my temples was an annoying reminder of last night's indulgence.

Dash bent down and plucked something growing in a small patch of wild weeds. "Here, chew this," he advised after seeing me massage the sides of my head.

I took the tiny green leaf, examining the texture and ridges. Lifting it to my nose, I took a sniff and scrunched my face. "It smells like a guys' locker room."

Dash grinned. "It does, but it will help ease the throbbing in your head. Take the edge off."

"Thanks," I mumbled and popped the herb into my mouth. It didn't taste as nasty as it smelled. In fact, it had a hint of mint flavor.

Hurst had been nestled deep in the woods, where wild things roamed and foxglove grew fat buds that spit poison. There were so many other oddities, too many to name. Basically, every cell had been mutated in some way, shape, or form. It was a world of wonder and danger, and I would be lying if I didn't say parts of it fascinated me. Other parts, like the insects the size of Jupiter, freaked me to the max.

"How far is the first holding house?" *And are there going to be any unexpected visitors of the creature kind?* I added mentally.

Dash's long legs expertly took him over the terrain with ease. "We have to cross territories first, over the boundary of the woods. We should reach the Plains of Despair by first light. As long as we don't run into any trouble."

We'd been walking for an hour or so, and I could already feel the burn in my lungs. "What kind of trouble?"

Dash gave me a chilling smile. "With you in tow, anything's game. Scorptran. Rattlog. Wild Borolf. Grasp. Or worse, the Night's Guard."

"Splendid," I said sarcastically.

"And that's just in the Grove. Things will get a whole lot trickier once we cross quadrants."

"Can't wait," I muttered, lowering my eyes to the ground. "How many holding houses have you been to?"

"In the last year. ..." he pondered. "I've lost count."

"So, you've been awake for a year?" I asked.

"Yeah, at least. The first few months I spent training before being assigned as a Night's Guard."

"What was it like? Being in the Institute?" I was curious. He'd been inside the lion's den.

"Which time?" he asked flatly.

Pine needles crunched under my boots. "There's been more than one?"

He nodded. "My grueling training and combing the land as a guard. Then the stint I did in their dungeons."

"Dungeons?" I squeaked.

His lips split into a grin, showing off a dimple. "You bet your skinny butt, Freckles. The Institute has a legit dungeon. And there is no way I am ever going back there—over my dead body."

"That bad, huh?"

Lifting a branch of leaves the color of deep garnet, he held it up as I walked under. "Remember the snyker that gave you a fright? Critters like that, and bigger, dwell in the dark corners of every cell."

I shivered as he ducked under the branch. "What did you do to end up in such a place?"

The squeamish chill didn't go unnoticed by Dash. "You really shouldn't ask questions you don't want answers to."

"What makes you think I don't want to know?" I challenged. I didn't like presumptuous guys. I wasn't one of those girls who appreciated it when a guy took it upon himself to know what I wanted, like ordering for me at dinner. Screw that.

"You know what, you're right," he agreed, and I immediately knew this was somehow going to get turned around. "You've been sheltered for too long, and if you're going to survive out here, you're going to need to deal with the harsh reality that we're not in Kansas anymore."

"Missouri," I mumbled.

"What?" he said, blinking in confusion.

"I'm from Missouri, not Kansas." I loved being a smartass. It was part of my charm.

He laughed, a rich and sexy sound. "Freckles, one thing is certain. This is going to be a journey neither of us is likely to forget."

I was under the impression he was somehow poking fun at me. "What did I say that was so amusing?"

He fell in step with me. "It's just been awhile since I've seen this place from the eyes of an awakened. I lived in Chicago before, close enough to feel the ground zero effects before the national warning went out."

"Where was ground zero?" The starting point of the mist. The start of the end.

"Word is, the mist originated in St. Louis."

I let out a quiet gasp. "That's where I live ... lived," I corrected.

We were silent for a bit, each absorbed in our own thoughts. I couldn't stop thinking about how close to the mist I'd been, and with it came those burning memories: the mist burning my skin, scorching my throat, scratching my eyes. A hundred years might have gone by, but since that day was my last memory, it was like yesterday, clear and vivid in my brain.

"I know what you're doing," Dash said gently. "And you can't keep reliving that date. I've seen what it can do to people. You have to find a way to shut it out. Forget the past. It will not serve you here."

I squeezed my eyes closed, forcing the horror from my mind like Dash suggested. "So what was it? What did you do that was so bad?" I asked, circling back around to him being imprisoned.

"I killed someone." There was no inflection in his tone. No remorse. No gratification. Just a blank expression, as if he didn't have a feeling about it one way or the other.

I called BS.

Dash was a master at hiding his emotions. Maybe it had been part of his *training*, or maybe it was something he had learned to do before all hell broke loose. Either way, he wasn't as unaffected as he wanted me to think.

I sent him a disbelieving stare. "So murder is a crime, even here?"

"I tell you I murdered someone, and you don't bat an eye."

I blinked a few times forcefully. "There, is that better?"

He shook his head, lips cracking a small curve. "You have spunk. Who knows? You might make it out here after all."

My eyes narrowed. "Thanks. That's very reassuring."

"The Institute has laws, similar to before, but not as structured or regimented the same. Killing a Night's Guard or a member of the Institute is pretty much a sure way to rot in a cell."

This place just keeps getting more welcoming.

We walked. And walked. And unfortunately walked some more. I lost track of how long we'd been traveling; all I knew was my legs were jelly, my lungs were going to collapse, and the air was starting to get warmer. I kept telling myself this was for a cause: to find my family. It kept my feet moving, one in front of the other.

As it does when I'm not yapping, my mind wandered, so I didn't notice the change in scenery until I stubbed my toe on a stupid tree stump. The pain propelled me back into the present.

Holy crap.

The first thing to catch my eye was the leaves on the trees. They varied in shapes—some hearts, others like stars—but it was the vibrant colors that stole the show: pink, purple, turquoise, vivid and bold like an artist's palette. Sparkles of yellow lights frolicked in between tall blades of grass, skipping off the water's surface. "What is this place?" I asked in awe, spinning in a circle with my head back. There were a few trees whose trunks were so tall it was as if they reached the clouds.

"The Wisps," Dash spoke softly, coming to stand beside me.

"It's beautiful."

"And beauty here is deadly."

In the distance, the rumble of thunder matched my mood. If felt as if we'd been roaming aimlessly and going nowhere. I didn't know how Dash knew what the right direction was. And if a storm was coming, that meant I was going to get wet.

Lightning struck across the sky in a bolt of blue, and I lifted my hand, mesmerized by the enchanting display. It struck again, but this time, something strange happened. The lightning didn't just strike in a flash and disappear. It came directly at me, and I thought for sure the spear was going to hit me, but it did something outlandish instead. The power of light encompassed me in a circle, static electricity humming all around me.

I stood in the center of an electric storm dumbfounded and in awe at the same time. It didn't make sense, but this time it hadn't been an accident. I had done this, summoned a bolt of lightning from the sky.

Once was a happenstance, but twice within forty-eight hours was no coincidence.

My entire body was charged, and the hairs on my arms were standing up. Reaching out with my hand, I touched the patterns of current dancing around me. The light bent around my hand, traveling up my arm like a ribbon.

Dash regarded me strangely. "Charlotte? Are you okay?"

"I-I think so," I said, gaping down at my hands and backing away from Dash. If he got too close, I might accidently hurt him. And that would be bad. I needed him.

Dash took a step forward.

"Don't touch me!" I hissed, retreating and throwing up a hand to warn him from coming any closer. Big mistake. Like an extension of my hand, the lightning burst from my fingertips, zapping across the forest in a javelin of light. Lucky for Dash, my aim was utterly horrible. It bypassed him, hitting a tree. *Kaboom!* The halo of light struck, cracking the trunk down the middle and dissipating with the impact.

I stood, feet planted, with my jaw on the ground and an expression of disbelief on my face. What. In. The. Hell.

"Charlotte," Dash spoke softly. "It's okay. This is normal ... probably."

"Normal?" I shrilled, my eyes slamming into his. "How can pulling lightning from the sky and hurling it across the woods be normal?"

He ran a hand through his hair. "Okay, it might not seem like it yet, but in Starling Heights, normal doesn't exist."

"So the mist gave me the ability to manipulate lightning?"

"Seems like it," he drawled.

"I guess there is worse abilities I could have been given."

"You have no idea," he muttered.

I bit my lip. "I don't even know how I did it."

"You'll learn," he assured. "But I think your eye color has something to do with it."

I angled my head to the side, still staring at the charred spots on the fallen tree. "How so?"

"The color turned again when you, uh, did that thing. They were bright purple, and. ..."

"And what?" I prompted impatiently.

"I can't be certain. It happened so quickly, but I think they were glowing. And before you get your panties in a wad, glowing eyes is a pretty common occurrence nowadays."

Dread settled like a cannonball in the pit of my belly, heavy and explosive. I struggled to keep my composure. There were about a million and one emotions coursing through me. I didn't know how I felt about this new development. Did I even want to learn to control it? "Is it possible to suppress the … gift?" I recalled Dash calling them a curse.

"Anything is possible, but whether you want the gift or not, it has a way of making itself known. Take it from my personal experience."

I still had no idea what Dash's curse was, but the truth of his words rang true inside me. The aftereffects of the lightning buzzed through my veins like a drug. One taste and I was ready for more. It scared me. "Wonderful, so at any time, I could electrocute someone or myself."

"Pretty much, Freckles. Kind of cool." He grinned.

I rolled my eyes. He just earned a few kiss-ass points. The dimples helped, and I'll be damned if he didn't know how to use them when it was convenient. "You know what I think?"

"You're going to tell me whether I want you to or not. So go for it."

I straightened my spine, hiking the bag higher on my shoulder. "I think you're mental."

His grin turned part sinister. "Glad we got that out of the way. You better believe I am taking shelter during the next storm. I don't want to risk being zapped."

I glared at his back, contemplating zapping him now.

We left the Wisps behind, and I was sad to see it go. It had been the only real beauty I'd seen here. I was a hundred percent sure the Plains of Despair were going to live up to their name.

One of the first things I noticed as the woods gradually began to dwindle was the change in temperature. In the woods, there had been a cool breeze, but that died, making the air warmer.

What I found most noticeable was the landscape. The lush and vibrant colors of the trees gave way to barren branches, dried and thirsty. The whole place looked like it could use a torrential downpour. Occasionally we'd pass a tree with leaves that looked like they were made of silver metal, similar to the color of Dash's eyes.

I cringed. Did everything I see somehow have to remind me of him?

Curious, and not really thinking about what I was doing, I lifted my hand as we passed under one of those silver trees. I ran my finger along a leaf, expecting it to be smooth and waxy. It was neither.

"Ouch!" I yelped.

Dash whirled around. "What?"

I sucked on my finger, trying to ease the pain. "That thing just cut me." I held out my hand, showing him the drops of blood pooling at the end of my finger. It wasn't a deep wound, but thin like a paper cut.

He had the sleeves of his shirt rolled up. "You touched the tree."

So what if I did? "I was curious. I didn't think it was going to assault me."

"You remember the saying, 'Curiosity killed the cat'?"

I gave him a dull glare. "I remember the phrase, 'Silence is the best reply to a fool.' "

His lips twitched. "I think you'll live."

"You never know here," I said, frowning and glancing around. The Plains of Despair were definitely living up to their reputation.

He scratched his jaw. "At least you're catching on. Come on, we need to keep moving. The sun is going to be up soon."

I could already see soft rays of amber and rose cresting over the horizon.

Dash's eyes moved upward, following my gaze. "It's going to be a scorcher today ... and every day as long as we are within the boundaries of the plains."

My eyes were drawn skyward, seeing streaks of cheerful sunbeams setting the sandy floor to flame. "I could use a little sun," I replied, thinking how pale my skin was after being tucked away inside for so long.

Dash snickered. "You've never felt heat like this. It can fry a chicken."

"Swell, I love this place already."

As the sun inched its way higher and we went farther into the plains, frustration prickled at my skin like a heat rash. "Is there no other way to travel in this godforsaken land?"

"Depends," he mused. "If you can tame a horsea, they might grant you permission. Of course, inside the walls of the white city there are refurbished recreation vehicles, but nothing that runs on gas. Petroleum hasn't been discovered here, not yet."

Sweat dotted my brows. Tendrils of red hair clung to my neck. My legs were achy. Blisters covered my feet, and I was pretty sure there was a waterfall of perspiration dripping between my breasts. I didn't bother asking what a horsea was, because I was sure I didn't want to know.

The day dragged on, making the air sticky and humid from the glare of heat. A bug of sorts landed on the tip of my nose, and I went cross-eyed looking at it. The desert-like temperature, the never-ending trek, and being hangry all soured my mood. I was close to either throwing myself over a cliff or slapping the dog shit out of someone.

Dash must have picked up on my weariness. "We need to find shelter before this heat kills us."

I didn't even bother asking if that was a thing. "Please tell me we're not looking for another cave."

"Uh, not precisely, but I doubt you'll find our accommodations any less appealing." His eyes scanned the area, several dark waves falling across his forehead. "Okay, stay here. I am going to check to see if the road is clear. This is usually the time when the Night's Guard start making their rounds."

"You're leaving me alone? Do I need to remind you what happened last time?"

"Freckles, this time, don't wander," he said, walking backwards with a twist to his lips.

I pulled out my bottle of water and pulled a swig. "Douchebag," I grumbled as he darted between the trees. I should follow him just to piss him off. Maybe it would be the last time he left me behind.

He *was* coming back? Right?

Déjà vu smacked into me, causing my heart to jackhammer. Only a complete asshat would drag me all the way out to the desert and leave me. Dash might be a jerk at times, but I had to believe he wasn't cruel.

After a few calming breaths, I shifted uncomfortably. This time it wasn't an abandonment issue. Instead, I got this feeling that wormed inside me of being watched, yet I stared down the empty path. No sign of life. Nothing but sand, tumbleweeds, and barren trees. Maybe it was my own delusional imagination, but I kept thinking, *I'm in the Plains of Despair. Disaster is its name.*

Stop being paranoid, I told myself.

The air became eerily quiet, like the calm before a storm. I leaned back against a bare tree and shivered, despite the hundred degree temp. Goosebumps covered my arms.

No joke, I wasn't alone.

I craned my neck upward, peering at the branches over my head. An enormous black bird was perched on the tip of the tree. His head angled from side to side, watching me with golden eyes the color of whiskey.

He was regal and pretty, perched with his head held high, regarding me with mirrored intrigue. His feathers glistened like raindrops after a storm.

Mesmerized by the way he watched me, I didn't notice the other danger that creeped around me, not until it was too late and it coiled around my arm like a python.

Chapter Nine

Fear rose in me like thin smoke. "Let go!" I screamed, jerking my arm free and trying to run before that *thing* caught me again. The *thing* being the tree. I was sure it had some epic name, but *thing* was the best I could come up with under pressure.

Its branches became arms, twirling and lashing in the air toward me. Instinct fired inside. Whipping out my blade, I slashed in the air the next time it reached for me, just barely nicking it, but giving me a window to escape. I whirled around, tensed to bolt, and bumped into Dash. His chest was firm. Too firm. Colliding into him rattled more than my brain cells.

His hands steadied me, on either side of my shoulders, but his silver eyes were zeroed in on the *thing*. "What are you, a magnet for every beast and creature out here? Put that thing away before you hurt yourself."

I wanted to tell him this was his fault for leaving me alone … again. But that *thing* was still after me. It managed to wind its limbs around my ankle, twining up my calf. "Are you just going to stand there? Do something!" I shrieked, shaking my leg to no avail.

Dash sighed. "Duck."

I pouted my sullen lips, unfazed by his tone. "Huh?"

"Get on the ground. Now," he hissed through his teeth, grabbing my blade.

I hit the deck, flattening myself in the sand and dug my heels in. My resistance did very little to keep the *thing* from dragging me, and I cursed Dash under my breath. "What are you waiting —?"

My blade whizzed over my head—so close, the rush of air whizzed over my face—before embedding itself into the base of the tree. A heinous sound screeched, piercing the air in decimals that could shatter glass. My body tensed, willing the horrible sound to stop.

And then it did.

I let a sweet sigh of relief. There was definitely going to be some eardrum damage.

Dash's lips moved, but I heard nothing.

"What?" I hollered above the buzzing in my ears.

He bent down at the knees and repeated, "I asked if you were okay."

Don't even get me started. I sat up, my gaze landing on his. "You could have killed me." The branches from the tree were no longer slapping in the air, but lying limp on the ground, shriveled and curled inward, as if the tree was hugging itself.

"You were never in danger." He held out his hands.

I placed both of mine in his, my skin tingling where our hands connected. Irritation snapped. "Are you kidding me?" I broke the contact as soon as I was on my feet.

Dash rocked back on his heels. "You're still alive, aren't you?"

My gaze narrowed. "How did you do that? Throw the blade like Rambo?"

He walked to the shriveled tree and yanked out my knife. "It's not rocket science. I aim and throw." Twirling it up in the air, he caught it by the hilt before offering it back to me.

I very much doubted that. His throw had been precise with hardly any aim. He literally picked up the blade and tossed it. The more I thought about it, the more I was sure he hadn't even been looking at the tree, but at me. Though it all had happened so fast. Whatever. And to think I believed him when he said he wouldn't lie to me. I took the blade and tucked it back against my thigh. "Did you at least find us somewhere to rest?"

The corner of his lips twitched up. "How do you feel about tree houses?"

"After what just happened ... not too comfortable."

"Well, Freckles, you got about a two-minute hike to get comfortable."

I grumbled and dragged my feet in the sand the entire two minutes. We arrived at the tree, another giant oak. I eyed it warily. If this thing even so much as twitched, I was out of here.

After eyeballing it for a good minute, I stood at the base of the trunk, wondering just how Dash classified this as a tree house. It was missing one of the key elements—the house.

All I saw was a truly tall tree draped in moss and vines. The air around it shimmered from the heat, making me think I was seeing things. Or not seeing things. "Where is this tree house you speak of?"

His answer was a wicked grin that never failed to give me those warm fuzzies, and I was so awestruck by his dimples, I almost missed the vines peeling away. They revealed a narrow opening into the tree, tangled roots supplying a floor.

"This is your idea of a tree house?" I mumbled, following Dash into the small doorway. As we stepped through, I looked over my shoulder, watching the vines knit back together, hiding the entrance and providing safety.

"The land here can be unforgiving, but you'll find it can also be an ally."

I ran my fingers along the bumpy bark, and I swore the tree purred. "You talk about it as if it has feelings."

"You'd be surprised," Dash replied, taking my hand as we climbed deeper into the tree, defying logic.

How could the trunk of the tree be so expansive? And if I wasn't mistaken, we were going up. At the top, the branches had woven together to make two hammock-like beds. "What is this place?"

"It's a hideout, only available to those the tree deems worthy of its safety."

"How do you know about it?"

He shrugged. "I've passed through before and heard the rumors. Turns out the rumors are true."

I rolled my eyes.

"Pick a bunk, Freckles. Relax, sleep, eat. By nightfall, we'll be back on the road, and the real fun begins," Dash said, hanging his bag on one of the branches.

Testing the weight of the twigs, I sat and sighed. It was amazing to get off my feet, yet slightly discouraging. I didn't know what I expected from this journey, but the slow pace was disheartening. I wanted to find my family, and it was beginning to set in that it might take me days, weeks even to do that. Or my worst fear: longer.

"I've seen that look before. It's why I travel alone."

Above my head, the branches came together in a canopy that blocked most of the sun. "Are you going to tell me it gets easier?"

He spread out in the other hammock, looping his hands behind his head. "No. I won't lie to you."

I respected that, admired it even. Still, it didn't make me feel better.

"There are holding houses scattered everywhere. And the disappointment after each can be crippling. I want you to be prepared," he cautioned.

"When does the thought of sleep no longer send your mind into a frenzy?"

The usually cynical lines around his eyes softened. "As soon as the reality sets in that this is now your life."

I shifted my head to be cozier on my hands. "I remember being at the park with friends, one of my favorite places in the city. We were sitting on a bench talking about starting our junior year and how great high school was going to be. There were swans swimming in the misty green pond, surrounded by towering pine trees. I remember kicking the fallen pinecones as we walked around the trails laughing."

The memory was so clear, as if I was living it now. "Sometimes I can't decide if I'm afraid to sleep because

I might not wake up or because I won't wake up from this nightmare."

"At least you have your memories," he mumbled, voice growing heavy with exhaustion.

"You don't remember anything?" I asked, prodding.

"Not the important stuff, like details. I remember faces: my mom and my little brother, even the asshole father who walked out us when I was ten. Tell me, how I can recall his face, a man I haven't seen since the day he left, but I can't drum up my own name?" Anger. It was there, among other emotions buried deep, but anger was at the top of the heap.

"A name isn't everything," I replied softly.

"It sure would be damn helpful when I'm scanning the list of names, hoping one of them will click. Both my mom and little brother could be out there and I wouldn't know, not without seeing their faces."

So that's who he was looking for—just like me.

I flipped my head to the side, toward him, to say something else, but similar to the first night, Dash was able to fall asleep within moments, his chest rising and falling in even movements. I, on the other hand, lay fully awake, staring at him. It was becoming a problem.

Sighing, I dragged my eyes from his flawless face, refusing to spend my downtime gawking at him constantly. I gazed at the intricate canopy of branches.

A short while later, the sound of wings flapping disturbed the silence, and a huge black bird soared down from the sky, landing on a branch just above my head. It eyed me with cautious golden eyes, turning his head from side to side thoughtfully, very much like a raven, but there was something ethereal about his wings. I didn't claim to be a bird expert, but I'd seen this guy earlier today before the *thing* attacked me.

Afraid to scare him off, I stayed still, only admiring. "You're beautiful," I whispered. "Unlike most of the creatures I've encountered."

He lifted his head proudly, and then he spoke. "I am quite dashing," he said in a distinguished voice.

My gaze darted back and forth, thinking this had to be a trick. "D-did you just talk?" I stammered.

"Unless the dark hunter is playing games with you."

"You mean Dash?" I asked softly.

"I refuse to utter the barbarian's name," he squawked, sounding outraged.

"But you're a bird," I blurted dumbly. In my defense, animals didn't talk, unless you were Snow White.

"I'm more than just a bird, human; I'm a blinken, to be precise."

"How is this possible?" I mumbled, scratching my head and sitting up.

The blinken hopped down a few branches so we were nose to beak. "Have you ever seen a parrot before? If memory serves, those colorful feathered friends spoke to humans."

I gaped at him. "I guess." He had a point. I forced myself to take a breath and calm down. Dash was still dozing quietly beside me.

The bird opened and closed his claws on the branch. "Well, there you go. Not so hard to believe."

Charlotte, stranger things have happened than holding a conversation with a bird. Occasionally, I talked in my head, usually when I was nervous or freaked out. I was both now. "Do you have a name?"

The bird stretched its wings before settling the black feathers against his body. "Blink."

"Creative," I muttered. The word spilled from my mouth before I thought about the bird, Blink, pecking my eyeballs out. I glanced up, attempting to judge if I had offended him. Did birds understand sarcasm?

"You're the girl the woods are buzzing about."

"Uh, I am?"

He twitched his tail feather. "Are you the one who plucked lightning from the sky?" he asked in a patronizing tone.

Blink was a bird with a dose of attitude. I wasn't sure I should be telling this creature anything. If word of what I could do got to the Institute, I wasn't naïve enough to think they'd leave me alone. Already I'd broken protocol. The Institute was supposed to screen each person after waking from the slumber. I had sort of skipped that process, and many others, I'm sure. "I don't see why that's important."

"I've never seen eyes like yours. You can hide from the humans, girl, but you can't hide from the land."

What did that mean? "My name's Charlotte."

"Ooooh, the princess remembers her name. You are much smarter than most humans already."

"What do you want?"

He fixed me with an unblinking stare, making the gold of his eyes shine. "I was sent to see what you were about."

"Sent by who?" I contemplated giving Dash one good kick. Was this bird harmful? Was he like all the other atrocious creatures occupying the lands?

"There is no need to wake the dark hunter. I got what I came for."

"And what was that?" I hissed, confused. I had admitted to nothing, but like everything here, the laws of nature no longer applied.

Dash rolled in his sleep, shifting so he faced me.

"Until next time, Charlotte. And do try to stay alive. I might like you yet." Regal wings spread wide; he took flight, and with a ripple of onyx, he vanished.

Something about his departure caused my skin to prickle.

I slept very little. There were a number of things to blame: the time of day, the unexpected visit from Blink, the fear to close my eyes and not wake up for another hundred years. Sleep was what my body needed, but without the aid of drugs or alcohol, my mind refused to shut down.

Eventually, it was going to catch up with me.

I must've dozed for an hour or so. When I opened my eyes, night had drifted in, dotted with millions and millions of stars sprinkling the sky. It was magnificent. Light spilled out of the stars like liquid silver, the wind whistling in an inviting song. I couldn't remember the last time I took a moment to appreciate the beauty nature offered. In my life before, I'd always been too busy with friends, school, shopping, boy gazing, cheerleading, and life in general, but never did I stop and appreciate what was right in front of me.

"It's breathtaking, isn't it?" a smooth and mellow voice whispered.

I tilted my head to the side, finding Dash looking at me. My skin flushed, and it wasn't from the heat. The look he gave was downright menacing and rattled my composure. He made me feel as if he wasn't talking about the sky, and when he flashed me those dimples, my brain went to mush.

Damn him.

My throat went dry. I don't know how long I lay gaping at him, but it had definitely been an awkward amount of time. The air thickened between us, sparking with a tension I didn't want to acknowledge. *You are not going to fall for him, Charlotte. You're too smart to be one of those girls who fall prey to the charm of Dash Darhk.*

"You're utterly distracting. I can't afford to be sidetracked," he said, sitting up and running a hand through his tousled hair.

I was distracting? Me! Was he kidding? I spent half the time thinking there was a chemical imbalance in my body. Every time he was near, my insides went haywire. The distraction was all him, and his swoon-worthy dimples.

If he would stop giving me those come-get-me glances, I wouldn't be left weak in the knees half the time. I'd never met anyone who gave more mixed signals than Dash did. He liked me. He hated me. He thought I was a nuisance. He thought I was distracting. Which was it?

He wrapped a finger around the end of my hair, the back of his hand brushing against my neck. "We should go," he said, tugging on the strand before pushing to his feet and making the trek down the tree trunk.

Whatever air was left in my lungs expelled in an unsteady rush. I shook my head and gathered my bag, tossing it over my shoulder. I wasn't sure how much longer I could lie to myself and resist Dash's wily charms.

The holding house was a stone structure able to withstand the harsh elements. Even though I'd woken up in a similar facility just days ago, things had been so hectic, I hadn't seen what the building looked like. There was nothing fancy or special about the place sheltering the last of the human race. If you really thought about it, it was kind of messed up. These holding houses were supposed to protect the extinction of mankind. Maybe they were made up of some kind of advanced material to withstand the mist, but to the eye, it looked like nothing more than a concrete shelter.

We had waited in the bushes for the Night's Guard to finish their rounds at this specific location. Propped against the outside wall, I scratched at my arm. The last thing I needed was to contract poison ivy here. I waited as Dash worked his magic on the lock. They were secured buildings, but not tight enough to keep Dash Darhk out. Within a minute, the lock clicked, followed by a series of beeps and green flashing lights.

"Voilà," he said, bumping the door with his hip and sweeping his arm out, giving me the okay to enter.

"If you're trying to impress me, it's going to take more than an amateur trick."

He smirked. "I knew you were a tough cookie. Good thing we have plenty of time. I'm bound to amaze you at some point."

I stepped inside, my boots hitting the concrete. *Clap. Clap. Clap.* The sound bounced off the corridor walls, echoing in a lonely chorus. The air had a stale smell—not death, but desolate. The bodies here had no idea what they were in store for.

It was all still fresh for me. The changes. The impossibilities. The hopelessness.

"You don't have to do this," Dash said. He had come to stand beside me while I had gone paralyzed in a flashback.

I blinked. "Yes, I do. There's no going back."

He nodded. "Okay. The guards post a list at each station of those who have already been identified and regained consciousness. It isn't always an accurate list because not everyone will regain his or her memories. We'll check the list, and then quickly make our rounds. We have approximately thirty minutes before the goons show back up."

"What are we waiting for?"

His lips curled. "After you, Freckles."

To the right of the door was a sheet stuck on the wall. I trailed a finger down the list of names, scanning for Winston, and felt the first tinge of discouragement. Baron, Peterson, Smith, and blah, blah, blah, but there was no one with my last name on the list.

"On to phase two," Dash mumbled, his boots clanking on the floor.

Systematically, Dash strutted down the halls, glancing at each of the nameless faces. "How many holding houses have you been to?" I asked, passing a woman with cinnamon hair like my mom's. My heart pounded as I moved to get a closer look, and just as quickly, it plummeted to my feet. She wasn't my mom.

"It sucks every time," Dash said, seeing my crestfallen expression. There was an edge of stiffness to his tone.

I quickly masked my emotions. It was easy to understand how, over time, Dash's heart had hardened to the constant disappointment; the alternative was heartbreak, over and over again. Even the softest of souls would eventually toughen. It was almost cruel.

Wrapping my arms around myself, I tried to chase the chill moving in my veins. Didn't help that this place was a meat locker. "I can handle it," I assured him, stiffening my trembling lip. I refused to give Dash the satisfaction of thinking he was right about me.

I was not a damsel in distress. He would not regret bringing me along, I vowed to myself.

"You might surprise us both," he replied, offering a coy smile as he moved on past me.

"You know, you don't have to be a jerk *all* the time."

He snorted. "*This* is me being nice."

I'd been prepared for disappointment, expected it even, but the rock in my gut was solid and burdensome. My family wasn't here, and seeing all those drugged people left an acidic taste in my mouth. "Is there no way to help them? Force them to wake up?"

"Not unless the Institute is keeping it a secret. Nothing we've done has worked, and if you try to move the bodies before they wake up, a silent alarm goes off, alerting the Night's Guard."

There goes that theory.

We were in and out in less than twenty minutes and back on the road with me dragging my heavy heart behind me. I didn't think I could feel any lonelier than I did at that moment. I kept telling myself things had to get better, get easier, but the problem was, no matter how many times I recited it, I didn't believe it.

The next two days passed in a blur.

And in those days, we hit three more holding houses, each leaving me emptier inside. Dash and I barely said five sentences to each other. I wasn't in the mood to listen to him telling me he had warned me, or how I should have stayed in Hurst to save myself the emotional pain. So I kept my trap shut. He didn't say anything either, but he didn't have to. It was written in every line in his face each time he looked at me.

Which, surprisingly, was often.

Or maybe I only noticed because I couldn't keep my eyes off him.

The longer I traveled, I realized it was like Jumanji out here, a crossbreed of every animal I'd ever seen at the zoo—the good, the bad, and the vicious.

Walking side by side, I remembered Blink, the talking bird. "Is it common for animals to talk?" I asked, breaking our silent streak.

"Only in fairytales," he responded.

I couldn't decide if he was being a smartass or truthful. "So, that's a no."

He glanced oddly at me. "Are you saying you can talk to animals?"

"Uh, no." At least I didn't think so. I was under the impression that it was a blinken thing, not a Charlotte thing. Maybe Dash had never encountered a blinken. I was just about to elaborate when a rustling of leaves sounded behind us. My steps faltered. "Did you hear that?" At first I thought I was just freaking myself out, but then Dash's body stiffened.

He glanced over his shoulder at me, lashes hiding his eyes. Trouble was coming. Suddenly, there were footsteps racing over the ground. It sounded like a stampede. A curse erupted beside me. "We got company."

"Night's Guard?" I guessed.

"A wild boarus."

Right. One of those.

Busting through the trees like a cracked-out linebacker, foaming at the mouth, was an oversized boar. It screeched like a gremlin; damn thing even kind of looked like one. The boarus' skin was tough and green, and its eyes burned red with black slits like a python.

I backed up, automatically moving closer to Dash. "You got a plan?"

"Yeah, dinner. This might be a good time to test your hunting skills."

I could tell by the stiff set of his shoulders, he wasn't kidding. His hand went behind his back, pulling out a bow and a single arrow. He better be a damn good shot. The tusks on that thing meant business.

The boar ground his feet into the sand and let out one long mad squeal as it charged straight for us. My brain stopped working, and instinct kicked in. I whipped out the blade strapped to my thigh, clutching it tightly in my hand. Most people's gut reaction might be to run when being rushed by a wild beast; mine was to defend myself. I needed to learn how to survive here on my own.

Planting my feet, I waited for the boarus to come to me. I sensed Dash at my back, poised to strike if I failed. The heat from the sun glared down on me, making my eyesight just a tad hazy. The next minute happened in a blur. I remembered the boarus' head coming up—pointy husks jutted from its jaw—and a puff of mist blasted the air at my face. I had raised my dagger, going for the exposed belly as it was up on two legs. But somehow I ended up flat on my back staring up at the clouds.

I blinked.

A second later, Dash's face came into focus, a shit-eating grin on his lips. "Don't say it," I hissed through my teeth as a dull ache fired along my spine. The air had been knocked from my lungs and came back in slow bursts.

"Did I fail to mention it spits a venom that knocks out its prey?"

My narrow gaze swung to his face. "As soon as I catch my breath, I'm going to kick you in the balls."

That got me a husky chuckle and a hand up. "I swear, I've never had so much shit happen the entire year I've been awake than I have had in the five days in your company. Christ. You're going to get us both killed."

"How is this my fault?" I spat. I'd actually tried to help. It would have been nice to know the damn thing spit some kind of sleeping venom. And what kind of teacher did that make him?

The pad of his thumb danced along my hand. "Beats me. It just is. Maybe it's your perfume."

The boar lay at my feet, belly up with an arrow sticking out. "I'm not wearing any perfume. And besides, I smell like sweat and musk," I grumbled.

"At least we have dinner." He walked to the boar, pulled out his arrow, and wiped the blood off the tip on his pants.

Gross.

He sheathed the arrow in his pack. "What do you know about skinning an animal, Freckles?"

My face turned green. I was going to hurl. "I don't think I'm hungry anymore."

Dash grabbed the hind legs of our dinner and heaved it onto his shoulders. The muscles on his arms tightened, and I momentarily forgot about the boarus, being bested by the beast, and Dash wanting to flay him up. Dash had pretty impressive arms; it was no wonder why my brain went loopy. Unfortunately, by the time we heard the rustling of feet moving around us, we were surrounded. My mind jumped to all sorts of terrifying conclusions. Another boarus. The Night's Guard. A vampire. Hell, at this point, anything was possible.

Dash froze, dropping the boarus back to the ground. "Nomads," he hissed.

A group of drifters circled us from all sides. "So this isn't the welcome party?" I muttered.

"Hardly," he griped, carefully moving closer to me. "They must have been hunting the boarus."

And they found us instead.

I opened my mouth to ask Dash how he was going to get us out of this mess, when something cool pressed against my neck and the sweat on my brow turned cold.

This couldn't be good.

Chapter Ten

Don't move, Grà," warned a not so friendly voice.

It only took a few seconds for me to understand I had a knife held to my throat. Any sudden movements would draw blood. My blood.

Dash spun around. The bow in his hand was drawn back and aimed just above my head. Anger radiated off him in waves. He was itching to let the arrow fly. Keeping the fear from my face became a strain, especially with the knife held at my throat, but I refused to let this nomad sense I was shaking in my boots.

Besides, my captor smelled like ass, and I found it hard to feel anything with the stench of a swamp permeating off him. They must bathe in their own funk. My nausea came back tenfold.

"So much as twitch and the girl gets it," the stinky douchebag informed us.

Dash's silver eyes hovered over me, glaring at the nomad leader with open disdain. He weighed his options, and I knew the moment he decided to not risk my life. His expression collapsed. "Shit," he breathed, lowering his bow. "If you harm her, I'll kill you," Dash growled, downright evilly.

Wow. I didn't think he cared that much. This was one of those times it was nice to be wrong.

"Is that a threat?" the leader asked, cocking his head to the side.

"Do you know who I am?" Dash prompted.

A humorless chuckle left his lips. "The slayer."

Dash shot him a merciless grin. "Then you know it's a promise."

The nomad shifted his other hand over my belly and yanked me back, securing me deeper in his clutches. "You're trespassing on our territory. Why?" And just in case Dash needed a reason to provide him the answers he sought, the nomad pressed the tip of the blade deeper to my skin.

I felt a sting and winced.

Murder leapt into Dash's eyes. "We're just passing through. I'm looking for someone."

"Aren't we all?" the nomad replied.

If Dash's plan was to taunt our captor, then he was doing a bang-up job being extra dickish. He excelled at it. "Then what is the point of all this?" he argued.

I wanted to tell him to chill, but one of the four nomads surrounding Dash grabbed ahold of his wrist and flipped it over, revealing a black mark on the inside of his arm. A series of three stars, interwoven together, had been branded into his flesh.

Dash sighed, yanking his hand free. "I'm no longer part of the guard."

The nomad didn't seem to believe him. "Don't move," he warned Dash. Lowering the blade at my back, he grabbed my wrist and spun me around. My breath was coming out in quick pants. I was finally able to see his face. His skin was bronze, darkening the color of his mahogany eyes. I had pictured someone younger from the sound of his voice, not that he was extremely old, somewhere around my father's age maybe. His black hair was secured in a man bun. There was gunk smeared under his eyes and down along his defined cheekbones.

Guess that could be what the smell was.

"You don't really believe that, do you? The Institute never releases one of its own," the nomad leader fired back. "And besides, this one intrigues me." He clutched my chin between his fingers, staring at my face. "There is something about her eyes. ..."

I was tired of being manhandled, so I did the first thing that popped in my head, I spit in his face before jerking my chin out of his grip. "If you don't let go of me, I'm going to string you up by your nuts and hang you out to dry."

The leader threw his head back and laughed. "See what I mean? There is spirit inside her and strength—qualities a woman needs to survive the Badlands."

His comrades chuckled and nodded their heads in agreement.

I didn't like the nomad's implication. There was something brewing behind his dark eyes, something that spelled t-r-o-u-b-l-e.

Dash's scowl deepened. The next thing I knew, Dash flicked up his arm at the elbow, fist clenched, hitting one of the sneering nomads in the nose. *Crunch.*

Blood burst from his nostrils, running down over his mouth.

"Why did you have to go and do that? We were just starting to get along." My detainer's hand snaked up into my hair and grasped a handful, jerking me back. The blade once again pressed to my skin—my cheek this time. "You better tell your boyfriend to behave."

I shrieked, tears of sharp pain stinging my eyes.

Dash held up his hands and backed off, but I could see the desire for blood blazing in his glare. "I wasn't kidding when I said I would kill you."

The guy Dash had decked spit a mouthful of blood before taking a cheap shot at Dash. He planted his fist into his gut. Dash barely made a sound, and I found his lack of emotion frightening.

"You're quite the killer, aren't you?" the nomad prompted. "Isn't that why the Institute is so interested in you, Dash Darhk?"

My hand itched to wrap around a very unladylike place and twist.

The nomad leader must have sensed my edginess. "Move," he ordered, pushing me forward. I thought Dash growled, but there was nothing either of us could do.

The nomads herded us through the desert. Not that I was allowed much personal space. The stinky pig kept my arms cuffed in his grasp as the band of misfits led us to God knew where.

I dragged my feet, testing his restraint. "Where are you taking us?"

A wry grin appeared on his dirty face. "You'll see, Grà."

"Stop calling me that," I hissed.
He just chuckled.

The longer we walked on foot, the more time my mind had to come up with gruesome situations. Rape. Torture. Murder. I didn't know what their agenda was, and the unknown that waited for me was feeding my fear. "I'm not going anywhere with you," I seethed, struggling to loosen his grasp.

His fingers dug into my skin, and I grimaced.

"Freckles, you're going to hurt yourself," Dash said evenly.

I shot him a cold glare. A lot of help he was being. How was he so calm, especially when I was freaking out inside?

It didn't seem fair.

After several unsuccessful attempts that only made trekking it through the desert difficult, we came upon a sand tunnel that hadn't been there a minute ago. I blinked and glanced around to see if anyone else found that odd. Nope. Just me.

Following the tunnel—a maze of twists and turns—it finally ended with a curtain of thorny, dry vines, opening up into a vast clearing of a hidden village. Tents were strung up in rows like a suburban cookie cutter neighborhood—all the same, just lacking the white picket fences and manicured yards. A few heads turned our way, checking out the commotion, but for the most part, everyone went about their daily business.

There was a lady carrying a bucket of water, and a group of children playing with wooden blocks. It all seemed … normal.

Good to know it was a common sight to see their leader bringing home hostages. It gave me no hope they would help us escape.

"Nice place you got here," Dash said dryly.

I tried unsuccessfully to keep the smirk off my lips.

"My daughter is a cloaker. It keeps us off the Institute's radar," the nomad offered—the first piece of insightful information we'd gotten on this expedition.

"Clever," Dash said, actually impressed.

What was going on here? Fraternizing with the enemy? I got that they had a common adversary in the Institute, but anyone who kidnaps me automatically gets put on my shit list.

We had come to the center of the camp, and our little group disbanded, dropping our bags on the ground and leaving Dash and me with the big chief. "Is she yours?" the nomadic leader asked Dash as his eyes roamed over me.

Ick. Gross.

"No, I'm not," I said swiftly.

"Yes, she is," Dash rapidly replied at the same time.

I glared at him. What was he up to?

The crooked teeth leader grinned. And then I remembered Dash mentioning something about the tribes rebelling against the Institute and how they abide by their own rules. My mind ran with a million different scenarios, all bad.

Dash and I exchanged looks.

"Yes," I said, changing my mind.

"No," the doofus said in unison with me.

OMG. We were so dead.

The nomad's grin spread. He enjoyed watching us dig ourselves into a hole. "There seems to be a little confusion. Is she, or isn't she, yours, slayer?"

Apparently, in this tribe, women were possessions. This time, Dash flicked me a pointed look. He wanted me to keep my mouth shut. "What's it to you?" He crossed his arms over his broad chest, not a single bone in his body intimidated by our situation.

The same couldn't be said about me. I was somewhere between bawling my eyes out or going berserk. It was a toss-up.

"My name is Brunlak, and it is my responsibility to ensure my son has a future. He needs a woman," he informed us.

I gulped. And this nomad thought I would make a good woman for his son? Ha. He had another thing coming. Talk about caveman. Me. Want. Woman. If he tried to drag me off by my hair, I was going to lose my shit.

Dash glowered, and the muscle along his neck pulsed. "Your son would be better off with someone else. This one is too much trouble."

Brunlak only seemed more intrigued. "She is spirited, no?"

Hell yes, I was. He didn't know the half of it. And if he kept talking about me as if I didn't have my own mind, I was going to show him just how *spirited* I could be. Brunlak wouldn't be having any more sons—that was for sure.

A glint entered Dash's gray eyes as if he could read my mind. "I guess you could call her that. Although I have a few other choice words; she has proven to be far more troublesome than she is worth."

I kicked Dash in the shin. The nerve of him. I should have stood there quietly with a sweet smile plastered on my face, but it was a kneejerk reaction. *Why doesn't he just hand me over now to the chump?* It was no secret he hadn't wanted me trailing along. Here was an easy way to get rid of me.

Dash's eyes narrowed.

I tapped my foot, back rigid, and gave him the stink eye.

The leader rumbled low in his chest at Dash's implication. "This one has a mind of her own. Good. She will do well in my tribe."

Shit.

That got my attention and Dash's too. Ruthlessness darkened his eyes like granite. "I think you misunderstood. She isn't available. Like I said, she's mine." He stepped in front of me, and there was no doubting the menace lacing his tone. He meant business.

I exhaled. Dash wasn't going to throw me to the dogs. If he wasn't such an asshat half of the time, I'd kiss him right now.

He moved protectively in front of me in case the nomad hadn't gotten the message.

Brunlak eyed him, weighing his options. "It's a pity. She would have made a great wife for my son. There is a warrior's heart in this one."

I choked. Wife? I wasn't even eighteen. Well, if you didn't count the hundred years I'd been dozing.

The arrogant half smile I was beginning to dislike tipped the corners of Dash's lips. "There's no arguing that."

He was lucky I didn't kick him again.

"Still, you don't act like lovers," Brunlak insisted, crossing a leg and leaning back against a wooden pole holding up a tent. Doubt lined every inch of his face.

Damn, he was persistent and perceptive. Dash and I weren't anything. We were barely friends, but I had a feeling I better start acting like Dash hung the moon, or I was going to find myself in an unwanted situation.

Dash slipped a hand around my waist, taking the nomad's resistance as a challenge. I willed my face blank, regardless of the fact that my heart thudded as

Dash pulled me closer to him. Blood rushed to every point in my body. "What are you doing?" I hissed through my teeth.

His head dipped, brushing just past my cheek. "Giving him what he wants. Kiss me," he whispered in my ear.

"What?" I muttered, lost in the sensation of his breath on my skin.

"You heard me. Now kiss me like you mean it." He traced the line of my jaw with his words.

This absurd discussion no longer became about my safety but telling Dash no out of spite. I wasn't sure a girl had ever refused him anything. Well, universe, I was about to be the first. The consequences at the moment didn't seem to matter. No one demanded I kiss him. And if we kissed … no way was I going to have to pretend. The tension between us was enough to tell me we would light the sheets on fire, but it didn't mean I jumped when he said, "Kiss me." Where was the romance in that? "I'm not going to kiss you, Dash. In your dreams—"

Dash kissed me.

Chapter Eleven

He swooped in, taking possession of my lips, and I stopped thinking. Excitement dazzled inside me, like the lights of a disco ball. And just like that, the desert, Brunlak, the little village, all faded around me, and there was no one else but him. I stepped forward, closing the space between us and pressed against the length of him. My fingers dug into his hair, keeping his lips right where I wanted them—on me. His hair was silky and soft, like his lips.

He shuddered, and there were fireworks of emotions sparking off inside me. Thrilling. Scary. Urgent. But one of them I hadn't expected was familiarity. It was as if we'd done this before—kiss.

His hand came up and tangled in my hair, the other at the small of my back. His tongue pressed between my lips, and he received no resistance from me. The moment our tongues danced, little shivers skipped down my spine.

I moaned, and the soft sound was swallowed by his kiss.

Separating our lips, he touched his forehead gently to mine. "I've never wanted to be alone with someone so much in my life."

Then why weren't his lips still on mine? I stared into his clouded eyes, caught up in the storm. As the seconds ticked by, clarity swept through my muddled brain, but it only left me more confused. "Why did you do that?" I breathed, stumbling toward him. My balance was off-kilter.

His eyes flared as his hands slipped to my waist, steadying me. "Because I'm saving your butt. Again."

If he wanted a thank you, my mind was too jumbled to form the words. Had that been real or an act for my benefit? I was positive I hadn't imagined him telling me he wanted me alone. My head was starting to hurt.

"Did you enjoy the show?" Dash snarled, his entire body tight.

The nomad's amber eyes narrowed thoughtfully, judging how sincere our little display of PDA had been. "You proved your point, slayer. It would be a pity if anything happened to you."

I didn't like the look on his face or the threat on Dash's life. Although he appeared satisfied, there was something sinister lurking behind his eyes. I didn't trust Brunlak and neither did Dash.

"I'm pretty hard to kill. Are you going to tell me why you've brought us here?" Dash asked.

"The safety of my people comes first. Once I am satisfied this isn't a ruse and you haven't led the Night's Guard to my doorstep, you're free to go."

My stomach twisted. "How long will that take?" I wanted to find my family. Each day that went by left me more anxious.

He shrugged, cocksure now that we were in the confines of his domain. "Time isn't important. Why don't I show you your accommodations? I think you'll find our little community quite homey, if you don't mind the heat," he said with a smile, in a sad attempt at a joke.

"We just can't leave the confines of your compound," Dash muttered.

Although we were no longer outnumbered and he wasn't holding a blade to my throat, I refused to let my guard down. "I don't get it. You're pissed because we encroached on your territory?"

Dash squeezed my hip.

I ignored him. Just because we shared a few mind-blowing kisses didn't mean he was the boss of me.

"You have much to learn, Grà. There have been whispers trickling down from the white city. The Institute has doubled their security."

Dash found this information enlightening. "Twenty-four hours," he conceded. "After that, I find my own way out of here, and I will take out anyone in my way. That's a promise. Oh, and Freckles here, she stays with me."

My head whipped around so fast. I figured he'd be dying to get rid of me for a night or two.

"No harm will come to her," Brunlak maintained.

"All the same, I'm not letting her out of my sight or this tribe will be minus a leader," Dash threatened, his voice dipping into dangerous levels.

Dash's unrelenting protection of me amused the nomad leader. "As you wish."

Brunlak ushered us through the camp. No one said anything as we passed, but they had friendly expressions of interest. They didn't seem to be savage but people trying to pick up the pieces, make a new life. Brunlak stopped just outside the watchtower, where a guard was stationed. I was sure it was a tactical move. He wanted us watched day and night.

Oh, goodie.

Dash kept a rueful eye on the guard as I meandered into the covered tarp. My first thought was: *Will I ever see a bedroom with four walls and a mattress again?*

I sighed.

"What? Not the Caesars Palace?" Dash sneered, coming in behind me.

Once again we were in close quarters with the scent of him tantalizing my senses, reminding me how incredible it had felt to be in his arms. My body instantly reacted, humming, which in turn got under my skin. I spun around and glared. "Don't ever do that again!"

"Which part? Save your ass?"

"Kiss me."

Dash's eyes surveyed the circular space. "It was the only way. Brunlak sees something in you. Power. And he wants you to marry his son, to use you as an ally against the Institute. I needed him and everyone here to know that no one is to touch you."

"How the heck did you get all of that?"

His lips twitched. "I'm perceptive."

I rolled my eyes. "What do you care what happens to me?"

"I don't."

"Of course not. That would require you to have feelings." I crossed my arms. Suddenly, sleeping in the same quarters as Dash no longer seemed like a fantasy but a setup for me to do something utterly stupid and reckless, like jump him in the middle of the night.

"Precisely," he agreed, eyes still scanning the tent for who knows what. There was nothing in here but a pile of blankets and a guard outside our door.

"It's a good thing. A relationship between us would never work," I said, pretending the air between us wasn't charged. It was only a matter of time before one of us got electrocuted.

"And why is that?" he asked.

My eyes dropped to his poetic lips, and I berated my weakness. "Because I'm allergic to assholes."

"I just saved your butt back there ... unless you want to marry his son? Go right ahead. You have my blessing. I'll even stay to attend the ceremony."

"You're such a jerk," I spat.

He arched a brow. "A thank you would have been nice."

"Thanks!" I yelled. Dash was a douchebag of the highest order.

"I'm going to check the perimeter; see if there is a way out of this place without setting off any alarm bells. Stay put," he muttered.

"You can't leave," I reminded him.

"Watch me." He slipped out of the tent, and a few seconds later a scuffle was followed by a thump.

Biting my nails, I gave in and snuck a peek outside. Dash was dragging the unconscious guard behind our tent. "Just great," I muttered.

If he got himself killed, I was going to be so pissed.

Flopping on a pile of blankets, I closed my eyes and let out a long exhale, intending only to relax for a few minutes while Dash played James Bond. What a freaking day! I didn't entirely understand what was going on or why Dash thought Brunlak had nefarious intentions about a gift I didn't know how to control. It made no sense. How would Brunlak even know what I could do? The question ran through my head on repeat as I dozed off.

I opened my eyes and found I wasn't alone.

The intruder wore a lacy halter that defied gravity and a colorful peasant skirt flowing to her feet. She had glossy, chestnut hair tied into two loose braids. There was something almost pixie-like about her features—dainty and soft.

Sitting up, I rubbed at my eyes. She was definitely real and not much older than me. My gaze looked left and right, scanning for trouble. Dash hadn't returned, and my worry radar went up ten notches.

Did the idiot get caught? Were they stringing him up by his feet? Was he rotting away in the desert?

"I didn't mean to wake you," she said in a voice that was sweet and charming. I detected a tinge of a southern accent.

"It's okay," I assured her, clearing the frogginess from my throat and keeping my fears for Dash under lock and key.

She stepped farther into the tent. "I hope I didn't startle you. It's not every day a gal close to my age strolls into the Badlands."

"I just bet," I mumbled, running my fingers through my rumpled hair. It was hopeless.

In the sunlight streaming from the opening of the tent, her hair had a russet sheen to it that I envied—pretty. Mine looked like the juice of a maraschino cherry—frightening. She smiled. "I'm Vee. I was warned that you had the tongue of a viper."

"Who do I have to thank for such a high compliment?"

She flashed me her hundred-watt smile. "My father."

I paused. "You're Brunlak's daughter."

"You sound surprised."

My first impression of my capturer's offspring was she was too beautiful to be tucked away in the desert. "I am."

The silver bangle bracelets on her wrist chimed together as she moved. "He isn't as ruthless as he portrays himself. He loves his family, and sometimes that love makes him do crazy things."

My definition and her definition of crazy were worlds apart. My Aunt Betty was crazy. Brunlak was missing a few buttons on the remote control. He'd had a knife to my throat one minute and was matchmaking the next. "So, has he tried to marry you off yet?"

She laughed, light and bubbly. "Every day. Let me guess. He thought you would make Dustyn an ideal match."

I nodded, assuming Dustyn was her brother. I never got the name of Brunlak's son.

Was it really the smartest idea, opening up to the daughter of Brunlak? Probably not. But there was something about her that made me trust her. She had eyes of an angel, and it was so nice having another girl to talk to.

I didn't realize how much I missed having a friend. I thought about Chloe and Bethany, wondering if they had survived the mist and if they were out here like me, struggling. The three of us had been best friends since diapers. Our parents had gone to college together, and we had basically always been there for each other.

Breakups. Divorce. Awkward adolescence. First kiss.

Would I ever see them again?

"You're too lively and female for my brother's taste," Vee said, bringing my mind back to the present.

My brows drew together as I put together what she was telling me. "Your brother's gay?" I hated to be presumptuous. Hopefully, she didn't take offense, because that hadn't been my intention.

Her head bobbed up and down. "My father refuses to accept the truth. He believes Dustyn's duty is to populate mankind before we end up extinct."

That was some old school thinking, but with the catastrophe that could have wiped out the planet, I could understand the concerns. "And you? Does he expect the same from you?"

"Absolutely. I'm positive he has your boyfriend cornered right now, praising his daughter's unparalleled beauty. By the way, where is he?"

Dash, you fool.

If he was, in fact, getting an earful from Brunlak, then he was in hot water. He was going to want to know where the guard was. I pushed aside my concern for the slayer. Vee was stunning, that's for sure, and I didn't think she'd have any problems finding a line of suitors. Just not Dash. Jealousy licked through me as I thought about how adorable their kids would be.

The image made me sick.

I could still taste him on my lips, and I reminded myself what Dash did with his lips weren't my concern. Finding my family was.

"He's not my boyfriend," I rasped without thinking.

Oops.

I squeezed my eyes shut for a few seconds. I sucked at secrets. I sucked more at lying. It was entirely my lack of filter inherited from my mother. Saying whatever was on my mind got me in trouble—hopefully not today.

Vee giggled. "Don't fret," she assured, seeing the blunder on my face. "I already have my heart set on someone."

I exhaled, thinking she hadn't realized my slip. Her next comment crushed that relief.

"You sure the mouthwatering tracker isn't your boyfriend?" she posed in a way that suggested doubt.

I bit my lip, knowing I couldn't backpedal now, and settled for a half-truth. "It's complicated."

"Everything here is complicated," she said sadly.

Amen. And it was time to change the subject before I dug myself into a deeper grave. "You're the one who has the ability to cloak?"

She nodded, taking a seat beside me and folding her legs underneath her. "Yep, that's me."

We were about the same height and build, but that was where our likenesses ended. Her complexion was a beautiful olive. Her hair straight and silky, mine wild and unmanageable. I fumbled with the spot where my ring had once been. "How did you learn to control it?"

Her shoulders gave a graceful shrug. "One day it just clicked. The darkness swirled inside."

"Darkness?" I echoed.

"Yeah. That's what it feels like—something dark running through my veins, whispering in my ear. The first few times it happened, it was a defense mechanism. I didn't even know what I was doing."

That I could relate to. "I imagine it being a ton of pressure, having an entire village's protection up to you." I couldn't fathom that kind of responsibility, especially at our age.

She leaned to one side, putting her weight on her flattened palm. "Honestly, I'm bored. The cloak stays in place until I remove it. However, putting a shroud of this size in place had me in bed for a week. It drained me completely."

"That sounds dreadful."

"It was, I can assure you." Her head angled to the side, staring at me. "You have the most unusual eyes. I think it's why you fascinate my father. What's your gift?"

"Um. ..." I wanted to confide in someone, and Vee was so easy to talk to. She could probably even help me, but Dash had warned me. If word got out what I could do, as meaningless as it was to me, he believed the Institute would snatch me up before I could refuse. Not that the Institute gave you the option to sign up. There was no refusing. "I'm not a hundred percent sure, yet. I've been awake for less than a week."

Was that all it had been? It felt like a month had gone by since I opened my eyes and saw Dash above me.

"You've got time. It will make itself known, but with eyes like those, you're definitely gifted. It's no wonder why *he* is so possessive."

I assumed we were once again talking about Dash. He could be the most delectable and disturbing topic at the same time. "I don't know what you mean."

Her almond-shaped eyes got bright. "I was watching you when my father brought you in. The way he constantly put himself in front of you."

Dash did that? I guess he had, but I'd grown accustomed to him saving me.

"I almost had a heatstroke when he kissed you." She air-fanned her face with her hand. "There's an intensity about the slayer, and my guess, he doesn't risk his life for just anyone."

Thinking about his lips on my mine left my mouth as dry as the air. "God, is it always so hot here?"

She grinned. "Every. Stinking. Day."

I picked the hair off the nape of my neck. "Another day in this heat, and I'm going to look like Bozo the Clown, not to mention I probably already sweated a pound off my boobs."

Vee giggled.

"How come you're not sweating like a pig?" I asked her. Talk about unfair.

"Before the mist, I lived in Louisiana. This heat is my bread and butter."

That explained the cute accent and hospitality. I wanted to hate her for just being beautiful, but I found myself with a friend, one I could desperately use. "Hmm. Bread and butter. I'd donate my left ovary for a whole loaf."

She tipped her chin back and laughed. "Maybe you *should* marry my brother. It would be so nice to have a friend."

I agreed it was nice to talk to someone other than moody Dash, but I couldn't stay. "I'm looking for my family," I told her.

"Ah, isn't everyone. So that's what you were doing roaming so close to our borders."

I nodded and opened my mouth to ask her how she had been reunited with her father, when Dash came barreling through the cloth flap. Our little girl talk had come to an end. A deep scowl was etched on his lips. Vee gave him a shy grin, but Dash barely spared her a glance. Nope. His signature glare was all for me. "Who is she?"

"Brunlak's daughter," I replied.

He turned around and looked at her and then stated, "Did anyone ever tell you that your father's an asshole?"

Vee stood up. "My whole life. I should probably go before the guard wakes up." She gave me a wink before leaving.

As soon as we were alone, Dash dropped enough f-bombs to bring down a city. His creativity was stellar.

"Wow," I said. "Are you speaking a new language? I'm not sure I understood any of what came out of your mouth. But judging by the grisly frown on your face, I'm taking it your scout of the area was detrimental."

"Are you trying to be cute?" he retorted.

"I don't have to try," I replied, taking a page from his ego book.

He snorted. "If you're done being a smartass, we've got problems."

Somehow I managed to refrain from saying the first sarcastic thing that popped into my head: When didn't we have a problem?

Dash began to pace in circles with his fingers shoved into his hair. "This whole place is cloaked, not just from anyone finding it, but from anyone wanting to leave."

My alarm pitched, reaching an all-time high. I had this unreasonable expectation that Dash would just fix everything. The idea that he couldn't get us out of here never really crossed my mind. "Are you saying we're stuck here?"

His eyes were guarded, but I knew he was concerned with our current situation. "Unless you know a way to break the shroud."

We both knew I didn't.

He eyed me closely. "What were you and Brunlak's daughter talking about?" he asked, brows furrowing together.

I folded my hands, craning my neck to look up at him as he towered over me. "Nothing. I think she was curious about us."

He plopped down on the bed of blankets, looking exhausted. My neck thanked him. "Yeah, well, we're here for the night. We might as well take advantage of the bed."

"What does that mean?"

He turned his head sideways at me, a one-sided smirk on his lips. "Get your mind out of the gutter, Freckles."

Lying down, I pulled the covers up to my chin, doing everything I could to not think about our tumultuous situation. I should have been more scared than I was. In the week we'd been together, I'd grown dependent on Dash. There wasn't a predicament he couldn't get us out of. My faith in him was becoming unyielding … and that couldn't be good. Even now, he was telling me he didn't know how to get us out, but I couldn't help believe he would—somehow, some way. He made me feel safe and secure; even with a knife thrust against my throat, I had known Dash would never let true harm come to me. I'm not saying I wasn't scared, because I had been. There was something unique about Dash. And the wondering was going to keep me up.

I turned restlessly on the quilted blankets. Left. Right. Left again. I pressed my face into my makeshift pillow and stared at the guy sleeping beside me. His hands were crossed over his broad chest, long lashes fanned out over his cheeks. His lips were slightly parted, and several dark locks fell over his forehead. If I closed my eyes, I could picture every inch of his face. Dash had a masculine beauty I'd never seen before. He was such a conundrum—prickly as a cactus when he was in a mood, but underneath all the needles was a sweet, protective side that I don't think many people ever got to see.

Which made me wonder, why did he choose me?

The heat made me groggy, and combined with the clusterfuck day I'd had, my eyes were heavy and my body ached. Yet, the idea of falling asleep still scared the ever-loving crap out of me. Would there ever be a time when it didn't? Definitely didn't help that I was sleeping in hostile grounds.

There was no denying it anymore. I was weary to my core, and after nights of fighting off sleep, my brain had had enough and closed shop.

I dozed and with it came the very thing I'd been trying to avoid: disturbing dreams. It started with those creepy laiders crawling over my body in great swarms of black hairy legs. Their beady eyes surrounded me on all sides. Screaming wasn't an option, for the hybrid spiders had covered me in webs, cutting off my voice.

Jerking in my sleep, the dream rolled from one nightmare to another, mixing with reality in a cloudy stage of unconsciousness. I knew I was dreaming, but it felt real, as real as when Dash had kissed me, and in the dream, I was chasing my family. Sometimes Dash. I could see their faces, hear their voices, but every time I thought I was close, I was only farther away. It was an endless maze, like the Dying Labyrinth. I yelled their names, scrabbling in the dark, in the woods, in the desert to find them.

The nightmare went on and on until the comfort of strong arms wrapped around my waist and the soft murmurs of a deep voice calmed my seizure of panic.

Dash.

His scent, it had followed me into a deep slumber, not the drug-induced kind, but the sheer exhaustion form. The soothing tone of his voice replaced the cobwebs of sleep with a hazy desire. It was instantaneous. His body molded against mine, and warmth flooded my senses as he trailed kisses along my jawline.

Dream or not, I was no longer afraid to never wake up. Dash made me feel things I'd only ever read in those trashy novels I would sneak from my mom's room.

"You have no idea how long I've wanted to kiss you," he murmured, his voice soft and dangerous.

Goosebumps crawled over my arms. I think I had a good idea.

Dream, fantasy, or somewhere in between, regardless of what it was, I was in pleasure heaven.

My back bowed off the bed as his lips latched on to the lobe of my ear, sucking gently. I curled my fingers through his dark hair and bit down on my lip to keep from crying out, but I had a feeling that was exactly what he wanted—to make me scream.

But it wasn't my scream that echoed in my head. It was Vee's. At least I thought it was her. The cry was pure terror and was followed by a dark voice. *Where is he?*

Vee's voice trembled. *I don't know who it is you seek.*

The one you hide. He calls himself Dash Darhk, and the Institute wants him. To house a criminal is against the rules, punishable by imprisonment. If you do not turn him over, others will die.

Vee whimpered, as if whomever the gruesome voice belonged to was hurting her.

Their blood will be on your hands, Charlotte. Can you live with that?

Every muscle in my body seized as the voice suddenly addressed me, and he was clear on his intent. They'd already killed and would do so until they got what they came for.

Dash.

The voice continued to taunt me, promising to kill everyone in the camp, including me, until they found Dash. And I believed him. Even in the realm of dreams, I knew this wasn't a joke. The murky voice had found a way to penetrate my mind when it was in its weakest state. It had the Institute written all over it.

I whimpered in my sleep, thrashed on the sheets.

"Charlotte," Dash whispered.

I thought I felt him gently run a hand along my cheek, but this time, his warmth didn't chase away the frigid chill of the ominous voice.

My head shook from side to side and another sob left my lips. I bit the inside of my cheek, and the metallic taste of blood filled my mouth. The longer I resisted, the more persistent the voice became. *If you surrender peacefully, we will spare your life.*

My heart pounded, nearly jumping out of my chest. Dash had risked his neck more than once for me. I wouldn't put his in jeopardy; I wouldn't let the Institute get their hands on him again. I might not know the details of what they did to him, but I knew enough to know he'd gone to great lengths to avoid the Institute.

With the intimidations came more screams.

"Freckles, wake up!" Dash shouted.

This time, there was no mistaking that voice—or the urgency. Something was wrong.

Chapter Twelve

I jolted awake, my heart pounding and my mouth dry.

Did I just have a nightmare? I dragged in a ragged breath and opened my eyes. Little white fuzzy particles danced in the moonlight as I glanced upwards, a cream tarp tented over my head. A strange tingle wafted over my skin. Why was I under a canopy?

Like almost every time I opened my eyes, I was disoriented, forgetting where I was or how screwed up the world had become. But as those fluffy particles shimmered and floated in the air, my memories slowly returned. And with the memories came the dream.

From daunting to steamy to core shaking, it had everything, an extreme roller coaster. It had been so vivid, so real, the screams were still echoing in my head.

"Charlotte." My name tumbled cautiously from Dash. His silver eyes met mine, glowing with alarm.

He was close, far closer than he had been when I went to sleep.

Did that mean—?

Did we—?

Had it not been a dream?

Good God almighty.

Was that why my skin tingled? From his touch? And were my lips swollen like I'd been thoroughly kissed? "What happened?" I asked, bemused.

"You were dreaming," he murmured, brushing a wild curl off my cheek.

It was humid still, regardless that the sun had set. My hair was crazy wild, no doubt looking like a family of forest creatures had decided to make a nest of it. "I had a nightmare."

His cool gray eyes studied me, face drawn with concern. "You were talking in your sleep. It was adorable until your eyes opened. They were pink. I figured you were sleepwalking or something."

Wait? What? How was it that my eyes could change colors? "Impossible," I said after a moment of dead air.

"That you talk in your sleep? I think it's pretty common."

I rolled my eyes. "No, the dreams. My eyes. Why do strange things keep happening to me?"

Dash tilted his head to the side. "Do you really expect an answer?"

I sat up. "Oh God. I think I had some sort of premonition." I assessed what happened, working through the ups and downs, trying to sort out what had been an illusion and what had been real—if any. It all came back in a rush. The more I thought about it, the more I was certain the warning from the Institute had been real. "We need to leave. Now." I untangled myself from the mound of blankets and scrambled to gather my bag.

Dash followed me with his eyes as if I was losing it. "What's gotten into you? Not that I'm rejecting the idea. I'm always down for a good escape plan."

"The voice," I whispered. In another time and place, I would have brushed off the wacky dream, but not now—not here—not after another eye-changing episode. It meant something. And I was deathly afraid I knew what.

"What voice?" Dash asked, watching me frantically throw my bag onto my shoulders.

Someone screamed, and my eyes flipped to the closed flap of the tent. A trickle of fear moved into my veins, forming a ball of unease in my gut. This was one of those times it sucked to be right. I whipped my head toward him, eyes hysterical. "They're coming for you," I hissed.

His brows flew together. Suddenly, I had his attention. "Who?"

Why wasn't he moving? "The Institute. They're coming. They found us." Fear consumed me.

To stress the danger I was positive was heading our way, another scream bellowed from the camp. This time Dash reacted. Bolting upright, he automatically reached in his bag for a weapon. "Shit." Unhappiness colored his voice as he remembered Brunlak had confiscated them. His body tensed as he raked a hand through his hair.

The cry for help was followed by another. And another.

He was on his feet, finally realizing the depth of our situation. "Freckles, I'm not even going to ask." He grabbed my hand, tugging me to the front of the tent. Peeling a corner back, he glanced outside.

I got up on tiptoes, peering over his shoulder. The camp was in chaos. People running around, frightened and screaming. The defense tower was unmanned, and I didn't want to think why. "What are we going to do?" I whispered.

He didn't hesitate or panic. "First, we're going to get our weapons. Then we're going to get the hell out of here."

Solid plan … if we pulled it off. There seemed to be a lot of details missing. Like how were we going to find our stuff? Did we even know where Brunlak had stashed our weaponry? And with the cloak blocking the camp, how were we getting out?

Dash didn't seem to be worried about the particulars. I worried enough for the both of us.

"Let's get this show on the road," he muttered, and like that, we were off.

We raced out into the open, warm air, the whipping wind swirling dust and sand in our faces. I don't know how he managed to see where he was going, but I held on tight, trusting him. Through the pandemonium, I noticed something different. Where the barrier of the camp used to be was gone. I could see the horizon in the distance, the three-quarter moonlight shimmering over the desert. "The veil is gone. Someone removed Vee's cloak."

"The Institute," Dash hissed, ducking behind a canvas structure.

The scent of fear seemed to rise up and surround me until my head spun. My heartbeat was fast, racing with the people seeking safety.

Dash, the voice whispered in the wind.

I shivered. "They're close."

Dash glanced at me, and whatever he saw sent him into action. Somehow we made it across the little village—near to where we had been snuck in—but we weren't the only ones. The Institute had arrived, their *gifted* military spreading over the camp.

Dash's hand squeezed mine, and he took a sharp intake of air. A group of them surged our way, and Dash froze. His eyes were dazed, pupils huge, and his hand turned clammy in mine. The close proximity of the Institute caused a reaction inside him. And not a good one. I have no idea how long I stood calling his name. In some ways, it felt like only a heartbeat passed, but at the same moment, it was as if we were suspended in time.

Then proverbial crap hit the fan.

A blazing wall of heat and flames shot from a female guard, appearing before me in a wall, and I barely had the presence of mind to back up, pulling Dash with me. The fire shot up from the ground as it circled around us in a ring. If we didn't move now, we would be trapped.

The fire was closing in, growing tighter and hotter. I screamed.

Dash blinked, and just like that, his ruthless demeanor returned.

"Get behind me," he ordered.

I raised my hand, instinctively shielding my eyes from the blinding bright light of the flames. The heat licked over my skin in a painful discomfort.

Beyond the fire was a dark outline. Dash reached through the flames, grabbing the shadow and ripping him into the circle of hell. "Hey, Ashton, I see you still like to play with fire. Ember must be tired of you dousing her flames. I told you one day you were going to get burned."

Ashton's eyes went wide, and before he could plead for his life, Dash had his fist planted in his face. The Night's Guard's eyes rolled back in his head as his body crumbled to the grass. Unconscious, the fire simply disappeared.

When Dash turned back to look at me, something a hell of a lot of primitive and aggressive took over. "You okay?"

All I could do was nod.

Boom! Gunshots echoed over the field, and the dark voice's promise echoed in my head. *One by one, they will die,* and the thought made my stomach twist. The voice had promised death, and it appeared they were living up to their end of the bargain. I, on the other hand, was not.

Panic ensued. I couldn't betray Dash. I wouldn't. But could I live with death on my hands?

The first signs of resistance sounded, even over the howling of the wind. The people of Eastroth weren't going down poo creek without a fight.

Wheeling around, Dash looked back the way we'd come. "We're sitting ducks out here, defenseless."

"Not completely defenseless," I replied, wiggling my free hand in the air.

"No. Absolutely not. You're not putting yourself in the line of fire," he snarled, drawing me alongside him.

Too late.

A whizz of light zipped by, hitting the tent beside us in a burst of sparks. Dash reacted immediately, rolling me into his arms and pulling me against his chest. He brought us to the pavement, curving his body around mine. I could feel the corded muscles of him as they tensed, the ground shaking under our feet.

A loud *crack* thundered, and I jerked in his arms, but he held onto me close. *Oh my God.* This was really happening.

"We need to find a way out," Dash growled.

The Institute continued to raid the camp, tearing through the homes of Eastroth and destroying what these people had worked so hard to build like it was nothing.

As Dash unfolded his arms around me, a shadow fell over us, spurring him to his feet. The muscle in his jaw clenched. Horror ate at my stomach. All I could think was the Institute had found him. I forced my eyes skyward and prepared to launch myself at the Night's Guard in crazy ex-girlfriend style. But it wasn't a guard. It was a six-foot, golden nomad.

Brunlak stood in our path.

This wasn't ideal, but it could have been worse.

Pushing to my feet, a horrible sense of betrayal wormed in my gut. Not that Brunlak owed us anything; I assumed his disregard for the Institute ran almost as deep as Dash's. But looking at him now, I knew he was the one who had contacted them and squealed like a rat, giving the Institute Dash's location. He had even risked the safety of his village for the bounty the Institute had on Dash's head. Caught in a tailspin of rage and despair, I didn't think about what I was doing until after the fact, and by then, the deed was done.

Swinging out, my fist connected with Brunlak's cheekbone. It wasn't a girly hit, either. I had the stinging hand to prove it. It hurt. A lot. But totally worth it. Every ounce of my frustration, fear, and pent-up anger was packed into that punch.

He deserved it for what he had done to us and so much more, as far as I was concerned. "You bastard! How could you?"

Brunlak let out a groan of part pain, part anger, which turned into a frightening laugh. "I knew I was right about you."

"Go screw yourself!" I yelled, springing forward, but I didn't get far.

"Whoa, Freckles," Dash said with a hint of amusement, wrapping a hand around my waist and keeping me from going She-Ra on Brunlak.

I couldn't pull myself out of it. All I could do was glare at the man standing between us and our freedom.

"Get out of the way, old man," Dash roared, pushing me behind him, "before I make you wish you never set eyes on me."

My gaze swung behind us, afraid the Institute's foot soldiers were going to come storming out of the dust any second, waving their guns and demanding us to hit the ground or they'd shoot. I placed a hand on Dash's shoulder just as there was a succession of several pops.

I gasped, but the sound was lost in the screams.

Dash's patience had run out. "I don't need a weapon to kill, and that's what I'll do before I let the Institute get their hands on her," he told a brooding Brunlak.

Me? He was worried about me? They were after him.

There was no doubting the conviction in Dash's voice. I believed him. Brunlak believed him. And if Brunlak didn't let us go, Dash would kill him. He wouldn't think twice about it. I wanted to hurt Brunlak, but I didn't want him dead, and I had to do something before Dash did indeed kill Vee's father. It wasn't Brunlak I was saving, but Vee, wanting to spare her the pain of losing a parent in a world where so many people were missing their loved ones.

"You just made my day," Dash seethed, grabbing a fistful of Brunlak's shirt. He rocked back on his heels. "I've been itching to smash your face."

Here goes nothing. I squeezed my eyes shut, blocking out all the wild emotions rolling inside me. I remembered what Vee had said—how she could sense the darkness. There was no darkness but a static of energy pulsing inside me. It fluttered over my skin, building the more I centered on the sensation. Lightning was energy. *Please let this work.* I didn't really have high hopes, but what could it hurt?

Leaning to the side, I opened my eyes and reared back, letting the collection of static soar. I threw out my arm, feeling foolish, but the foolishness quickly turned to success. A charged bolt of lightning flew from my hand like a spear, striking the ground at Brunlak's feet before fizzing out.

I'll be damned. My mouth dropped open.

Brunlak's eyes went wide as he stared at the charred ground. White smoke billowed at his feet, blowing away with the wind. My fingers tingled. That. Had. Been. Amazing.

Dash shot me a look over his shoulder.

Brunlak faced me, a gleam of triumph in his mahogany eyes. "The Institute is going to have a field day with you two."

Dammit. I'd gotten his attention all right and probably every Night's Guard in a mile radius. Swell. *Bright idea, Charlotte.*

"That's what you think," Dash rumbled, right before he planted his fist into Brunlak's gut. He was extremely hands-on today. I could only imagine what he could do with a weapon.

My concentration was solely on Dash, and I didn't hear anyone come up behind me until a brisk voice ordered, "If you want a chance to survive, you must come with me. And hurry."

I swung around. It was Vee. Her hair was piled on top of her head in a loop of braids, and the loose shawl she wore slipped off one shoulder.

I sighed in relief. Finally, someone with estrogen.

Dash's keen eyes took in her presence and used it to his advantage. He shoved aside Brunlak and latched onto Vee's arm. "If you want to see your daughter again, keep your mouth shut," Dash warned.

Brunlak crumbled to the ground, doubled over in pain.

I didn't agree with Dash's methods, but I told myself he wasn't actually going to hurt Vee. Then he turned to her, and I was no longer sure she was safe from Dash's vengeance. "Don't screw me over. You won't like the results."

I wanted to tell Dash to be nice, but I didn't think it would be well received, so I kept my mouth shut and followed Vee, happy to be moving.

"You can use the tunnels," she advised as we raced along the edge of the village. "It will give you a head start, a chance to possibly lose them."

Vee paused at a crate and gave Dash an impatient glance. "I won't run. You don't need to keep me on a leash."

Dash growled before freeing her arm.

She made haste, pulling on the lock and swinging open the crate door. "Here, you're going to need these."

Dash grinned and removed his bow and arrow, along with three knives. "Come to papa."

I rolled my eyes and reached in to grab my dagger. It no longer felt awkward or clumsy in my grasp. "Thank you," I breathed.

Vee gave a tip of her head. "You can thank me by surviving. ... I have a feeling about you two."

There wasn't time to ask what she meant. The Institute was breathing down our necks.

Chapter Thirteen

Dash swung the bow over his arm. "If you get us out of here, I'll be in your debt." It was a big deal, Dash offering a debt. A flash of blue light flew over our heads, narrowly missing him. His eyes narrowed.

Another blast went off, causing my heart to pound like a jackhammer. If it hadn't been for the high wind making their visibility impaired, we wouldn't have had the advantage. Slinking along the edge of a circular structure, we stayed low, keeping conversation to a minimum. Sandwiched between Vee and Dash, I gritted my teeth and tried to block out the screams. It felt as if we were never going to make it to the tunnel.

Regardless of the fact that my legs were shaky, I made myself push on, one foot in front of the other. And when Vee came to a sudden halt, I walked right into her. I could have blamed the dust in my eyes, but it was just my absent-mindedness. Recovering my balance, I saw what had her stopping in her tracks. Three Night's Guards blocked the path to the tunnels— two men and one woman. We were so close, the hairs on my arms stood. All we had to do was get through three Night's Guards. No sweat.

Who was I kidding?

For a moment, my breath faltered, and I didn't know what to do. "You've got to be kidding me."

"I hope one of you has a plan," Vee said, backing up a step or two.

"Duck!" Dash yelled.

Two seconds went by before Vee and I hit the ground. Dash stepped in front of us, bow drawn and prepared to strike. I counted the arrows whooshing over my head. Two single arrows. That left one.

Lifting my head, two of the guards were on the ground, moaning and bleeding. Not life-threatening injuries, but enough to keep them incapacitated and out of our way. It was the last guy I was worried about. The moment the thought left my brain, a hand grabbed a chunk of my hair and yanked me backward. I fell on my butt, sprawled out on the ground.

Curse this stupid hair.

It was a fire engine beacon, begging for attention, and in this situation, it was costly.

Dash spun around. "Hands off the lady, amigo."

I grabbed the guard's wrist and sent him an electric shock strong enough to make the hairs on his arm singe. He yelped, releasing the death grip on my locks, and gave Dash the opening he'd been looking for.

The arrow sunk straight into the guard's heart.

Pushing up on my hands, the guard's mouth dropped open in a silent cry of surprise. He clutched the air, blood oozing on his hands and dribbling down his arm. Like someone had yelled *timber*, he planked to the ground.

The guard was dead.

Dash had singlehandedly dispatched three Night's Guards. I didn't know whether I should be impressed or terrified. There was a quiet calm on his handsome face. Killing didn't faze him.

The same couldn't be said about me.

There was a good chance I was going to hurl.

"So the rumors about you are true?" Vee said, eyeing Dash. "This is one of those times I'm glad."

"What rumors?" I asked, testing my legs. I was still a little shaken. Seeing Dash kill someone was not as cool as it looked in the movies.

Vee stepped over the dead guard. "He hasn't told you what his gift is?"

I looked to Dash.

"We don't have time for this," he grumbled. "We need to go. Right. Now."

Part of me wanted to dig my feet in and demand he tell me, but we really did need to leave the camp. Sighing, I told myself that Dash and I were going to have this conversation once we got out of here.

We reached the tunnel, and although I couldn't be happier to leave Eastroth behind, I got a little choked up about saying good-bye to the only person I felt a kinship with.

Vee gave me a quick hug. "We'll see each other again. I'm sure of it."

"Only under better circumstances I hope," I said, returning her embrace.

Dash cleared his throat, my cue to get my butt moving.

"Stay safe," she whispered.

"You, too," I replied over my shoulder, following Dash toward our freedom.

The tunnel was dark and winding. More than a dozen times I managed to scrape myself on the jagged walls. As we squeezed past a narrow stretch, I cursed my shitty luck. Since the moment I'd woken up, it felt as if all I'd been doing was running from something or someone. When did I get the chance to catch my breath?

Not today.

Our pace was grueling, and the murmurings of the Night's Guard carried through the passageways, letting us know they hadn't given up. Dash must have an internal GPS. He seemed to know what turns to take. I wanted to chalk it up to blind luck, but there was something more to Dash Darhk than I knew. Vee had pretty much solidified my suspicion, and if we were going to continue to travel together, I think I deserved the truth of who he really was.

A ripple of joy danced inside me at the first sight of light. Only a few more steps and we'd be out in the open.

Dash slowed, allowing me a moment to catch my breath. I collapsed against a tree, my muscles relaxing and my heart rate slowly returning to normal from the frantic getaway. Breaths shallow, I closed my eyes, letting my lungs enjoy the air and my peace drift through my muscles. A hundred years asleep had really done a number to my body, or I wasn't as fit as I thought I'd been.

"Do you think we lost them?" I panted.

Dash's sharp eyes continued to stare into the opening of the dark tunnel. "Not for long. They won't ever stop hunting us. You exposed yourself, allowing them to see you're gifted. It won't take them long to realize you haven't been charted."

The Institute kept a running tab of all the people who woke up and those who were classified as gifted. "I hope I never see another tunnel again."

He swiped the back of his arm over his sweaty forehead. "Yeah, I've had enough of this desert heat to last me a lifetime."

The back of my shirt was dripping with gross, smelly perspiration. So attractive. I had a theme going—unkempt and wild. If my parents saw me now, they probably wouldn't recognize their daughter. "Tell me about it. I didn't think it was possible to sweat so much." And the sun wasn't even fully up.

"We need to keep moving."

I nodded, knowing he was right, but that didn't mean every bone in my body didn't protest the slightest movement. Hopefully, the Night's Guard got lost in the network of tunnels.

Staying off the path, we walked in silence, until I could no longer take it—about five minutes. "What did Vee mean when she said the rumors about you are true?" I thought back to what happened. It was obvious his gift had something to do with killing. I'd heard of expert marksmanship, but this went beyond that. He hadn't even looked at the guy, and yet the arrow sunk dead center in his chest. Dumb luck? I don't think so. Not in this world.

With a hard set to his jaw, he said, "I never miss, Freckles. It's my curse. There isn't a target, moving or standing still, that I can't hit. Eyes closed, upside down, backwards, it doesn't matter how I make the shot. It goes exactly where I want it."

I stared at him. He wasn't kidding. And I saw a side of Dash I hadn't let myself see, the side he kept telling me was there: his dark side. Dash was a mob boss's wet dream with the ability to never miss his intended target. No wonder the Institute was so intent on capturing him.

"Holy shit balls," I whispered. "You're like Robin Hood," I commented.

He snorted. "I'm not taking from the rich to give to the poor. I just killed that guard without hesitating. And I'd do it again if it meant saving my life."

It hadn't been his life he saved; it had been mine. "But if you hadn't, he would have tried to kill you or me or Vee."

"You can't justify everyone I've ever killed."

"Have there been many? Is that why the Institute has put a warrant on your head?"

He made a guttural sound in his throat. "Hardly. The Institute taught me to kill. The warrant is because I refuse to do their bidding. They didn't take well to my rejection, and I suddenly was no longer their star pupil."

I scuffed my foot on the sand. "That's ... horrible."

Dash stopped at a funny-shaped tree, similar to a cactus, and I snuffled a giggle. It was childish, but after the stress we'd just encountered the last day, it felt good to laugh at something as stupid as a plant that favored a part of the male anatomy.

He plucked a round fruit the size of a coconut and flashed me his dimples. Cracking the sphere open on his knee, he handed me half. "Drink this. It will keep you from getting dehydrated."

I sniffed and wrinkled my nose. It smelled like honey and melons. I took a generous gulp, wiping a dribble off the side of my mouth. It was sweet, but tolerable. "You're nothing like I first thought," I informed him, handing him back the shell.

"And what, Freckles, was your first impression of me?"

An almost shy smile curved my lips. "You're going to laugh."

He tossed aside the empty pod. "Probably."

I was going to regret this. "I thought you looked like a prince." I crumpled my nose as soon as the admission left my mouth.

Dash busted out laughing.

I whacked him on the arm. "Hey."

"That is classic. And do you still think I'm a prince?"

"I haven't made up my mind yet."

He took a step forward, eyes flashing like a silver bullet. "How does it feel, knowing you've kissed a killer?" The texture in his voice had gone low and ruthless.

Was that how he saw himself? A killer? I couldn't understand that. From what I could tell, the walls he built around himself were sky high, not allowing real friendship or love. He thought of himself as a dirty, no good killer. Unworthy.

Bullshit.

I'd assumed he was one of those guys afraid of commitment, didn't want to be tied down, hell, even that he was afraid to be close to someone, but to think he wasn't good enough for me, that was poppycock. I didn't care if he had killed a hundred people. He didn't do it for shits and giggles or sport, but for survival. The Institute was hunting him. It was instinctual to protect yourself. And I knew for a fact, he didn't always kill. How many of the Night's Guards had Dash only wounded since the night he found me? Way more than he'd killed.

That didn't make him a ruthless murderer in my book.

The Institute had done a number on him, and I wasn't sure why, but I wanted to be the one to crack those walls. There was a lot I didn't know about Dash, but what I did know was that he was no murderer.

I tipped my chin, meeting his warning glare, and leaned toward him so our bodies brushed. "I'm not afraid of you. Nothing you could do or say is going to make me think you're the bad guy."

His eyes searched mine, and as I held his gaze, the iciness began to thaw. He didn't really want me to hate him. "Being near me is going to get you hurt. Just look around."

My eyes dropped to his lips. "You would never let anything happen to me," I whispered.

The pad of his thumb traced a line along my bottom lip. "What is it about you?"

"Maybe I see *you* for who you are."

A slow grin curved his lips. "Nah, that's not it."

I nudged the tip of my nose against his. "Then it has got to be my sparkling personality."

He framed the side of my face with his hand. "That's it."

Warmth swept across my cheeks, his breath tickling the spot just below my ear.

His eyes deepened to a smoky gray. "You have the softest pair of lips, and I can't get the taste of you out of my head."

He amazed me. Who would have thought that the big and tough tracker had a soft and chewy center? As I stared at him, caught in the spell his words brewed, I wanted to tell him not to play games with my heart … and to stop being so damn tempting and charming. I wanted him to kiss me.

My heart stuttered blindly as I kept my eyes centered on his, lifting up on my toes. Our lips were now aligned, and all I had to do was lean in a mere inch. There was a fire of anticipation in my blood, a curiosity to see if the kiss would be as earth-shattering as I remembered. He wasn't the only one who couldn't stop thinking about it. His chest rose under my hand as I moved in to close the distance between our mouths.

His head snapped up, leaving me hanging. "Shh."

My eyes narrowed. "Did you just—"

He threw a hand over my mouth.

I bit the inside of his palm, not hard, but enough to draw his attention. Inside, I was achy, disappointed, and pissed off.

His brows slammed together, the silver hue of his eyes churning restlessly. "We're being followed," he mouthed as his gaze went skyward.

A bit of the sting eked out of my body. Too bad I couldn't get rid of the molten lava simmering in my veins still. I followed his line of vision. There, just below the clouds, was a black bird circling over our heads. His wings spread wide as he swooped majestically in the air, head held high and proud. There was no mistaking him. "It's just a bird," I said, disregarding the blinken.

"That so-called bird has been trailing us since we emerged from the tunnels. A friend of yours?" he proposed, jesting.

I swallowed. "Blink."

"You named him?"

I rolled my eyes. "I'm not lame. It's his name."

His brows arched. "He told you his name was Blink?"

"Did I stutter?"

"Freckles, are you sure you didn't hit your head?"

"I'm not delusional. He's a blinken," I said, assuming that would clear things up.

He gave me a confused half-grin. "Okay. I'll take your word for it."

I put some space between us. "I know it sounds crazy, and it probably is, but that bird flying around up there can talk."

"If what you say is true, that isn't a bird. It's a weapon of the Institute."

I craned my neck up, fighting the glare from the sun as I let my eyes trail after the bird. "What do you mean, like a drone?"

"Possibly."

"How can you be sure?"

A dark shadow of suspicion crossed his features. "I've seen all kinds of shit in this world but talking animals is not one of them. In the last ten years, since the first group of settlers awoke, there have been many advances within the Institute, privy only to those within the walls of Diamond Towers. If there were a way for the Institute to have eyes on the Heights, this would be the perfect tactic. It reeks of the Institute."

Dash pulled out his bow and grappled in his pack for an arrow. He was going to shoot Blink from the sky. Considering his skill set, Blink didn't stand a chance, and I didn't think it mattered how high he flew.

"No, don't," I said, resting a hand on Dash's forearm, stopping him from killing the potential scout. "We can't be sure."

"And if I'm right?" he suggested. "You're willing to take the chance?"

I wasn't sure if the chatty bird was a spy or just another victim of the mist, but the idea of him reporting our location to the Institute made me nervous. "I don't know."

Blink squawked once and then broke his flight pattern, flying off.

Dash lowered his bow, regret lining his forehead. "If I see him again, I shoot." It was a promise.

I sighed. If the bird knew what was good for him, he'd stay clear of Dash and his lethal arrows.

Time elapsed as we continued to put as much ground as we could between us and the guards. Now that they knew Dash's general location, they weren't about to ease up on their hunt, not when they'd been so close. Since there was still a huge section of the Badlands we hadn't explored and multiple holding pods, Dash thought it was best if we switched quadrants.

I didn't really care one way or the other, as long as we continued to search. Each day that went by my hope of finding my family diminished bit by bit. In a place like the Badlands, it was hard to find optimism and keep it. Dash, regardless of his dark past and brooding personality, had a presence about him that made me want to not just live, but thrive. He awakened feelings that reminded me of all the good in life.

There was a gradual change in temperature as we got closer to the edge of the Badlands and near the border of Somber Mountain—the quadrant southwest of Diamond Towers. We came across a bridge, if you could call it that, and my internal daredevil was skeptical of crossing. Half the wooden planks were missing, and the ones left were rickety and decaying. I stood behind Dash, staring at the bridge of doom. "No."

Dash laid on hand on the rail and shook it. "I don't really think we have a choice in the matter, Freckles."

FML.

"I hate this place," I muttered.

"Ladies first," Dash said, making a swooping movement with his arm.

"You picked a shitty time to suddenly go gentleman on me." With more bravado than I felt, I moved in front of Dash. Balancing wasn't a problem for me, thanks to being a rah-rah cheerleader. It was the sturdiness of the wood I mistrusted. My feet felt like iron as I lifted them to take my first step onto the bridge. I froze. The bridge creaked and groaned under my measly hundred and twenty pound weight. "I have a really bad feeling about this."

"Where's your sense of adventure?"

The muscles in my legs quivered as I attempted to gain my balance. "I left it back in the twenty-first century."

With only a single rope on the rail for support, each shaky step caused the bridge to swing. "I hope you can swim," Dash joked in bad taste.

"Jerk," I hissed through my teeth. I could swim, but my biggest concern was the hundred-foot-plus drop to the water and what lived in it.

You can do this. Just don't look down. It's like walking the beam in gym. No biggie. Except there was no safety net. I made it about a quarter through without looking down, and then of course, I made the stupid mistake. My eyes rejected the warning my brain kept sending it, and the consequence was paralyzing fear, freezing me in my tracks.

Way to go, Charlotte.

Now how are you going to get out of this mess?

Chapter Fourteen

Dash to the rescue—again. It was becoming a bad habit, relying on him to constantly get my sorry butt out of sticky situations. If I wasn't careful, leaning on him was going to become a crutch.

Directly behind me, he rested a hand on my waist and coaxed me in his calmest voice, a challenge for him, but it worked. I concentrated on the smooth texture of his words, forcing myself to put one foot in front of the other, and crawled across the bridge. I was cautious, testing the sturdiness of each plank. He was patient, and I gave him credit, but my carefulness might have just been my downfall.

We had reached the halfway point, and with each step closer toward the other side, I gained control over my trembling body. Exhaling a breath, I put my foot on the next plank. It made a funny noise, like when my robust Uncle John plops into his recliner—a groan followed by a creak. And then it happened—what I'd been dreading. It was as if I'd psyched myself up for failure.

My foot slipped as the wood began to split. There was no stopping the chain of events. The decomposing plank broke into pieces, leaving me with nothing to stand on. I saw my life flash before my eyes as my arms flailed in the air. This was it. I was going to plummet to my death and look like a chicken with its head cut off while doing so. My scream echoed over the valley.

A strong arm wrapped around my torso, cutting off my shriek of terror and knocking the wind out of me. "I got you," Dash assured me with a grunt, pulling me against his chest.

My dangling feet stretched to touch a flat surface. I wanted to cry. I wanted to hold onto him forever. I wanted to get the fudge off this bridge.

But one disaster led to another.

"Don't you dare let me go," I said, angling my head to the side to peer at Dash.

"I swear, some days with you feels like my own personal trial," he grumbled. Grabbing my wrist, he spun me around. My breath was coming out in quick pants. He had saved me from a disastrous situation, but did he have to be such a jerkwad about it?

I was about to tell him to take it easy when I heard the voices.

This way!

They're on the bridge.

We got them now.

"Do you trust me?" Dash murmured.

My fingers were stiff and clammy as I gripped the front of his shirt. "You're asking me that as we're dangling a hundred feet off the ground." There was no hiding the sheer outrage in my voice.

Dash examined the ravine below. "Now seemed like a good time."

"What makes you—?" An arrow sunk into a wooden plank directly in front of me, and my voice faltered.

"Them," he replied, scooping an arm around my waist.

The Night's Guard were coming down the hill.

Ugh. These asshats don't give up. Dash and I exchanged looks. I knew what was going on inside that head of his. We were only halfway to the other side. There was no way we were going to make it without one or both of us getting an arrow to the back. "Isn't it just as dangerous in there?" I asked, glancing over the edge into the churning waters below. The waves whooshed over the rocks. The sun's reflection tinged the water gold, but beauty was only surface deep. Under those waves lived another horror.

"Dammit," Dash growled, surveying our limited options. "Yeah, but I'll take my chances with the sea creatures rather than with the Institute."

My brain balked at the idea.

"Hold on tight, Freckles." He secured me in his arms and jumped.

"Dash—!"

My scream was cut off, caught in my lungs as the rush of wind cascaded over my face, whipping through my hair as we fell. I buried my face into Dash's shoulder and held on for dear life.

Water rushed over my head.

The moment I hit the river, we were thrust apart. My body got caught in a whirlwind of waves, spinning me around and around as it carried me downstream. I was disoriented, unable to see Dash or get my bearings.

Something brushed against my leg, and I made the mistake of screaming. Water rushed into my lungs as I flailed in the turbulence, trying to make a break for the surface. If the Institute caught me, at least I'd still be alive.

I didn't know how he did it. Dash was always just there when I needed him. His fingers touched mine, and I reached out, interlocking our hands. He hauled me to him. I threw my arms around his neck like a hysterical monkey.

This time, Dash couldn't talk me through it, but his silver eyes ensnared mine, telling me to keep my cool.

Trust him.

He pointed a finger toward the surface, and I nodded. Already, I could feel the burn in my lungs.

Our heads bobbed over the water at the same time. Although we'd been tossed around in the water, we hadn't traveled as far as I had hoped. The Night's Guard were waiting for us with weapons ready. A series of arrows showered the water surrounding us, and we had no choice but to go back under again.

I took an enormous gulp of air and let myself sink into the water.

I was trapped like an animal—nowhere to turn, no way out.

It was a feeling I hated—helplessness.

Anger slowly began to tingle like a low fire in my belly. I was fed up with being chased. I was tired of being shot at. And I was damn sick of being scared.

Giving up wasn't the answer. It would only let them win, and I wasn't a quitter. Screw the Institute. Screw the Night's Guard. Screw the entire Heights.

I let the anger consume me, fueling my strokes as I swam deeper, scrambling to avoid the arrows pelting the water.

Whoosh. Plop. Plop. Ping.

The little spears cut through the river.

I didn't know what came over me. It was as if I was possessed by a ninja with a death wish. Time seemed to slow in the sludge of the water, but contrary to the time glitch, my senses felt heightened. Rolling to my right, I positioned myself in front of Dash. Behind me, I could hear his protest muffled by the water. There was no stopping the split-second decision, and honestly, on some greater level, I believed I timed the maneuver just so Dash wouldn't be able to prevent the arrow heading straight at me.

I closed my eyes, no idea what I was actually doing, and braced for the arrow that was going to pierce my gut. The seconds ticked by. And I waited. ...

"Freckles, you can open your eyes," Dash prompted. "We're safe ... sort of."

What did he mean, sort of?

How is he talking?

And why can I suddenly breathe?

My wet lashes fluttered opened. What the—

Confusion swirled inside me as I stared through an iridescent barrier. I followed the rainbow-like substance with my gaze, curious and alarmed. It was in the shape of a globe—a giant bubble might be a better description—and Dash and I were inside. The bubble provided an air pocket for us to breathe.

I was a little dizzy with the waves sloshing on either side of the magical globe. "How is this possible?"

He watched me carefully. "You tell me. You're the one who created this force field."

"I did?"

He thrust the wet curls plastered to his forehead off his face. "What were you thinking?"

I shook my head, unable to believe what I was seeing. "I didn't think."

"How the hell did you do this?"

"I-I don't know. It just happened."

"You seem to be able to do all kinds of things that just happen."

"So what color were my eyes this time?" I asked, knowing there was a pattern developing between my eyes and the strange things I could do.

His lips thinned. "I wasn't going to say anything. They were blue."

"Fabulous. Another problem to work through." I couldn't ignore the unusualness of my eyes or what they meant.

We floated downstream, the current pulling us farther out of the Badlands. Break out the streamers and confetti. If I hadn't been stuck in a bubble underwater with Dash, I might have done a little happy dance.

Dash outstretched his arms, flattening his palms and testing the durability of the material. "Whatever you're doing, don't stop."

The thing was, I wasn't doing anything. Not now. Once the barrier was created, my *abilities* or whatever, were no longer needed. On the flip side, apparently this *thing* I made was impenetrable, which made me a tad nervous. How were we going to get out of here?

Space was going to be a problem, especially with someone Dash's size. His head almost touched the top. To make things more comfortable as we drifted under the surface, Dash circled his fingers on my waist. Unsure what to do with my hands, I laid them on his shoulders. It was like we were doing an awkward floating dance in the water. Our bodies fit together, and I was immediately aware of the hard breadth of his chest.

Tension sparked.

It couldn't be helped.

Deny it all we wanted, there was something concocting between us.

Two shadows moved at the edge of the water, and I stiffened against Dash, knowing it was the Night's Guard. Swallowing, I wondered if they could see through the murky waters. "Crap."

Dash's hand curled around the wet material of my shirt. "We might get to test out the durability of your bubble."

"This was your grand idea, tossing us over the edge," I so pointedly reminded him.

A glimmer of light entered his expression, and he pressed his cheek to mine and whispered, "We're still alive."

I shivered, a blend of being soaking wet and Dash's warm breath on the skin of my neck. My hands tightened on Dash's shoulders. "The day's not over yet."

There were threats all around us, and now, caught in our own personal bubble, all I could do was dwell on Dash and the magic of his lips. Every time I thought about kissing him, my senses came alive.

An unfriendly looking fish with razor teeth cut through the water, making circles around us. And I hadn't forgotten about the two guards patrolling the water's shoreline, but a rocky wave brought my body closer to Dash's, and I couldn't ever remember feeling like this. He made the air in my lungs still.

"They haven't noticed us." Dash's voice was soothing in my ear.

I wished he would stop talking … or not stop. I couldn't make my mind up. Gathering courage, I draped my arms around his neck, easing the strain of my muscles as I leaned into him. "Who?" I blinked, my head scrambled.

His silver eyes twinkled. "The guards."

Face palm. "I knew that."

Dash's gaze turned arrogant and amused, a combination I found both irritating and tempting. "I think maybe the heat is getting to you," he mused, his lips brushing the sensitive skin below my ear.

Was it ever. My pulse skyrocketed. I swear the temperature inside the bubble hiked fifty degrees. Holding his smug gaze, I twined my fingers in his hair and tugged just hard enough to cause his gaze to meet mine. "I know what you're doing."

He chuckled. "Freckles, you have no idea what I'm capable of." To prove his point, his hand slid along the base of my spine, trailing up and then down, leaving a wake of tingles in its path.

His challenge backfired. "When are you going to get it through that thick head of yours that it doesn't matter to me what you've done?"

Smoky eyes snarled mine. I wasn't the only one feeling the energy igniting between us. "Careful," he said.

That was the thing: I didn't want to be careful. I wanted to be anything but. I wanted to not think for once and act on these emotions churning inside me. Expanding my fingers in his hair, I made a slight movement with my hips, fitting our bodies closer together. There was something exciting about our situation—being stranded underwater—and also a bit naughty.

A shiver of awareness jolted through Dash, and the arrogance from earlier was gone, replaced by stark emotion. Our bodies were virtually one. The feel of him turned my insides to molten mush and gave me a rush of confidence. He didn't make me feel like a girl. He made me feel like I was sexy and irresistible. I tipped my head up. When he didn't move away, I pressed my mouth to his.

Just one kiss, I told myself.

The moment our mouths met, I knew I had lied. One would never be enough.

His lips were warm and decadent as they moved over mine, and it was easy to drift into the kiss. "This is going to complicate things," he murmured, lips brushing over mine.

He was kissing me again, not so patient now, not so gentle. Clever fingers found a bare patch of skin at my hip, above my waistline. Things were quickly escalating, and I loved every second. "I've never wanted a bed more in my life." His voice took on an air of desperation.

A breath left my lungs in an unsteady rush. He pressed a kiss to the corner of my mouth. We were safe, and the reasonable thing to do would have been to stop and go on our way, but his fingers were skimming just under the swell of my breast. My entire body reacted to the intimate touch. *Yes. Yes. Yes,* I thought a second before he sealed his lips to mine.

He kissed me as if I was the single most important person in his world. If I could sink any deeper, I'd be halfway to China. Against his mouth, I moaned.

There was a *POP!*

The bubble burst.

I don't why or how, but once again we were immersed in the dark waters, the drop pulling us apart. Kicking toward the stream of light, I laughed the moment my head broke the surface, the sound rippling over the water and into the cloudy mist hovering above the river. A rush of adrenaline trilled through my veins.

That had been the most insane thing I'd ever done to date.

I pulled myself up on the ledge and flopped on the grass. Dash lay beside me, water dripping from his hair as black as a moonless night, framing a face of male beauty. "I love the sound of your laugh," he said, eyes smoldering. "No one laughs anymore. I've missed the sound."

I turned my head. "That's sad. Without laughter, there's no happiness."

Dash got quiet, his shoulders going tense. "There hasn't been much to laugh about."

My smile started to slip. I wanted to make Dash laugh. It suddenly became my personal mission to see the serious tracker let loose, do something silly. "Maybe once you find who you're looking for, you'll see things differently."

"I've been searching for a year."

I lifted up on my elbow. "You can't give up."

His gaze captured mine, and the look settling into his features had my heart racing. I couldn't look away. In the pit of my stomach, a flock of butterflies congregated, completely hopped up on Red Bull. I was back in the bubble with Dash kissing me until my toes curled.

Dragging in a deep breath, he finally looked away and stared at the sky. "I shouldn't have kissed you."

I blinked. "Because you're seeing someone else," I rationalized. Why else would he regret something that had been so amazing?

He shoved both his hands into his hair, his gaze avoiding mine. "You took me by surprise. No one's made me feel as much as you do."

Holy hot dwarf babies.

A hot flush crawled into my cheeks, and my stomach cartwheeled. I didn't see what the problem was. There was obviously something between us. "Why do you make that sound like a problem?"

"I'm hazardous, Charlotte." Our eyes locked, and if I didn't know better, there was regret. "If you don't get as far away from me as possible, you're going to get hurt. I couldn't live with myself if anything happened to you. I told myself I wouldn't touch you. It can't happen again. I can never give you what you deserve."

Every fiber in my being was saturated with raw emotions. He couldn't keep doing this to me, kissing me and then giving me the cold shoulder. He wanted me. He didn't. But in this moment, I didn't care about his reasons. They were insignificant to me when all I felt was the sting of his rejection. "No," I dug in, refusing to listen. "I don't believe that." It had only been one kiss—two if you counted the one at Eastroth—but I knew he felt something.

A moment passed, and he worked his jaw as he sat up. "Us being together would be a mistake. One you can't ever change. You might not understand now, but I'm doing you a favor."

I pushed up, forcing him to look at me. "Everyone thinks you're so tough, so dangerous. But you're a coward. You're too scared to let someone in. That's why there is no laughter in your life, Dash Darhk."

He drew in a harsh breath. "You say that now. I didn't ask for this. For you. I don't want the hassle."

A breeze kicked up, tickling over my arms as pain sliced across my face. "A hassle, am I? Well, this hassle just saved your ass."

"Look, once we find your family, and we will find them, you won't have time to think about me. You're gorgeous and sexy. There will be a hundred guys lined up for your attention. You won't remember my name."

Hardly. He wasn't giving himself enough credit. The only one I cared about wanting me was him. "But what about you? Do you want me?" I hated myself for asking. Afterward, I could have kicked myself. I didn't want to come across as needy or clingy.

For a brief second, I swore the mask cracked and uncertainty contorted his face. "I'd be dead or stupid to not want you. I'm neither, but that doesn't change the facts."

I didn't know whether to be insulted or flattered. It didn't matter. "I don't understand you. Why are you such a dick one minute and kissing me the next?"

He frowned. "I don't like the way you make me feel."

I cast him a sideways glance and swallowed thickly. "How do I make you feel?"

I wasn't sure he was going to answer me or that it would be an honest one. He surprised us both. "Like I want to care about someone. I haven't cared about what happens to anyone other than me in a long time."

"Why is that a bad thing?"

"Until I find my mom and brother, I don't have time for feelings. They get in the way."

I threw my arms up in frustration, pushing the tears that were building aside. I refused to cry in front of him, to give him that kind of power. "You know what? Screw you." I jumped to my feet.

Dash was right there with me, looming down over me. "What happens when you find *your* family?" he tossed at me. "You think they're just going to welcome me with open arms? A killer?"

I hadn't thought about it. Truthfully, my parents were rigid. Dash wasn't far off in thinking I'd grown up with a silver spoon in my back pocket. Yes, I went to uppity prep schools. Yep, my parents had more money than I probably realized. I hadn't wanted for anything, and I knew, a hundred years ago, I wouldn't have given Dash a second glance. We came from the opposite side of the tracks. I wasn't proud of who I'd been then, but I had a chance to be something different—someone better.

Why couldn't he?

I crossed my arms. "I think my parents will just be glad I'm alive. They want me to be happy."

"I'm not going to make you happy, Freckles."

I groaned and started walking around Dash. It was only a matter of seconds before the tears started. I knew it.

"Charlotte, wait—"

"Stop talking," I hissed.

He put a hand on my shoulder, stopping me, but I refused to look at him. "You're being unreasonable. We're both here for a purpose. My mom and brother are out there. I won't stop looking for them. Never. It could take years. Are you willing to wait that long? Longer?"

I hated that he was making me think about not having him in my life. Pressure clamped down on my chest. "I don't know, but you're not even willing to give me the chance."

"It would be better if we didn't get involved—less messy. We can't start something that is going nowhere."

Wow. That hurt. More than I expected. It was a smack in the face. Only worse. "Too late," I muttered. He had made up his mind about us, and no amount of talking or pleading was going to change that. We could talk circles around the subject all day. Short of busting out the tears, this topic was over.

"You might think you have feelings for me, but it's only because of our situation. You'll see things differently. You'll realize I'm not the guy you think I am."

Blinking away the rush of angry tears, I brushed at my cheeks. "Karma called. She said, 'Suck it!' " I yelled, tossing wet hair out of my face.

His chin jerked up. "Original."

Seething and hurting, I stormed off before I let my emotions get the best of me. I didn't need Dash Darhk. I didn't want Dash Darhk. He could fall off the face of the earth, and I wouldn't care.

It was safe to say there would be little conversation between us. He wanted me to separate my feelings. Fine. I turned the lock and threw out the key. In the distance, lightning cracked across the sky.

Great. Just great.

I stumbled once or twice on the uneven ground, tears blurring my eyes. *Shit.* I was doing the very thing I said I wouldn't: cry.

Just keep moving.

Dash yelled my name, but his voice was drowned out by another round of thunder and lightning as it whipped across the sky. My hands curled into fists. If he caught up to me, there was a good chance I'd hit him.

For the well-being of his health, he didn't follow me as I traipsed off to nowhere in particular, just away. I wanted to be free of him, to take a minute to gain control of what was churning inside me. I picked up my pace until I was almost running. It didn't matter that the wind had kicked up and I was slapped with tree branches; I didn't feel the sting.

That was the problem.

I felt nothing. Numb. Raw. Alone.

My eyes were glassy with tears. What I wouldn't do to see my mom right now. She might not have always been the most affectionate mother, but in her own way, she'd loved me. And I could really use a shoulder to cry on, but that would have been my little sister Monroe's shoulder. We'd been closer than thieves, and I missed her something terrible.

I continued to run, dodging trees and zigzagging over the hilly terrain, until I could no longer hear the rushing of water. When I slowed down, I began to realize how foolish it had been to have taken off on my own, and as I glanced around, I was no longer angry at Dash ... but myself.

Hugging my arms around my middle, a chill had settled in my blood, cooling the flush of anger. A section of my brain told me I should be terrified, however the other part knew if I stayed here at this spot, Dash would eventually find me.

He always did. And I was counting on him to continue being my guardian. There were many things we might not agree on, and we might never see eye to eye, but Dash never let me down when it mattered most ... except with elements of the heart.

But as I sat on the edge of a bluff with the wind rushing over my face, I told myself not to think about the pain slicing through my heart or what it meant. I mean, how could I possibly have such strong feelings for a guy I'd only met a little more than a week ago? It wasn't rational. I wasn't a fanciful girl. I didn't believe in love at first sight. Lust, sure, but not love. It was too soon to throw such a word around, but I couldn't say that the emotional roller coaster Dash put me on wasn't powerful.

Who knew? Maybe it was part of this screwed-up world, aftereffects of being exposed to the mist, being drugged for a century, or being mutated. Take your pick.

Getting out of my head, I took in my surroundings, seeing what lay ahead of us. I already knew what we had left behind. The river had taken us out of the Badlands and tossed us somewhere in between the mountains and the desert. I could see both of them on either side of me, and in the middle stood a series of towers, glistening like crystals in a patch of sunlight, tall and spellbinding.

Diamond Towers. The heart of the Institute.

It lived up to its name.

I gazed at the city below, half-hypnotized, and was transported to a different world, one very unlike what I'd grown accustomed to. What I'd seen of Starling Heights paled in comparison to Diamond Towers. It was a fortress, and as I gawked at its sheer mass, my curiosity piqued. A wall of white stone surrounded the perimeter with defense towers placed every so often, providing eyes from all angles. The guard towers were several feet taller than the already high wall. From my position, I was able to see down into the city. The towers were at the hub, surrounded by a community.

In the distance, rough mountains peaked below puffy, white clouds. Mist gathered midway, making a section of the mountain disappear. Thick fog spread out around the outside of Diamond Towers, swirling toward the jagged rocks. Sunlight glinted along the edges, and dark shadows formed beyond the mountains.

I rested my chin on my knees. That was where we were going—away from the bright glowing light of the city, and toward the darkness.

Chapter Fifteen

My mind rebelled at the idea. It was instinctual to move toward the light and run from the darkness, but I had to find my family. So if that meant I had to check my feelings for Dash and embrace the dangers of the darkness, I would do whatever it took.

A curse sounded close behind me, and I let my hair fall forward, shielding my face. Footfalls echoed, snapping a twig. It was Dash. I didn't have to look up to see. The tingles radiating down my spine were validation enough.

When Dash took a seat beside me, my body rejoiced. I'd known he would find me, but there was always that tiny slice of doubt.

"Freckles," he spoke softly.

"I don't want to talk about it. I just want to find my family," I replied, hugging my legs tighter to my chest. I missed the sweet, unshakable love that families had for each other, the kind of love that kept me warm at night and my belly full during the day.

"We will," he assured me with conviction.

I closed my eyes for a moment. How long had we been apart? Thirty minutes? An hour? Such a short time, yet I missed the sound of his voice as if I hadn't heard it in days.

His shoulder lightly touched mine. "Look, I'm sorry. I swear the last thing I want to do is hurt you."

"You can take your sorry and choke on it." Guilt arrowed through me. I hadn't meant to snap at him, and the words had flown out of my mouth in a gut reaction. I took in an awkward breath, my defenses crumbling. "I don't want to fight with you."

He offered a rueful smile. "Good, because I got us dinner."

While I'd been sulking, Dash had been hunting. The mere mention of food sent my stomach growling. Except when I saw the road kill dangling from a stick, the rumble turned to queasiness. "We're eating that?" I shrieked.

"You'll thank me later, once it's cooking."

Dash built a small fire, and he was right. The scent of grilled meat sent my stomach into a tizzy. I watched him over the flickering flames as he seared our mysterious dinner. From my pack, I dug out a bottle of water and took a sip. "What is it we're eating?" I asked.

He turned the skewers. "Chicken."

"You mean there are actually chickens here?" I was stunned. The mist was supposed to have mutated everything.

"No, but it helps to think of it as chicken."

I cracked a smile.

"Friends?"

"Yeah, we're friends," I agreed, a wisp of a smile on my lips.

"It's something, isn't it?" he asked, following my gaze to Diamond Towers.

Surrounded in warmth, I nodded. "There are so many lights."

"When I first saw it, I thought the same thing too, and for a while, I was captivated. Not everyone within the Institute is bad. There are those who truly do want to make this world a place worthy of living in again. The problem is those people didn't wake before the circle of trustees was created."

"Trustees?"

"Within those walls is a select group of people who govern the Heights. They were among the first to wake. Theories are it was no coincidence. They in some way were all connected in the world before. The Institute paints themselves to be the good guys, protecting the people, rebuilding the world to be a safe place, and all the while they are constructing an army of mutated humans." He removed one of the stakes and handed it to me.

Holding it in my hand, I waited for the meat to cool before burning my lips. "And since you escaped the Institute, you've been looking for your family?"

"My mom and little brother." Other than the few times I'd caught him looking at me, I hadn't seen affection in his eyes.

"What about your dad?"

His entire face changed, darkening, and his posture stiffened. I had touched upon one of those sore subjects Dash never wanted to talk about, and I instantly wished there was such a thing as Wite-Out for words.

"I'm sorry. I don't mean to pry."

"You're not. We're friends, remember?"

How could I forget?

"My father invented the word asshole. I don't think there was ever a day he loved my brother or me. We spent our entire childhood avoiding him and protecting our mother, until she finally got the nerve to leave the bastard. For more than a year, I spent my nights expecting him to come kicking down the door."

"That's horrible."

"Don't feel sorry for me, Freckles. I survived. It made me a stronger person."

It might have, and maybe that hard shell gave him an edge here in this world, but I wept inside for the little boy who never got the chance to be one, who never knew a father's love.

Dash was more than a survivor. He was also a protector. His father's abuse made Dash shield the weak.

I couldn't quench the sympathy.

He ripped off a hunk of mystery meat. "What about you? Do you miss your little sister?"

"Every day. It gives me nightmares thinking of her being out there."

His slanted eyes shot me a knowing look. "The chances of her being on her own are slim. She, like most everyone, will probably get picked up by the Night's Guard."

I nibbled on the meat, testing the taste, but once my stomach got wind there was food, it didn't care what it was. "And that is an even more frightening thought. What if she is like me? What will they do to her?" I asked, taking a bigger bite from the skewer.

His gaze moved to the white city. "Then she's gone."

He wasn't trying to be mean or discouraging. He was being straightforward, from personal experience, but it didn't prevent a seed of sadness from rooting deep in my belly. "If the Institute is so horrible, why don't more people rebel? Overpower them?"

"They're afraid. They feel trapped. They fear for their families. Pick a reason. It doesn't matter which. The Institute finds your weakness and exploits it."

"It's not fair. Haven't we all suffered enough?" I didn't just escape a catastrophe that wiped out the Earth only to be a puppet in a group of power-hungry control freaks.

"You're like a rare gem. The Institute would stop at nothing to have someone with your gifts. I've never met someone who had more than one ability."

"My eyes change with each one."

He nodded.

"So if that theory is true, there is still one more I haven't discovered."

"Green," he replied, nodding.

I swallowed, the meat feeling like sandpaper on my throat. "I don't know that I want to find out," I whispered, staring down at the half-eaten skewer.

"We need to be even more careful now that they know I'm traveling with someone and that they've gotten a glimpse at what you can do."

He had only killed one of the three guards. The other two were probably squealing like pigs to whomever they reported to. "Is this going to be my life now? Running from the Institute?"

"It doesn't have to be. You've seen people make lives for themselves outside of the Institute. As glitzy as

Diamond Towers is from here, inside those walls, the glamour is only surface deep. Out here, it's like a snow globe, and we're all outside looking in, slumming it in the Heights."

My nose wrinkled. "I get it. It's only as good as you make it. You sound like my dad."

Dash cracked a smile.

Night had descended. Cool moonbeams cast from the sky above, and the stars glimmered like points of ice. "The moon is out," I said, sighing. "It looks beautiful, untouched by all the ugliness of the mist."

"No one knows how far the mist was able to travel or how it originated, only that it started in St. Louis." The thin crest of moon offered little light, but his eyes were keen. "You still afraid to sleep?"

I tossed my stick into the fire and watched the flames lick over the wood. "I'm not afraid to sleep. It's what happens while I'm sleeping that gives me hives."

"The dreams?" he guessed, seeing the unease enter my expression.

I pressed my palms into my thighs to keep from bouncing them. "I find myself submerged deeper in the dreams. They stay with me, nagging at me, as if I'm supposed to do something, but I don't know what."

"Snapshots."

"What does that mean?"

"I've heard of people being able to get flashes of events to come." His eyes narrowed. "Kind of like how you knew the Institute was coming."

"Premonitions."

He nodded.

I didn't know what to say after that. The idea of being able to get glimpses of the future left me with a funny feeling. Acutely aware of Dash's intense stare, I kept my eyes averted on the fire as my brain attempted to process this new development. How was I going to learn to control four abilities when I couldn't even control one?

Dash leaned back against a tree, letting his eyes drift shut. The long fringe of his lashes fanned over his cheeks. "We should get some rest."

I blinked slowly, knowing I needed sleep, but my mind was twisted up, striving to work through all the crap. Sleep was where the alarming and vivid dreams would come, where the screams and pain would wrap around me, sucking the life from me. The tatters of them would linger in my mind long after I woke.

Whether it was my abilities or memories from the mist or a combination, it made sleep difficult, for I never knew what I would see.

Fog and fear. Mist and misery. The flash of my sister's wholesome face. The gleam of Dash's silver eyes. A blur of both the past and present.

If I was indeed getting snapshots, did I want to block them? Did I want to know the future? One thing I'd learned was the visions weren't set in stone. The future could be altered.

My mind wasn't the only thing burdened as I lay on the ground, watching the firelight dance. So was my heart.

I'd told Dash we were friends, and I wanted that, but I also wanted more. I wanted the chance to see if there could be something between us, but I wasn't going to push myself on him. If he didn't want the same, it would be his loss.

My eyes eventually grew too heavy for me to keep them open. I wasn't exactly sure when I drifted off, and in the darkness I dreamed.

Visions of sugarplums danced ... *sugarplums my ass.*

In the dreams, the mist surrounded me, filling my lungs, torching my eyes, and incinerating my skin, but there was no pain, not physical. My whole being was solely concentrated on the events unfolding before me. Monroe, my kid sister, was standing in a field, her hands engulfed in flames. I yelled her name, but it was as if she couldn't see me. My cries went unheard.

Realizing I wasn't getting anywhere by exercising my lungs, I turned my efforts elsewhere and found what I was looking for. Dash stood on the other side of the field, bow drawn and arrow positioned to strike.

Five seconds went by as my mind processed what was going on, eyes rotating back and forth between them.

OMG.

They were going to kill each other.

I couldn't let that happen. I stopped thinking about the mist, about anything rational, and bolted out toward the middle of the field.

"Stop!" I screamed, throwing my arms out.

I could have been invisible. Neither of them batted an eye; however, I'd put myself in a dire predicament. As if someone had just yelled *fire*, Monroe and Dash both discharged their weapons, a blazing fireball and an accurate arrow. And I was the intended target.

I woke up covered in sweat, a scream caught in my throat.

Orange-blue flames sputtered from the fire, swathing the ground in an eerie glow, but there was no comfort. Gasping, I rolled over on the bedroll, the nightmare ebbing away into reality. But like a bloodstain, no matter how hard I tried to scrub it from my mind, it was impossible to get rid of. It would plague me day and night. When I woke, the dream stayed with me—the life I used to have and would never be mine again, or in this case, the possibility of the future.

If that had been a snapshot, were Dash and Monroe destined to kill each other? I refused to believe the two people I cared about most would ultimately hurt each other and in the process destroy me.

But ... if it was, what was I going to do about it?

There was something more to my dreams, more than I wanted to admit. I didn't want them to mean anything, because none of it was good. I didn't want to be haunted by things to come or what had passed.

Why did my subconscious have to be so screwed up?

Running a hand over my face, I sat up, cutting those bleak thoughts off. No reason to go there. Not today. Not tomorrow. Not any day. The past couldn't be undone; the future was uncertain, and it was time to decide what I was going to do now in this primitive world.

"You'll gain control of the dreams one day."

My head whipped up. The voice was a familiar one, and I hadn't been sure I'd ever hear it again. Above Dash's sleeping head, perched on a low branch, was a black bird with glowing gold eyes. His head was cocked to the side, eyeing me with an inquisitive gaze. Blink.

"Everyone starts out rocky and wakes up an emotional basket case, but eventually, you learn to steer the snapshots, instead of letting them rule you," he told me, as if he could read my mind.

"Ooookay." My eyes thinned as I stared at the bird. Dash thought he was a spy, an Institute drone. I'd admit the bird was a mystery. "Why are you here?"

Blink stretched out his wings and gave them a ruffle. "To make sure you escaped the guards. I provided a bit of a distraction, you know. Lost a few feathers in the process."

"I suppose I should thank you."

He raised his beak. "That would be the polite response."

"My mom always told me to mind my p's and q's."

"Sounds like a smart woman."

"Yeah, well, I didn't always think so." One of the things about hindsight, it sucked. I was beginning to wonder if I would ever get the chance to be the daughter she deserved.

"Is that regret I hear?" the all too perceptive bird asked.

I tucked a strand of hair behind my ear. "Maybe. You'd be surprised how much time you have to think out here."

"Especially when you don't sleep."

I nodded. Bull's-eye.

"You know there are plants here that can aid your insomnia. The rascally tracker has knowledge of medicinal properties. Part of his stint as a white city goon."

It was apparent Blink was no fan of Dash, and it made me want to know details. "And why should I trust you?"

If a bird could look offended, Blink did. "Saving your life isn't enough to earn your trust?" He snorted.

What is it with everyone saving my life?

How did I really know he had distracted the guards? They had ended up finding Dash and me anyway. He could have just as easily informed the guards of our location. "I don't know what or who to believe anymore." He was a freaking talking bird, for goodness' sake.

"You better decide soon, before it's too late," he warned.

He was telling me.

The bird started pacing up and down the branch, his little claws clamping on the wood as he went. "I can help you find your family. The tracker is good, I'll give him that, but he is not a blinken."

Whatever that meant. I glanced over at Dash as he rolled onto his side, shadows of firelight playing over his face. "What about him?"

Blink shook his feathery head. "Nope. No way. Not in this lifetime. The tracker stays put, and when he wakes, he'll think you took off or that the Institute got you. Either way, it's a win-win."

My brow furrowed. No deal. I didn't want Dash thinking I ditched him or that the Institute got its paws on me. And I think the bird underestimated Dash. If I just disappeared, he would be compelled to look for me—to save me. Something told me he wouldn't stop until he did. I couldn't put Dash through that, thinking he'd let the Institute snatch me from right under his nose. It was wrong. He might be an asshat most days, but it didn't erase the attachment I felt toward him. My feelings grew stronger the longer we were together. "Thanks, but I'll take my chances with him."

He puffed out his feathery chest. "Suit yourself." Blink hovered in the air, large wings flapping and blowing air over my face. "Do try to stay out of trouble, little human."

I rolled my eyes. He did know who he was talking to, right? Trouble followed me like a dog glued to a cat's butt.

"Did you have another snapshot?" Dash mumbled, his voice thick from sleep, and he looked over at me with half-slit eyes.

"What color are my eyes?" I asked, turning so he could see. I was pretty sure the dream had been a snapshot but was hoping enough time had elapsed that my eyes would be normal. I wasn't ready to talk about what I'd seen.

He squinted. "Orange."

"What?" I squeaked, hands flying to my face.

The tilt of his lips spread into a smile, revealing his oh-me, oh-my dimples. "Kidding."

I chucked a pebble at him. "That wasn't funny."

"Hey. That hurt," he complained, rubbing his arm with a grin on his lips.

"Good."

"I knew you had a wicked side."

A slow smile pulled at my lips. "Doesn't everyone?"

Stretching out his long legs, he sat up. "Oh, Freckles, you've no idea. In this world, people don't just have a wicked side, most have a dark, seedy side."

Joy. "You don't have much faith in mankind."

"Why should I when the world has done nothing but crap on me?"

"Well, I will definitely not crap on you."

His lips twitched, and our eyes entangled.

Uh-oh.

That feeling I was trying hard to pretend wasn't there snuck up, and I found I couldn't look away. There was something incredibly sexy about Dash, all rumpled from sleep, that made me want to curl up next to him.

And if he kept looking at me like I was the last piece of chocolate, I might be tempted to do just that. I didn't realize how much I craved human touch. A hug. A kiss. Holding hands. I missed all those simple gestures.

After what was certainly the longest and shortest minute of my life, he averted his gaze, breaking the intense moment. "We should probably go. Being this close to the Institute makes me restless."

Right … before things between us moved from steamy glances to awkward pining.

I cleared my throat and began gathering up my supplies, stuffing them into my pack. The moon was beginning to disappear, and the first morning light would crest within an hour. While Dash did his thing, I snuck off behind a tree and changed my shirt.

When I returned, Dash scattered the remains of the fire. "We'll fill our canteens and eat on the road."

I stood straight and gave him a mock salute. "Aye-aye, captain."

He looked at me, shoving his hands into his pockets. "Just try not to get us killed before midday."

I cracked a grin. "I can't make any promises."

Chapter Sixteen

I had never been so happy to be out of the desert, but roaming from one holding house to another on a mission had its own downfalls.

Unlike the Badlands, the Somber Mountains was cooler, not Chicago winter cold, but it was a relief from the melt-your-skin desert. The terrain was rough and bumpy. It was all about the jutting rocks and hilly ground. Ringlets of white smoke billowed over the top of the mountain peaks, evaporating into wisps of darkness.

Similar to the Badlands, there was a desolate loneliness hidden in the crevices of the hills. The wind howled in an almost cry of a weeping woman, instilling a sadness in my belly.

I rubbed my palms up and down my arms, generating warmth.

"Are you cold?" Dash asked. There was no denying the concern there. He swung his pack off his shoulder.

"No, not really," I assured him before he did something chivalrous. Wouldn't want him to tarnish his ominous reputation. "It's just this place. It gives me the chills." My eyes bounced from one rocky wall to another.

"The change in temp can be a shock to your system. Don't play the tough guy," he advised, kneeling down at the edge of the river flowing along the quadrant borders. He filled our canteens with one of the only natural water sources that wasn't toxic. It ran clear and blue, no bubbling green mist or glittery gold surface.

We were still teetering on the border of the Institute and the Somber Mountains. Straight ahead, I could just make out the mountain this quadrant was named for. It appeared to touch the sky, and at our backs, the Institute glittered in the moonlight. "Tell me more about the founding trustees. Have you ever met them?"

He handed me a bottle of water. "Once. After Jaxson, the commissioner to the Night's Guard, saw what I was capable of, I was brought to the trustees for an offer."

I took a swig, coating my parched throat. "What kind of offer?"

A frown marred his face. "They wanted me to help patrol the pods and bring in the new recruits, keep everyone in line. Not everyone wakes up so peaceful and trusting as you did, Freckles. Sometimes, things get out of hand."

"And you refused?"

He shook his head. "No. I took the job."

My eyes widened. "Why?"

"I saw it as an opportunity. If my family was in a pod, I could locate them. Eventually, it turned into a way for me to escape. It didn't pan out so well considering I ended up in an underground jail." He tried to keep his tone light, but under the façade, there was anger.

I started to scowl. "Is that how you know where to search?"

"Yeah. I know the general locations of all the pods in the Heights."

"How many are there?"

"Inside the quadrants, there are at least a few hundred. Outside the perimeter …" he shrugged, "…who knows? If anyone has woken beyond the boundaries, the mist that still lingers would have probably killed them."

I stumbled, tripping over my own sore feet. "The mist isn't gone?"

He shook his head. "No, not completely. Outside the borders of Starling Heights, the mist plagues the air. Each year it grows a little bit smaller, but at the rate it's shrinking, it will be decades before it disappears completely."

"So no one knows what is beyond the Heights?" I questioned.

"Death, that's what."

Dun. Dun. Duuun.

Leave it to Dash to end things on a dark and forlorn note.

Nestled into a debris of rocks, we came upon a holding pod that looked as if there had been an earthquake knocking rocks and rubble on top of it and partially obscuring the building. Intentional or not, it hid the entryway, and if Dash didn't have eyes as keen as an owl and the general knowledge of its location, we would have passed it right by.

I went through the front door with hope, knowing I was probably setting myself up for heartache, but I couldn't stop the tingling of optimism. My little sis, mom, or dad could be lying asleep within these concrete walls.

Once again, the coldness of the facility smacked me in the face, causing the tiny hairs on my arms to stand up. The air tasted of iron and sorrow. I didn't know what it was about these frozen chambers, but immense sadness rushed in me for the souls lying on the metal tables, like the place was a morgue.

I ran my fingers along the wall as we went down the hall. Dash's warm body beside me was the only thing making the chamber tolerable. I wanted to take his hand. He must have read my mind. His fingers threaded through mine.

Friends hold hands. It is totally normal.

Dash led me through chamber after chamber, and I did everything I could to keep my face expressionless. It wasn't easy. I wasn't made of stone, yet seeing the empty slabs gave me a wee bit of hope. I couldn't figure out which was the lessor of two evils—waking up, or being blissfully asleep.

"Any familiar faces?" Dash whispered.

"No. Not yet," I replied, scanning the sterile room. Two rows of bodies, lying there, placid and tinged with blue. The drug used to induce such a slumber was powerful and innovative stuff.

"Story of my life," he grumbled.

I squeezed his hand.

"We've only got an estimated twenty minutes until the next round of guards come strolling in. Let's do a quick sweep of the remaining rooms and make ourselves scarce. What do you say?"

I couldn't answer him, because I was staring at a face I recognized. Moving closer, I gaped at the girl who had been my friend since second grade. I couldn't describe the feelings racing through me at seeing a familiar face. My lips split into a silly grin.

"Chloe," I whispered. "Oh, my God. I can't believe it's you." My friend, with her blonde hair and doe eyes, didn't so much as twitch. "Chloe, wake up. It's me." I wanted to shake her, scream at her, slap her, anything to make her wake up, but it wouldn't have made a difference. Didn't stop me from trying. She just lay there motionless, her arm flopping over the side of the slab from my efforts.

Tears pricked at my eyes, but I blinked them back.

"Freckles, she can't hear you." He rested a gentle hand on my shoulder.

I sniffed and placed her hand over her chest. "I'll come back for you," I murmured.

"We need to go," Dash said, giving my shoulder a squeeze.

I nodded, allowing him to usher me through the holding house like a zombie. I could feel the control on my sanity snapping one fragile thread at a time. Seeing Chloe like that, frozen in a coma-like slumber, pale and lifeless, had a deeper influence on me than I'd expected. If seeing one of my friends in such a state had me a shaky mess, what would I feel at seeing my little sister like that?

My stomach sunk like an anchor to the bottom of the ocean as the crisp mountain air rushed over my cheeks. The disappointment spinning inside me was great knowing there was nothing I could do for Chloe, increasing the hopelessness I was trying so hard to squash. It was a losing battle.

A maelstrom of emotion swept through me, finally cracking the thin barricade I could no longer keep in place. My face crumbled, tears streaming down my face. I couldn't stop it, didn't even try. What was the point?

Dash took one look at my stricken expression and gathered me up in his arms, tucking my head against his chest. I buried my damp face, not able to care about my ugly cry.

"I'm sorry," I hiccupped. There wasn't time for me to have an emotional breakdown. We needed to be moving, and it meant something to me that Dash took a minute to comfort me in his own way. He might not want to admit there was something more between us, but it was moments like this that told me he cared.

Dash made a strangled sound from deep within him, and his arms tightened around me. "You have nothing to be sorry for," he murmured into my hair.

He continued to hold me until the tears ran dry, all the while whispering soothing words. I lifted my head, and he swept his thumbs over my cheeks, erasing the remaining tracks of tears. "You okay?"

On the spur of the moment, I stretched up on my toes and pressed my mouth to his. It was nothing more than a brush of our lips, a thank you, but there was an undeniable spark that radiated between us. It lit up every nerve ending in my body, and from the darkening of his eyes, he felt it too.

I lowered myself to the flats of my feet, staring into his stormy eyes. At another time and place, I might have taken advantage of the flare of need churning in his expression, but I wanted Dash to be receptive. I didn't want to trick him, so I pretended my body wasn't flushed, and I didn't want him to kiss me senseless.

With the tears dried, we left behind the holding pod and Chloe, heading back into the sporadic thickets of trees and cliffs. I had meant what I said. I would come back for Chloe. The vow triggered something inside me, and I began to pay attention to the details of where we were. Someday, I would come back here, and I would find a way to save Chloe from being another pawn for the Institute.

A patch of wildflowers caught my eye. Such a vibrant shade of purple, their velvety petals rained on the ground beneath the shrub. It was frivolous, but I wanted to pick one of the enchanting flowers. The sweet smell that fragranced the air around them caused a tinge of longing for the fanciful things from my life before. Perfume. Makeup. Prom.

I never got the chance to go to my senior prom or graduate high school. Just add that to the long list of crap I never got the chance to do. Bending down, I stuck my nose into the center of the flower and inhaled the scent of spring. It was lovely. I plucked a bud at the stem, failing to notice the thorns until one stuck me, piercing my skin.

"Ouch!" My blood, red as a freshly picked rose, trickled over my nail, running down the side of my hand. "Dammit," I swore, popping my finger into my mouth and attempting to suck away the sting.

Dash was suddenly at my side, barking orders. "Let me see that," he demanded, getting all pushy on me. He plucked my finger from my mouth, examining the puncture. It was a deeper cut than I would have ever imagined a tiny thorn could cause, and it hurt like no one's business.

I scowled. "Hey, I wasn't done with that."

"This plant is poisonous."

"Of course it is," I grumbled. Why wouldn't it be? Everything here is either venomous or rabid.

Dash watched me as he put pressure on the wound. "You might start to feel dizzy or sick. I'm going to try to drain out the poison."

Uh. What? Drain? With his mouth? He wanted to suck on my finger? I tugged my hand from his grasp. "You are not putting my finger in your mouth."

"Trust me, Freckles, this isn't a twisted attempt at foreplay."

I did the unthinkable. I glanced down at the cut. Ugh. This might have been a good time to mention that blood, more specifically, *my blood*, made me queasy. As usual, he had impeccable timing. Before I could mention my affliction, nausea came up out of nowhere, rolling in my stomach in angry waves.

Oh, God. I was going to vomit.

Like all over the front of Dash's black T-shirt.

"I need to sit down," I groaned. Hurling wasn't my only concern. I was having trouble breathing as I lifted my gaze. "Dash," I muttered.

His brows furrowed together. "You look like crap."

Any other time, I would have jumped down his throat for a comment like that, but at the moment, I didn't have the energy to mince words with him. My skin felt clammy and gross, dizziness swarming me as the wet warmth of blood cascaded down my finger.

There were two Dashs frowning at me. "Freckles, don't you dare—"

Too late. I swayed forward toward him. Blackness consumed me.

Chapter Seventeen

"Charlotte," Dash whispered.

My eyes fluttered open.

A sense of Déjà vu overcame me as I stared up into Dash's silver eyes. Why, oh why, did he always have to be so close? My body could only handle so much excitement in a twenty-four hour period, and I was past my point of controlling my ability to keep myself from doing stupid things.

"What happened?" I asked. I was on the ground, flat on my back, staring up at a dark sky strewn with glowing stars.

Moonlight sliced over his face, picking up flecks of gray in his eyes. "You fainted, that's what happened."

"I did not. I never faint."

The sides of his lips twitched. "Hate to break it to you, doll, but you most certainly did. And would've cracked your head on a rock too, if I didn't have ninja-like reflexes."

"I'm guessing you want a thank you?"

Dash tugged on a strand of my hair, grinning. "What do you have in mind?

I angled my head to the side. "Come a little closer, and I'll show you." I couldn't help myself. There was something almost fun and thrilling about making Dash uncomfortable.

"I'm beginning to think I didn't get all the poison. It could be causing delusions. Are you feeling well now?"

I gave him the finger.

He laughed.

And I really didn't want the sound to send butterflies through my belly.

"I'm going to take that as a yes. I never would have pegged you for the 'faint at the sight of blood' type of girl," he said.

"I'm not."

"Good. Don't ever do that again."

There he goes. I wasn't even on my feet, and he was ordering me about. Slowly, I stood up. Dash was right by my side in case things went topsy-turvy again. "I don't intend to. I find that fainting is not my thing."

He arched a brow.

"Shouldn't we be putting distance between us and that dreadful place?" The Night's Guard must patrol the nearby vicinity, and we hadn't gotten far before I'd decided to swoon.

"We're far enough; besides, I think you could use a bath," he said, wrinkling his nose.

He did, did he? "Me?" I gasped. "I'm the one who has to stare at you and that scruffy face of yours." I rubbed the palm over the underside of his chin.

He chuckled softly. "It is getting a bit hairy."

I plucked on a patch of scruff. "You think?"

"Fine. You want a bath; I might have an answer to your wish."

"Oh yeah, you know where a shower is with hot water and a whirlpool with steaming jets?" I asked, being a smartass.

It backfired ... sort of.

Dash delivered in a way that was post-apocalyptic approved.

"Another cave?" I said, angling my head suspiciously.

"Just wait," he grinned.

"If this one has any snykers, I'm out," I warned.

The narrow cave expanded to a circular grotto with a small, natural hot spring. Steam billowed from the water, rising up to the rocky ceiling. A waterfall cascaded over the side of a cave wall. Warmth flooded the room, but it wasn't an uncomfortable heat like the desert. From the mouth of the cave, a soft, cool breeze blew in, the combination making the room an idyllic temp. Blue lightning bugs fluttered in the air, skipping over the surface of the water. Their wings looked as if they were made of glass.

"What are they?" I asked, taken by their beauty.

"Glassflies," he answered, eyes on my face as he watched me absorb it all.

Wow. This place was a secret treasure, and I couldn't wait to take a dip. "Thank you for bringing me here."

He shrugged like it was no big deal, and maybe it wasn't for him, but for me it was phenomenal. "It was either this or continue to smell you."

I gave his shoulder a shove, not that he moved. Dash was an immovable force when he wanted to be.

I liked the drama of the view—the dangerous drop into the bubbling spring, even the ribbon of rocky path winding around the room and disappearing deeper into the cave. It was serene. The fact it was hidden in another cave, surprisingly, had very little impact on its splendor, which could only mean I was actually getting used to living like a mountain man.

What is happening to me?

Dash set down his bag and rummaged through one of the pockets, pulling out a bottle of soap and a straight razor.

"You're kidding. You had a razor this whole time?" My legs were starting to look like a gorilla. "I'll rock, paper, scissors you for first dibs."

"You're on, Freckles. Prepare to lose." There was a sardonic twist to his lips.

I grinned.

Let the games begin. Pounding my fist on my hand three times, I threw down scissors. Why not? I was feeling a bit sharp. Looking over at Dash's hand, I let out a squeal. "Scissors cut paper," I said, cutting his paper with my finger scissors.

"I don't know how, but you definitely cheated."

I won, and my grin said it all. "Thank you," I sung, plucking the razor and soap from the ground. Slipping my feet out of my boots, I walked to the water's edge and dipped a toe. I sighed, and then I remembered the usual nasties that prowled in the waters. "Are you sure it's safe?" I asked, lifting my head. I really hoped so, because it looked ultra-inviting, and I really wanted a bath that didn't involve being shot at. Not to mention, the chance to shave my legs and armpits … I'd died and gone to heaven.

Dash was more of a show than tell guy, but when he whipped his shirt off in one smooth motion and begun unbuttoning his pants, I was torn between gaping and glancing away.

Holy Mountain Dew.

Boy was stacked.

He kept on his boxers, and I was relieved and a tad disappointed. I'd seen my fair share of half-naked men thanks to my summers at the beach. I practiced cheerleading every day after school on the field, right next to the sweaty football team, but da-a-nm, seeing Dash shirtless, my pulse sped into unchartered territories.

It shouldn't have been a big deal. I already knew I had a teeny crush on the guy, so it made complete sense that seeing him nearly naked would send my hormones buzzing. He had a build that appealed to me—not too big like a steroid junky—but there wasn't an ounce of fat on him.

He dove over the side of the edge into the water with fluid grace. I stared after him with drool on the side of my mouth.

Get a grip.

Easier said than done. I exhaled.

Dash broke the surface laughing, water dripping off his face and glistening on his lashes.

"How deep is it?" I asked.

"Why don't you come in and find out?"

Oh boy. We'd come to the part where I had to take my clothes off. In front of Dash. I'd never been self-conscious of my body, but the idea of stripping suddenly filled me with awkwardness.

"What are you waiting for? You haven't gone shy on me, have you?" Dash challenged, knowing it would appeal to my rebellious side.

With a bravado I wasn't feeling, I grabbed the ends of my shirt and took a deep breath. His eyes were on mine, air in the cavern spiking. *Just do it. The longer you prolong, the harder it will be.*

I yanked the shirt over my head and quickly shimmied out of my pants, tossing them both on the cave floor. Forcing myself to keep my hands at my sides, I walked to the edge and made a point to meet Dash's smoldering gaze. "Satisfied?"

"I haven't been satisfied since I met you."

"Ditto," I muttered before jumping in.

Warm water rushed over my face, providing little relief to the flush overtaking my skin. But after a few moments, it didn't matter. The water was refreshing and invigorating, giving me a sense of joy.

Popping up out of the water, I laughed as I whipped my head back, pushing my long, tangled hair out of my face. I wanted to do that again. Forgetting about my modesty, I treaded water, moving toward the edge to test the depth of the lagoon. Based off my height, the shallowest part of the spring was around four feet. I was able to stand with the water hitting my chest.

Dash was watching me in a way that made me want to move closer. I made myself stay where I was and stumbled for something to say. "The water is nice."

"Why don't you come closer? The water is warmer over here."

I splashed a wave of water at his face. "No way. That is the last thing I'm going to do. Besides, what happened to you wanting to be just friends?"

He waded through the water, coming toward me with a mischievous glint that warned me to tread with caution. "I'm thinking friends with benefits might be more our thing."

"Oh, you are? I've got news for you: I'm not interested."

He flashed me a pair of identical dimples. "Liar."

"Maybe. Or I just don't want to get my hopes up for you to crush them again."

"Smart … and safe … but not very fun." Water lapped around my shoulders. "You're nothing but a tease."

"That's a first. I've been called many things, but never a tease."

"Okay. Correction. You're a man-whore *and* a tease."

He laughed. "If you're done gawking and ruining my good name, toss me the soap."

I rolled my eyes and lifted myself up onto the edge, leaving my feet dangling in the water. Grabbing the bottle of soap from the ledge, I opened the top and took a sniff. It smelled of sandalwood and vanilla. "Ladies first," I said, squeezing a glob into my hand. Securing the top, I flung the bottle a few feet across the water.

Dash caught it midair. "Nice throw, slugger."

I smashed my hands together, dispersing the soap before working it into the mop I called hair. "Actually, I was aiming for your head."

He gave me a shit-eating grin. "We'll have to work on your accuracy."

"You'd know all about that."

Dash lathered his hair and body, turning the water around him into suds. "I would."

That got me thinking. "Does that skill only apply to arrows? Or is it anything you touch?"

"Trust me. The Institute put me through the paces. There isn't a weapon I can't handle. There isn't a mark I can't hit."

"I understand why the Institute thinks you're an asset, why they're going to such great lengths to find you."

"Yeah, well, it's becoming tiresome. I've grown bored of this mouse and cat game."

Squeezing the suds out of my hair, I asked, "What does that mean?"

Dash chucked the shampoo bottle into the open flap of his bag. Show off. "It means, after I find my family, I'm going to find a way to deal with them. I don't want to spend the rest of my life running."

And who could blame him? I'd only been at this a short time, and I could attest that it was indeed exhausting. "If anyone can do the impossible, it's you."

A moment passed, and a curious, almost confused look crossed his expression. "You're nothing like I first thought."

I twisted around, kicking my feet under the water. "You mean, you still don't think I'm a spoiled brat?"

"No, I do … but you're more than that."

"Thanks." I grinned and then dunked my head underwater, rinsing off the bubbles from my hair. When I resurfaced, Dash was in front of me, the bubbles gone from his hair. He was so close, I could see the water droplets on his lashes, making them thicker and darker.

"Feel better?" he asked in a hushed voice.

Define better. I was feeling different—that's for sure—but better? I wouldn't go as far as to say so. If he'd just stayed on his side of the grotto, I'd be peachy-freaking-keen. "What are you doing?"

He brushed past me, lifting himself out of the water, and stood at the edge of the pool, looking down at me with beads of water dripping over his bare chest. "Drying off."

Hubba-hubba.

I gulped.

Would I ever be able to control my thoughts around Dash? Because right now, all I could think about was his abs and how delicious he was. And ... having his babies. His offer of friends with benefits was becoming more and more appealing by the second. "Any chance you got towels in that magic pack of yours?"

An arrogant smile spread across his face. "Afraid not, Freckles. We're going to have to air dry."

What is happening to me?

Everything he said enticed an emotion inside me, usually the desire to toss myself at him and kiss him brainless. When I was around Dash, it was as if someone else took over my body, making me do and think crazy things. How was I going to stop myself from ogling him like a total creep if he was going to be strutting around in wet boxers? It really left almost nothing to the imagination. I forced my gaze to stay centered on his face. "Did you plan this?"

He stood dripping water over the rocky floor and ran a hand through his hair, smoothing it back. "To get you naked and at my mercy? Absolutely."

"You're deplorable," I stated without much heat.

He strutted over to his bag and pulled something out. "Don't worry. I'll stay on my side of the cavern, and you can cover up with this. I'm not a complete tool," he said, offering me one of his shirts.

What other choice did I have? If I stayed in the spring much longer, I was going to end up shriveled like a raisin. I lifted myself out and reached for his shirt. The moment I gripped the material, Dash jerked it back, bringing me with it.

I tilted my head back and gave him a bored look. "I thought you said you weren't a tool."

He wasn't fooled by my lack of interest. "I lied."

Dash would be so much easier to resist if I didn't find his egotism charming. "Hands off, Darhk. Unless you're admitting you feel something for me," I said, angling my head to the side.

He took a step forward, our bodies grazing. "I definitely feel something."

My cheeks stained pink at his implication. "Other than lust, you jerk," I pointed out, shoving a finger in his chest.

Wrong move.

Touching Dash when he was more or less naked sent my senses into a whirlwind.

And I wasn't the only one.

"Is this about respect? Because I completely respect you." The husky quality of his voice hit me in the feels.

"You're so confusing," I muttered, yanking the shirt away from our weird game of tug-of-war. I slipped into his shirt. The hem reached my thighs, offering the coverage I sought.

Dash rocked back on his heels, lips lifted. "I'm a guy. My needs are pretty basic."

I rolled my eyes.

He pulled on his pants, and my eyes were disappointed, but my heart was relieved. "I'm going to get us some firewood. You think this one time you can stay out of trouble?"

I sat on the edge of the water, letting my toes skim on the surface. "I'll be good."

Watching the aqua glassflies making lazy circles in the air, I let my mind wander, reflecting on the craziness that had become my life. My normal schedule of waking up, going to school, cheer practice, and doing it all over again, day in and day out, seemed monotonous.

To think I'd always longed for adventure and excitement, to see the world and all it had to offer, and now that I had, I yearned for my old boring, quiet life.

A trail of tingles tapped up my spine, alerting me that Dash had returned. I spun around as he strolled through the narrow path into the opening of the cavern with nothing on but dark jeans. I might not understand the vast majority of things about this world, but I was lucky to have escaped the Institute and that Dash had found me. I shuddered to think where I would be otherwise.

Setting up the branches in a pile, he looked over at me. "Think I could get a spark?"

I gave him a funny glare. "You want me to produce a bolt of lightning? In here? Have you lost your mind? I could hit you."

His eyes glimmered. "Or ... you could hit the wood."

"That's *if* I can even summon the spark."

"You need the practice."

Frowning, I shook my head. "It's your grave."

He chuckled. "I trust you."

"What am I going to do if I miss and electrocute you instead? Not all of us have your perfect aim," I reminded him.

He dusted off his hands, removing any wood particles. "Simple solution: Don't miss."

Sighing, I stood up and walked closer to the mouth of the cave. "Your logic blows," I mumbled under my breath. "I should hit you just out of spite."

"You wouldn't dare," he said with a saucy grin.

That's what he thinks. Stretching my fingers, I crouched down beside the pile of wood and took a deep breath. I harnessed the electricity inside me, letting it stretch out to the tips. I felt it rattle and wake. A tiny glassfly buzzed near my ear, and I swore I could hear it urging me to summon the spark of lightning. I gave in, releasing the pent-up static. It raced down my arm, shooting from my fingers straight into the center of the stack of branches.

I liked the rush it gave me—potent and addicting, and I wanted to do it again.

A small stream of smoke floated from within the wood, and Dash rocked back, sitting on his butt. "See. I knew you could do it. No sweat."

"I almost had a panic attack." Curling my legs underneath me, I waited for the spark to turn into flames. I lifted my eyes to find Dash looking at me. "Why are you staring at me like I'm on the wrong side of special?"

His lips twitched. "I can't get over your eyes. When they shift colors, it's the most mesmerizing thing I've ever seen."

Not what I'd expected him to say. It was nice ... but uncharacteristic, and I wasn't sure I trusted this charming side of Dash. "I always figured they were my best feature."

"That and your legs aren't bad."

I wiggled my toes. "I guess all that cheerleading practice paid off."

He snorted. "I knew it."

"Are you telling me you weren't the captain of the football team?" I asked, feigning utter astonishment.

"Not by a long shot," he scoffed. "I spent more time ditching classes than I did attending."

No surprise.

I combed my fingers through my wet hair as we sat by the roaring fire, munching on a new version of trail mix and talking about our lives from before. What kind of school we went to. What our friends were like. How we never would have even spoken to one another in our previous lives. His little bro. My little sis. I could tell it was difficult for him to reveal parts of his life prior to the mist, and I didn't push. I just lent him my ear. No judgment. I wanted to know everything about Dash—what shaped the person he was today.

My hair was mostly dry when Dash stretched his legs, standing up and tossing me a wad of material from his pack. "I borrowed these from Eastroth. They should fit."

"Define 'borrowed,' " I asked, eyes narrowing.

"After the trouble Brunlak caused, I figured they owed us some clean clothes."

Translation: he stole them, but I couldn't fault his logic. And I really, really didn't want to have to put on the same clothes I'd been wearing for days. Not that I condoned stealing. Desperate times, desperate measures. "Are you going to put a shirt on now?"

He flipped on another black T-shirt. "Is my bare chest bothering you?"

"You could say that," I mumbled, slipping my legs into the black pants that were very similar to leggings.

God, what I wouldn't give for a shopping spree at Macy's. "I can't believe I feel halfway human again," I commented when I was fully dressed in my *borrowed* clothes.

Dash lifted a single brow. "Do you know what would make you feel completely human?"

I shoved my old clothes in my bag. "If you say having sex with you as friends, I'll kick you in the balls."

Dash chuckled. "That's … kind of hot."

"And you're demented."

He raised a single brow. "You ready to go?"

As much as I wanted to stay tucked away in this little slice of paradise, we couldn't. There were more holding pods to ransack, and we both had a reason to leave utopia behind. "No, but what choice do we have?"

"That's the spirit."

On the road again. It could have been our theme song. The winding path out of the cave was longer than I remembered. As we got closer to the exit, the wind picked up, whistling through the tunnel. We turned the corner, and I was feeling pretty good about going back out there. I had Dash by my side and a confidence that if anyone could find my family, it was him.

But the glow of faith didn't last more than a few minutes.

It never did in the Heights.

As we rounded the corner, we bumped into a pair of unexpected visitors, and all those good vibrations went to shit.

Two Night's Guards stood lounging at the opening, their blue uniforms stretched across their arms. At our untimely approach, they both straightened up; twin grins of cockiness flashed over their lips. "Well, what do we have here?"

Chapter Eighteen

———————— ❦ ————————

The tracker and his whore." One of the Institute douchebags sneered.

Dash and I sort of stood staring at each other like two doofuses caught in headlights, and then we sprang into action. He took a step back, positioning himself in front of me. "The way I see this going, you have two options. You either apologize to the lady, or ... I kick your ass. Actually, now that I've had a second to think about it, I'll probably kick your ass regardless. So why don't you apologize, and we can move straight into the ass kicking?"

"Glad to see your ego hasn't deflated while you've been living like a savage," the blond-haired guard said, clearly thinking he was clever.

I begged to differ. Lame-o.

"There are only two of them," I whispered, standing on my toes so I was close to Dash's ear.

His body was taut. "These are trained soldiers, Freckles," he muttered, keeping his eyes focused on dingleberry one and two.

"That's right, toots. We're bona fide killing machines. Ain't that right, Dash-y boy?"

"My fist is begging to be in your face," he growled, eyes flashing with dark promise.

The blond grinned in anticipation. "Now we're getting somewhere."

"Our orders are to bring you both in alive," the taller guard informed us, eyes darting between Dash and me. There were strands of red running through his auburn hair, but it was the strange color of his veins that caught my attention. They were black and stood out against his pale skin. "But I'm sure the boss won't mind if we have a little fun first."

Dash's cheeks were highlighted in the silvery moonlight. "Just like old times."

"Except you're no longer the commander's pet," Blondie said, flexing his fingers. The motion caused bone-like nails to extend, coming to a sharp serrated point, similar to Wolverine.

Dash gave him a half-grin, revealing one deep dimple. "Maybe not, but I bet you still can't hit a moving target."

Blondie didn't like that. His aqua eyes flashed with hatred and jealousy. There was no love there for Dash, not even a teensy bit, and regardless about their orders to bring us in alive, Blondie wanted to get in a few shots of his own to satisfy his urge to hurt Dash. I could see it in the malice behind his eyes, and Dash did too.

Shit hit the fan.

Spidey-vein made a grab at me. Instinct fired within, and I darted out of the way, avoiding his attempt to get handsy with me. Blondie took a swipe at Dash with his claws. Dash ducked and rolled his shoulder into the guard's side, knocking him back a few feet, but Blondie was quick on his feet, avoiding a tumble over the cliff.

A damn shame, too.

Anger settled over Dash like a blanket, and I saw a different side of him—fierce and ominous. He cracked his neck. "Let's hope I'm not getting rusty."

If that was a joke, I didn't find it funny.

The next thing I knew, Dash's arm struck out, smashing into the other guard's jaw. "There's more where that came from."

Spidey stumbled back, spitting a mouthful of blood as he lifted his head. "That was pathetic. The girl makes you weak."

"I don't need powers to wipe the ground with your blood, and realistically, I think Freckles here could take you both."

What the hell was he doing?

Offering me to fight Beavis and Butthead singlehandedly—he was going to get me killed. I poked Dash in the side, drawing a sideways glower. "Just what are you doing?"

"Buying us time," he replied, shoving me behind him and away from the edge.

"Oh. Good plan." My voice was fringed with sarcasm.

Dash returned his attention to the guards watching us intently. "I'm surprised the commissioners kept you guys around, let alone send you two after *me*. Not the most effective choice. I didn't think he underestimated me that much. Or … maybe he sent you both on a suicide mission, hoping I'd do him a favor and put an arrow in your hearts."

Blondie was back up on his feet and came barreling at Dash like a cracked-out linebacker, roaring with rage, hands slashing through the air. Dash leapt back, dodging swipe after swipe, narrowly missing being diced and lanced like a kebab. The guard did, however, manage to slice the front of Dash's shirt. Blondie ceased his kung fu and charged. A nanosecond before impact, Dash sidestepped to his left and stuck out his arm, clotheslining the poor sod. He went down like a sack of rocks, wheezing and gasping for air.

Ouch. That had to have hurt.

Dash stepped on the tips of his claws, leaning over the groaning guard. "I hope that felt as good as it did for me." Unfortunately, it was going to take more than a hit to the throat to take out Blondie. His leg swiped through the air, catching Dash in the back of the legs. He went down to his knees, stringing together a truckload of f-bombs.

Dash's head snapped up, his gaze finding mine, silver eyes glowing like orbs. I could feel the power radiating off him. "Run," he growled low in his throat.

There was no way I could leave him alone. Not with Blondie pointing his boney blades at Dash's heart.

Spidey laughed, a gloating sound, reminding me the fun wasn't over. I turned my head away from Dash to locate the second guard. Unfortunately, he was too close for comfort. The devil was in my face. "Shit," I swore. Spinning around, my shirt flapped in the wind as I tried to run.

"Charlotte!" Dash screamed.

Spidey's hand went into my hair, grabbing a fistful at the scalp and twisting me around so my back was to his chest. "Don't worry, doll. I'll be gentle," he murmured in my ear. "I mean, it can't be worse than letting Darhk touch you." He chuckled, his rancid breath on my neck. Just when I thought things couldn't get worse, his hand moved roughly around my hip and up my side, skimming just under my breast.

Revulsion rose up like bile in the back of my throat. "Listen, you piss-ant," I hissed. "I'm not going anywhere with you. Take your hands off me." I yanked back.

Big. Fat. Mistake.

Jarring pain shot through my head, and I squeezed my eyes against the sudden sting of tears. Concern blossomed. I struggled against him, but it did very little other than hurt me more.

"Fight all you want, sugar. I like it rough." His tone made my skin crawl.

I wanted to punch him and might have tried, if I just hadn't had my ass handed to me.

Dash glared at Spidey with murder in his eyes. "If you touch her again, I'll kill you." A muscle jerked in his jaw as he ground his teeth in disgust.

My captor pulled out a gun, and I was pretty sure it was a Taser, not the real deal. It still wouldn't feel good if he touched me with it. "You're in no position to make threats," he told Dash, gloating. "Or do I need to have Saber remind you?"

Saber was all too happy to comply. "I thought you'd never ask." He raised his hand, all five claws extended, with a devious grin on his slimy lips.

"No!" I bellowed.

Twisting and turning as if my hair was on fire, I tried to loosen his grasp, struggling to break free. All I managed to do was knot my hair and look the jerk in the face. Over his shoulder, my wild eyes found Dash. Rage seeped from his pores at seeing me struggle with the other guard.

I cried out when the douche tugged my head back, severing my brief glance at Dash. My hands flew to my head, and I thought I was going to scratch his eyes out. It also occurred to me that this might be it.

I might not survive this attack.

Saber swiped down his claws, grinning the entire time as he lacerated the flesh on Dash's chest. Dash reacted fast, moving an inch out of the way, minimizing the depth of the claws, but he didn't make a sound as the tips cut away at his flesh. Eyes closed, every muscle in his body clenched.

Seeing him at the mercy of Saber cracked my heart into a million pieces. "Dash," I sobbed as tears filled my eyes, going lax in the other guard's arms.

Everything felt surreal on my end.

Dash and I might end up in the Institute's clutches after all.

Or worse.

He must have had the same thought, because the next thing I knew, his eyes met mine and something transpired between us. I didn't know what it was. It was as if he could transport his thoughts into mine, and he was telling me to fight—to not forget the power I had, the power just at my fingertips.

Pulling from the light inside me, I held out my hands, ignoring the crackling of heat dancing along my skin. A spear of lightning launched from my fingers. This time I hadn't aimed for the ground as I had with the others. I went for his heart. Not having Dash's precision, the charged light hit Saber in the center of his stomach.

Impact knocked him back, and the shock of electricity vibrated throughout his body, causing him to shake uncontrollably. In my blind rage, I had wanted to kill him, stop his heart, and I might have, if my aim had been true.

"What the—" Spidey jumped, releasing me quickly as if he'd been zapped, and he probably had.

My skin vibrated with an electric current, making my hair fly out around my face. Dash shot to my side, grabbing Spidey as Saber twitched on the ground. "I told you I was going to kill you," Dash roared with a fueled rage that even frightened me. He had drawn the knife from his boot.

The guard's eyes went wide at the sound of Dash's threat, and his blade pressed against the guard's throat. A drop of blood trickled down the guard's neck, disappearing into the blue material of his issued uniform.

Yay for team Dash!

Without thinking, I twisted out of the guard's grasp and slammed my knee into his groin, instinct guiding me. I didn't know why I saved his life. Dash struggled with trying to be a different person than the Institute had trained him to be, and I didn't want there to be more blood on his hands because of me. My knee might be throbbing, but it had been worth it.

Air expelled from the guard's lungs in a rush. "That. Was. A. Stupid. Move," he wheezed.

A giddy satisfaction danced inside me, and I smirked. "It was my pleasure."

Dash whacked the guy on the back of the head, and it was lights out. "Charlotte," he groaned. "How many times can you stop a guy's heart in a day?"

I shot him a glare. "Do you really want to find out?" I had just been threatened and groped; I electrocuted someone and had seen Dash bleed. I was not in a good mood. The reminder of him getting shredded by Saber sent an instant concern streaming within me. "Are you okay?" I asked. Not waiting for him to respond, I tore open his shirt to look at the wounds. Five marks sliced across his chest broadside, close to the old scar. This hadn't been the first time he'd been lashed open.

My heart ached for him. There didn't seem to be any fresh blood flowing, but I ran my fingers along his chest. I wanted to touch him and fulfill the need to make sure he was okay. Somehow having my hands on him reassured me he was going to be fine.

He winced at my touch. "It's just a scratch," he said, grabbing my hands.

I tipped my head up. "You don't have to play the tough guy."

"I've had way worse, Freckles. I'll live." He threaded his fingers with mine. "Now, come on. You can play nurse later, once you're safe."

It was no longer when *we're* safe, but when *I* was safe. My eyes softened. When had his concern shifted entirely to keeping me out of the Institute? When had he suddenly made the decision he would put my life before his?

I didn't know what to say, but I really wanted to kiss him at that moment.

"Move your butt, hot cheeks"—a hand smacked me on the butt—"before these two decide to wake up." Obviously he wasn't in jeopardy of bleeding to death.

I jumped, giving him an exasperated look.

Dash let out a low chuckle at my expression and gathered up his discarded pack.

I didn't need to be told a second time. My legs were moving, climbing over the guards before either of them could regain consciousness.

"Thanks for what you did back there," he said. "Restraint has always been my biggest problem."

Did I hear him right? Dash was actually thanking me? "I thought I was your biggest problem," I added sweetly.

He groaned. "You might be right."

We worked our way down the mountain, careful not to lose our footing on the gravel and tumble down. There was an air of urgency that followed us. The guards wouldn't be unconscious for long, and who knew if they'd been alone? There could be an ambush waiting for us.

Someday, I was going to learn to keep my ominous thoughts to myself. They seemed to have some kind of voodoo power of coming true.

Rounding the edge of the cliff, Dash grabbed me and pressed me into the wall, sealing his body to mine.

Holy smokes.

It was unexpected, and the immediate contact from the length of him sent a thrill of tingles, but through the haze of feelings, voices traveled from below us—more guards. I glanced up at Dash for confirmation. He laid a finger to my lips, listening. I held my breath and pretended to be stone; all the while, my heart was pounding in my ears as he smashed me against the rock wall, and I wasn't certain who was more dangerous to me—Dash or the guards. Both had the power to drag me under.

Chapter Nineteen

His muscles flexed under my hands, and the thud of his heart beat against my chest. The goal was to blend in with the night and keep quiet, and hopefully the guards would move on. We were cheek-to-cheek against a dip in the mountainside, shadows surrounding us. Rock dug into my back, but with Dash so close, I could barely think about anything past the feel of him, let alone that I had a slight fear of heights.

Dash rubbed his stubble against my skin, breathing in my freshly bathed scent and whispered, "Don't move."

As if I could.

He had rendered me immobile, the length of his body rocking my composure. There was something stupidly hot about being in danger and having his lips drifting over my skin. Below us, a trio of guards and their lighted torches moved slowly, searching the region, for us no doubt.

"They couldn't have gone far," said a voice I recognized as Blondie or Saber. What a stupid name.

"Yeah well, if you two hadn't flubbed up, we wouldn't be out here playing hide and seek. Pathetic." The voice was female—which surprised me—and full of superiority and disapproval of her two comrades.

"I thought you liked games," Saber scoffed.

"If we don't bring them in, the commander is going to send you two to the dungeons," the female voice snarled. There was something youthful in her tone, but a hardness that implied she was older than her voice suggested. "I heard the ratice down there are bigger than your head, Trist."

Whatever a ratice was, I shuddered to think about sharing a cell with one. Every creature in the Heights was hopped up on steroids. Trist must have been the name of Saber's partner in crime, the one who had gotten a little too friendly with his roaming hands.

"Sorry, not all of us eat off a silver spoon, Captain Kiss Ass."

A glow lit the ground below us, and Dash's body went still; the even in and out of his breathing halted.

"If you have a problem with me, let's get this over with. Me and you." She was a tough chick, and I wasn't looking forward to ever meeting her face to face.

"Keep your panties on, Ember," one of the dipshits griped.

"Whatever. Just find them, and I'll take care of the rest," Ember said with a condescending bark.

The bickering continued below us, but I stopped hearing what they were saying. Dash nuzzled my neck, causing my body to relax into his. "You make me lose my head, forget the danger that lurks in the shadows below us. I don't like it."

I shivered. "I don't do it on purpose."

Our noses brushed. "Maybe not, but it doesn't change the fact that having you this close is hazardous." His silver eyes gleamed under the stars. "How the hell can you smell so good?"

I instantly felt the change and arched into him, sighing.

The sound was like dynamite over the valley. He pulled back, pressing a finger to my lips, silencing me. Moonlight splashed over his face, and my breath caught at the passion I read in his eyes. It was impossible to glance away, my face transparent. I wanted him to kiss me.

In one fluid motion, his mouth was on mine, drowning out my moan and one of his own. I couldn't believe I was kissing Dash on the edge of the mountain. Talk about being on top of the world. There was nothing sweet or gentle about his kiss. It was born from suppressed longing and the adrenaline of being caught.

My brain clicked off as his fingers tightened on my waist, skimming just under my shirt. As my hands slid up his chest, looping around his neck, I kept telling myself not to get emotionally involved. It was just a kiss—a very deep, scorching kiss that left me breathless and heady.

But there was no stopping now. I was sunk.

And I couldn't keep lying to myself.

I cared about Dash. A lot. I would have to deal with whatever did or didn't happen between us.

My teeth caught his lower lip, and he pulled back, ending the hottest kiss of my life and leaving me unstable and dazed. I would have been content to stay right here, overlooking the valley and the sparkling lights of Diamond Towers as long as Dash held me in his arms. But as I glanced into his eyes, I knew it was a dream not likely to happen.

Nothing had changed.

Other than giving into a moment of weakness, the troubled expression that crossed onto his face was clear. There still could be nothing between us.

And my heart hurt.

I forced myself to step out of his arms and shifted my gaze to the ground. "We should move," I whispered. The coast was clear. No guards. No voices. It was a miracle we hadn't been discovered making out on the side of a mountain.

"Freckles," he said, bringing my gaze up to his, but I didn't want to listen to him make any more lame excuses about how he shouldn't have kissed me. His scowl was enough.

"Save it. There's no need to make a big deal out of this. Let me worry about my feelings." I didn't wait for him to say something. Flipping my hair, I brushed past him, edging my way along the rocky path back down the mountain.

Dash moved a whole lot quieter behind me, but he followed, and he didn't press me to talk. Thank God. If I opened my mouth, I couldn't be held responsible for what ridiculousness came out.

We reached the bottom of the rocky incline, and I assumed we'd had our last brush with the Institute and their puppets, at least for the night. I was wrong.

Dash had instincts like a panther. Crouching behind a bush, he assessed the situation laid out in front of us. I scooted down beside him, pushing aside the large leaves. There was a line of guards standing in the field before us that made me wish we were back up on the mountain.

"How do you feel about spending the night in a bush?" he whispered.

"Are there bugs?"

"Uh, no?"

"That was so not convincing. How long do you think they plan on standing out there?" I asked.

"All night."

"Fabulous." I squinted my eyes, scanning the face of the guards. Trist and Saber were talking with another guard, and beside them was a female. I assumed it was Ember. Her back was to me, but she reminded me of someone, and it wasn't only her snobbish and self-righteous behavior. I'd known plenty of girls like that. It was the glint of her reddish-brown hair against the light of a torch that struck a chord of recognition.

Then she turned around, and the air stalled in my lungs. The world stopped spinning. I couldn't believe what I was seeing. A burst of happiness followed the shock. "Monroe," I whispered.

"Charlotte, don't move," Dash hissed.

I heard him, but what he was saying didn't register. All I could think about was getting to my little sister. I had found her.

"Dammit," he growled.

I didn't even get a full step before Dash tackled me, pinning me to the ground with his body.

Chapter Twenty

❖

"Let me go!" I seethed. "I'll scream."

His hand covered my mouth. "There is nothing you can do, Freckles."

Nothing I could do? That's what he thought. I jerked against the weight of his body, but it was a waste of effort. There was no way I would be able to move him, so I resorted to a dirty tactic. I bit him.

"You little minx," he growled, eyes luminous.

Dash could call me all the names he wanted, but it had gotten the job done, and I wasn't about to lose the opportunity to make him see reason. I had to save her. Didn't he see? "That's my sister out there! She needs me."

He caught my flailing wrists, pinning them to the ground. Silver eyes burned into mine. "Stop fighting me! You have to listen. That girl out there, she is not your sister, not the one you remember. And trust me, Ember needs no one. She is under the control of the Institute. Nothing you can do will save her."

I didn't think there was anything he could say that would make me think of Monroe as anything other than the pesky, lively, kindhearted—and yet stubborn when she believed in something—little girl. Monroe was only two years younger than me, but from the time she'd been born, I'd looked out for her.

"You don't understand," I argued, feeling desperate and frantic. "I know her. She would never hurt me."

"That might have once been true." The doubt was so obvious in his voice I wanted to prove him wrong. How could he possibly know anything about Monroe?

Since the moment I'd woken up, I'd longed to see a familiar face. And now she was out there. The only thing separating our reunion was six feet two inches of muscle. "Isn't the whole point of this expedition to find my family? Well, we have, and now you won't let me talk to her?"

Dash held me still, ignoring my protests. "I've never met a more obstinate female in my life. I'm trying to keep you from getting killed."

I wiggled underneath him. "Why do you care?"

He released one of my wrists and grazed my cheek. "Beats the shit out of me, but I do care."

I jerked at the warm zing his touch produced. "If that's true, then let me at least try to talk to her."

"No."

He tried to touch me again, but I wrenched my chin away. "God, you're so full of yourself. What would you do if it was your brother?"

His eyes bore into mine.

I stopped struggling and let him see how important this was to me, making myself vulnerable. All the fight went out of me, my body going lax in his arms. "I'm okay now."

He lifted a brow.

"I promise."

He paused, exhaling roughly. "If something goes wrong. ... If I can't protect you. ..."

I laid a hand on his arm. "It's okay. I know the risk. And Monroe's worth it."

"Is she now?" said a voice from the other side of the bush.

Dash rolled off me, snatching his bow off the ground beside him and kneeling on one knee, arrow pulled back against the string. "You move ... you twitch ... and I won't hesitate to shoot," he thundered lowly.

The voice laughed. "Still as jumpy as ever."

Our little scuffle in the bushes hadn't gone completely unnoticed. While Dash and I had wrangled over who was the boss of me, we had attracted the attention of the Night's Guards. I blamed Dash. If he hadn't gone all cavemen on me, we wouldn't have found ourselves surrounded by six of the Institute's finest. Not an absurd number, but I didn't know them; however I knew Monroe.

Here was my chance, and what was I doing? I was sprawled out on the ground gaping at her.

Collecting myself, I pushed to my feet and brushed off the leaves and dirt. I looked at Dash as I left the covering of the brush, and I swear I heard his voice in my head. *Be careful.* Of course, that was insane, and for a moment, a trickle of fear moved through my veins.

With sweaty palms, I stepped into the clearing and whispered her name. "Monroe."

I wasn't sure what I expected. Maybe for her to come running into my arms, or for her to shriek in surprise. My eyes were trained on her, waiting for the glow of recognition to beam in her expression.

I couldn't stop staring at her face. She had changed. I guess a hundred years would do that to you, but it wasn't just the angles of her cheeks or the extra inch of height; it went past skin deep. The green eyes that had once mirrored mine looked upon me with a haunting scorn, instead of the big sister admiration.

It was hard to admit, but Dash might have been right. I took a step back, feeling as if I'd been sucker punched, my mouth going dry. "Monroe," I called again. "Don't you remember me?"

Dash was behind me, and I could feel the tenseness coming off him. Someone was ready for a rumble. Out of the corner of my eye, two guards shifted their stance, and for a second, I thought they were going to bum-rush me.

"Don't," Monroe ordered. It was her voice, but not—sharp and clipped, unlike that of a fifteen year old. But I guess, depending on when she had woken, it was possible she could be my age ... or older. Thinking about it screwed with my head. Monroe stepped forward, looking me over. "My name's Ember. And you're in violation of the Institute's intake law."

I forced myself to breathe slowly. "Look, I know things are different now, but you can't trust these people, Monroe. Come with me."

"You know her?" Trist accused, eyes bouncing to me.

Ember cut him with a sharp glare. "Does it matter?"

He snickered. "Wait until the commissioner hears about this."

"Grab her," Ember ordered.

What?! Was she kidding?

"What about him?" the guard to her left asked. He had the eyes and fangs of a lion.

My mouth gaped as Monroe's hands were engulfed in flames, a wicked smile on her faerie features. "Leave the elusive Dash to me."

Ember, as she was calling herself, angled her body toward Dash. "Miss me?"

His mouth twisted into an ugly shape. "I wouldn't say that is the emotion I'm feeling."

I took another step back and found I couldn't go any farther. Two guards had moved in behind me.

"Keep your paws to yourself, or I promise you'll regret it," Dash thundered. The trigger on his temper was about a centimeter long.

The two guards hesitated, seedy eyes boomeranging between Dash and Ember. They seemed confused. It dawned on me that once upon a time, Dash would have been in Ember's place, barking the orders.

"What are you waiting for?" Ember hollered.

"Monroe, please. You don't have to do this," I begged, trying to reach the little girl who had once been my best friend.

"Stop calling me that. You know nothing about me."

Maybe not, but if she gave me a chance. ...

It didn't take me long to see that was not going to happen.

The guards, obviously more afraid of my little sister than Dash, grabbed me by the arms.

Bozos.

I would have feared Dash ten out of ten times over Ember. Before I could wrangle myself free and try this self-defense move I'd learned in gym, the guards set me free. Correction: as I glanced down, they hadn't been given a choice, because neither of them were breathing anymore, their eyes lifeless.

I tried not to freak out as the ground soaked up their blood, an arrow embedded into each of their chests.

"I warned you." Dash got to his feet, looking really, really angry.

A twisted smile cracked the corners of Ember's lips. "You just had to go and do that, didn't you? Always were a show-off. My turn." I'd forgotten about the flames flickering from Ember's hands. Apparently, I wasn't the only one in the family who got the superhero gene; except staring at Ember, I determined she might have gotten the villain chromosome.

With a flick of her wrist, globes of fire drifted between Dash and me, separating us as we darted away, barely avoiding our faces being incinerated. The flames sent shards of fractured light over the land.

Chaos ensued.

I hit the ground, shielding my face as cinders danced around me. The nickname suddenly made sense. My sister was a pyro.

Chapter Twenty-One

"Charlotte!" Dash cried, leaping through the towering flames. He reached me in two long strides.

"Are you insane?" I coughed, a mouthful of smoke clogging my lungs.

He pulled me to my feet. "Stay close."

Uh, if I could have glued myself to his side, I probably would have. My pulse was all over the place, and apparently when I got panicky, my defenses went haywire. Little prickles of electricity danced up and down my arms.

"We're going to get out of this," he murmured.

I didn't know how he always knew what I was feeling, but in times like this, it was encouraging.

He ran a hand through his tousled hair. "Hey Freckles, maybe do that thing you do."

I got the message. He wanted me to bring the storm. "I-I don't know that I can." As the flames died down, I once again found myself looking eye to eye with Monroe. I mean Ember. Whoever. No matter what she called herself, she was my sister.

A shadow pooled to my right, and as I took a step closer to Dash, the inky mass built itself into a shape, an outline of a man. I'd never seen anything like him, but then again, my sister had just shot flames from her hands.

"Crap," I muttered.

Dash's whole body tensed. "Um, Freckles, how about that storm?"

No pressure.

The shadow took the form of a human male. What was with the Institute and recruiting teens? He might have been twenty at the most, but he was built like the Hulk. The dude looked like he ate steroids for breakfast.

"You keep an eye on your sister," Dash instructed. "I'll keep beefcake and the others busy while you figure out how to get your mojo back."

"Dash, are you insane?" I squeaked. "He'll kill you."

Dash smirked. "Haven't you learned yet? I'm pretty damn hard to kill."

What a fool. There wasn't time to argue. The tall tank with icy blond hair was strutting our way.

What had I done?

This was entirely my fault. If I had listened to Dash when he'd tried to warn me about Monroe ... And now we were here, once again outnumbered by the Institute, but this time, I wasn't so sure we were going to slip away. Eventually, luck ran out.

Ember appeared beside me, and I jumped. "You scared me," I scolded, forgetting for a second this wasn't my little sister, but Ember crazy-pants.

"You *should* be scared of me," she replied, right before she swung her leg out, catching me in the stomach with the heel of her boot.

I went up into the air, landing on my back. Jarring pain ricocheted through my bones. I wanted to curl into the fetal position and groan but forced myself to roll onto my side, clutching my belly and gasping. Having the wind knocked out of you sucked llama balls. "What the hell, Monroe!?" I wheezed, shoving the hair out of my face.

"How many times do I have to tell you? My. Name. Is. Ember."

Okay. Point made. But I still didn't understand why she'd hit me. An insidious shadow crept into my line of vision. Dash was dealing with his own problems.

I wanted to defend myself, but how could I hurt the one person I had protected most of my life? Not that she seemed to care about my well-being. And if I waited for Dash to finish taking care of the other guards, it might be too late. I'd seen Dash do remarkable things, but if we were going to escape this time, he was going to need my help.

"Don't make me fight you," I said, shoving to my feet. Light filled my veins, moving through every cell in my body. Behind me, lightning snapped in the dark sky. Looked like someone got her mojo back.

"I can't wait until the commissioner sees you," was Ember's response. She went to grab my wrist but jerked back immediately after contact. Lips turned down, she stared at her hands. "Did you just shock me?" she accused, her glass bottle eyes sharpening.

I flicked out my hands. "It's probably not a good idea to touch me."

She chuckled, gaze moving to the light show happening overhead. The flash of yellow lit in her irises. "Big sister got morphed. Always did have to steal the spotlight."

We circled each other. Behind me a grunt was followed by a thump. Dash sounded as if he had his hands full. … I sympathized. A glow burned behind my eyes, purplish in color. "I'm electric … when I want to be."

"Oh good, this is going to be fun."

Dry lightning crackled across the sky in a burst of white light. Oh, yeah. I was feeling pretty badass right about now. Spreading my feet apart, I centered my gravity. "What happened to you?"

"Let's make a deal, sis. You come with me, and I'll tell you," she countered.

That sounded like a double-cross if I'd ever heard one. "Why? So the Institute can make me into a killer?"

"I see Dash has been filling your head with lies. He has that effect on people. There are reasons the Institute exists. Humankind wouldn't have survived if it wasn't for the existence of Night's Guards."

I didn't like the way she said his name. It made me wonder how well Ember and Dash knew each other. A flare of white-hot jealousy rippled inside me, and I hated it. The last thing I ever thought I would be doing was fighting over a guy with my sister. That wasn't the relationship we had … or used to have.

"Charlotte, we need to wrap this up," Dash interrupted.

I risked a glance at him. It was weird watching people fight with abilities. It was a mixture of hand to hand and stuff only found in movies. He ducked just as beefcake swung. Dash used his size as an advantage, recovering quicker than the giant-sized guard, and planted his fist into his ribcage.

I winced at the sound of a bone crunching.

"Still haven't changed your name, I see. How long have you been awake, wandering around with a fugitive?" Ember asked, drawing my attention back to her.

"A few weeks."

Surprise flickered across her face. "That's impossible."

"I think in the scheme of things, nothing is impossible."

"You might be right." She flicked out her wrists, letting them submerge in flames. "How about we make a deal?"

"What kind of deal?"

"If you come with me, I won't incinerate Dash. I'll even let him go."

I swallowed. Dash had warned me that as soon as the Institute got wind I had abilities, their interest in me would be unyielding. My instinct was immediately to refuse, but as I let my gaze slide to Dash, he was wearing down. I had to do something. Talking was getting me nowhere, and I had to come to terms with the fact that Monroe was gone.

Dash had been there from the moment I woke. And here he was fighting for me because I had wanted to save Ember, who clearly didn't want to be saved. I wasn't giving up, but this fight would have to wait for another day. We needed to go.

And I needed to pull my weight. Dash and Ember couldn't have all the fun.

It started with a crackle. A bright blue light flared from the sky, shining straight toward a guard—the one who looked like Hulk. It flew like a bullet, hitting the guard in the chest.

He went down, his body going all twitchy, and he didn't get back up.

A second bolt of lightning hit the ground, causing a fissure and ripple through the earth, knocking the other guards and Ember off balance.

I couldn't breathe.

I'd just killed someone. Knowing that the guard would have killed Dash, or was doing his damnest to, didn't make me feel any less horrible.

Dash's bright eyes held mine, understanding melting the hard flecks of flint. "It's going to be okay," he assured me.

His voice barely registered through the roaring in my ears.

"I-I hadn't meant to kill him," I said, trying to convince myself more. "Oh God."

"Get over it," Ember snapped.

Waves of electricity returned to me, and the purple haze behind my eyes began to fade. When the source of my power died, so did my energy level. There was a void inside me where the power stemmed from.

I backed up, away from Monroe, with a heavy heart. Inside, I was torn. I had only just found her, and here I was trying to escape with no idea if or when I would see her again.

I glanced over my shoulder at Dash. The shock to the earth had shaken things up, allowing us an edge.

Flames engulfed her hands. She wasn't going to let us walk away.

Ember was persistent. I'd give her that, exasperatingly so.

"Don't make me put an arrow in you. Remember, a good leader knows when to cut their losses, and you, Ember, can't take on both of us." Dash was behind me, a hand under my elbow, guiding me backwards.

Ember grinned. "You know I can't just let you go."

And that wasn't the answer Dash wanted. He shot an arrow. It swiped through the air in a clean arc, and I held my breath. OMG. It was headed directly at my sister. He wouldn't, would he? I get they had some sort of history, and it had ended badly, but he knew how much she meant to me.

My heart lodged in my throat, and I stood frozen. He never missed. How many times had he boasted about his precision skills? Emotion clogged my throat, tears gathering at the corners of my eyes. There was nothing I could do to stop it. All I could do was watch in astonishment as the arrow sliced through the air and. ...

I couldn't believe it. Exhaling the breath I'd been holding, I stared as the arrow sunk into the material of her left shoulder, missing her flesh, but pinning her to the trunk of the tree. The only thing he had injured was Ember's pride.

Ember laughed. "I thought you never missed."

"I don't," Dash said in a low voice of warning. If they tried to follow, he would bruise a whole lot more than their egos.

He had deliberately missed, and my shoulders sunk in relief. "Thank you," I whispered.

Bending down, he grabbed our packs and inhaled deeply. It came out in an unsteady rush. "Can we go now?"

Exhaustion lined every muscle in my body. "I thought you'd never ask."

He slipped a hand to the small of my back. Tattered and bruised, we limped like an old couple out of the clearing and toward the misty mountains. There was a primitive and essential feel to my future.

I missed the Charlotte that I was, back when things were normal, and I wondered what she would think of the Charlotte now—what I'd become. The Charlotte who was a weapon. The Charlotte who kills.

Had I known it then—that it would be the last normal day of my life—what would I have done differently?

Everything.

Dash ran a hand through his jet-black hair. "What you did back there, it doesn't get easier, but you did the right thing."

Had I? I kept telling myself I didn't have a choice, but I wasn't so sure. There had to be another way than killing. "Nothing makes sense anymore." I swayed on my feet. Suddenly, I wasn't feeling like hot shit.

Dash was in front of me. "Whoa there, Freckles. You okay?"

"I'm fine," I said. The words were weak, probably due to the ground spinning.

"Fine my butt." His jaw set in a firm line as he swept me into his arms moments before I hit the ground. "I've got you," he murmured. At least I think he did, because after that, I remembered nothing.

When I came to, my head was pulsing and my mouth was dry. I'd felt like this before: the day I'd woken up in Hurst after indulging on way too much cheap alcohol. I lifted my head and glanced up. Dash had me in his arms and was carrying me across the mountainous terrain. Looping my hands around his neck, I rested my cheek on his shoulder. "Holy crap. I did it again, didn't I?"

"Did what?" he asked, stepping around a sizable boulder.

"Fainted."

His lips twitched. "Maybe."

I played with the hair curling at the nape of his neck, too comfortable in his arms. "What's happening to me? Why do I keep blacking out?"

"I'm not sure," he admitted, but from the expression on his face, he wasn't liking it.

"You don't have to carry me," I offered, though I was content being off my feet, particularly since my head felt as if a drummer was practicing on my brain.

"Maybe not, but I like how you feel in my arms." His voice lowered to a sexy whisper.

I rolled my eyes, telling myself to not get swept up in his sweet words. "Seriously. I can walk. It's not like I broke a leg."

His lips curled into a small smile. "Yet."

He set me slowly on my feet, my body brushing against his. A wave of dizziness assaulted me, but I wasn't entirely sure it was all from fainting.

And he knew it, giving me a devious grin.

I dropped my gaze to his mouth. Wrong move. I shifted left, staring at the mountains. "Now what?" I asked.

"I got a plan."

My eyes flipped back to his. "That always scares me."

"As it should, but this one, I think you'll like … at least for the night."

I cocked a brow. "Now I'm terrified."

He didn't rush me at a grueling pace, regardless that the Institute could be on our heels. I was wrapped up in my own thoughts, and the conversation lagged. So much had happened in a short span; processing the dismal change in my life was difficult to swallow. For days, all I'd thought about was finding my family, how everything would be okay once I saw them, and now I wasn't certain of anything. I clung to the bit of hope that my parents weren't corrupted by the Institute like Monroe was.

I slid a sideways glance at Dash. "Did you hook up with my sister?"

"What?" he coughed. "No." I'd never seen him flustered, but I would say he was looking a tad guilty right about now.

"I don't believe you. I mean, it's clear you knew each other." There had definitely been some underlying tension.

"Where is this coming from?" he asked, the tips of his ears flushed.

I shrugged. "There was something about the way she looked at you." Monroe might have reinvented herself into Ember, but deep down, I still knew my sister.

"We did know each other," he admitted. "She was one of the first people I met when I woke. Actually, she was on patrol that night."

Now it was my turn to be rendered dumbstruck. I tucked the flyaways of my hair behind my ears. "You were right. She's not the same person. The Monroe I knew never would have hurt anyone, let alone me."

"She's been brainwashed, Freckles. We all were. From the moment the Institute finds you in the holding pod, they immediately start conditioning you, convincing you the only safe place is within the white walls of Diamond Towers. Those of us who showed gifts were put into the training program, and a few of us were transferred into a special division—those with exceptional skills." Distaste lined his words. Dash harbored some deep wounds and hatred toward the Institute. Who could blame him? I myself was feeling pretty damn jaded.

I wrapped my arm around my middle. "I don't know what to do next."

"I've got an idea." He draped an arm around my shoulders, drawing me to his side. "How about a night in a bed?"

I looped a hand around his waist. "Is this some weird game of make-believe? If so, I'm not in the mood."

He ruffled the top of my hair. "Guess you'll just have to see for yourself."

I blew the hair out of my face. "You're cruel. If there isn't a bed waiting for me wherever you're dragging me, I'm going to shock you."

"Torture. Nice. I like a girl who isn't afraid to get her hands dirty."

"You're weird."

"And you like it."

Maybe. And that was my problem. I liked Dash too much.

He stopped walking and pointed my shoulders to the northeast. "Do you see it?"

I looked in front of me, but my eyes kept sneaking glances at his face. "You mean that hunk of weeds over there? It's hard to miss."

He leaned down. "Look closely," he whispered, his warm breath on my ear.

If he would just stop distracting me, I might be able to concentrate long enough to focus. Squinting my eyes, I almost didn't see it, but a moonbeam caught on something shiny—a piece of glass. "Is that—?"

"A house." He grinned.

Just over the knoll stood a cabin that looked as if it had been through World War III, and maybe it had. Covered in moss, only a corner of a window peeked through the concealment, but it was a welcomed sight. "Does anyone live there?"

Dash winked. "Let's hope not."

"Great," I muttered, following behind him. "Now we're breaking and entering."

"Trust me, no one is home and hasn't been for decades."

"How did it survive this long?"

He shrugged. "Who knows? But don't expect Buckingham Palace."

I knew what to expect, all right. More bloodbugs, snykers, and other fun critters.

Taking out his dagger, Dash cut through the overgrown vines, but it was almost a fruitless endeavor. Like everything in this primitive place, the laws of nature had changed. Moments after he chopped off the tops, the vines regenerated, making getting to the house nearly impossible.

But somehow we managed to claw and hack our way through. "This thing isn't going to strangle me in the middle of the night, is it?" I asked, wrestling with a plant taller than me.

Dash's head swung my way. "Uh, probably not. Depends on how intact the windows are."

Wonderful. He promises me a bed, but how could I possibly get any sleep knowing a plant might kill me while I slept? "Did you know this was here already?" I asked, stepping on a stem to make a path to the door.

He placed the blade into his boot. "Yeah. I laid low here for a few weeks after escaping the dungeons."

"I'm shocked you were able to get out. What kind of freaking plant is this?"

"A Venus flytrap."

"I hate nature."

Chuckling, Dash put a shoulder to the door. It took three tries before giving way with a groan. Dust particles rained down from the doorway as he wedged it open. "Ready to play house, Freckles?"

I rolled my eyes and stepped inside.

Besides smelling like my great grandma's attic, the place wasn't nearly as atrocious as I'd imagined. It was a small cabin with a kitchen and living space open to one another. In the corner was a stone fireplace with a pile of black ash in the hearth. Everything was covered with an inch of dust, but I couldn't have cared less. It might have been sparsely furnished with what would now be considered antique furniture, but to me, this place reminded me of home.

Well, with a lot of imagination. Regardless, it beat sleeping in a cave or in a tree.

At the end of the wall was a set of stairs, leading to a small room with a low-lying bed. I sighed. "I never thought I'd see one of those again."

Dash stood in the archway, a rather dangerous smile on his face, watching me with intense, mercurial eyes. "Told you there was a bed. I think I deserve a reward."

I was unable to move. "What did you have in mind?"

"Just a kiss." His eyes were solely fixed on mine as he moved into the room.

"Uh-huh. I thought we were friends."

His gaze didn't stray from my face, and I knew we were standing on the edge of a vast abyss, looking down. If I didn't pull away, a line would be crossed, and we could never go back. There would be nothing *friendly* about the way we kissed, yet I couldn't make myself look away. "*Friends* can have a *friendly* kiss."

"Yeah, well, you're a handful, and more trouble than you're worth."

"If you're trying to sweet talk me, it's not working."

"You didn't let me finish," he said. "You're also beautiful."

"Better." I pushed closer to Dash, tilting my head back. "The thing is, I don't want just a kiss."

His eyes were dark, churning with emotion—so much conflict as his heart tried to decide what was right. "What do you want?"

"I don't want to be alone. Not tonight." *Not ever*, I added silently and stepped forward, slapping my fingers across his chest. If he didn't want me to touch him, he could walk away. I drank in the warm contact that I'd missed so much.

His hands framed my cheeks and brushed aside the stray curls. "Whether I want to admit it or not, every time I look at your face, I know I would do it all over again. I wouldn't take back the first kiss."

There was too much talking, and then I processed what he had said. "What are you talking about? What kiss?"

"The one that woke you up."

"You kissed me?"

"That's beside the point. Are you listening to me?" The pad of his thumb swept over my bottom lip.

"I'm trying, but I'm not sure I'm following." Being pressed against him left me a little scattered.

His eyes shifted degree by degree, the silver hue deepening. "To hell with morals and good deeds. I've survived just fine without a conscience before. Why do I need to start now?"

My thoughts exactly. I grinned. "What are you saying?"

"I don't know. I. …" He leaned in, and his lips hovered over mine, sharing the air between us. "Maybe this will clear it up for you."

He kissed me.

Dash angled his head just enough that our lips brushed. One turned into two before he increased the pressure. And just like that, any pretense of control or reason melted away. Everything around me—the noise, the smells—it all faded, leaving only Dash and me in this moment. After the first touch of his lips, fire leaped up inside me, roaring to the surface, and my heart constricted. A powerful, electric feeling coursed through me, almost like when I pulled lightning from the sky. I dug my fingers into his hair, yanking him close, and his arms crushed me to him.

We'd shared other kisses, not many, but this was different. There was urgency between us, as if this night might end before either of us wanted it to. His lips scorched mine as he deepened the kiss, taking it to a new intensity. My fingers trailed down his chest, gripping his arms and holding onto him.

I wasn't sure what had come over me, but I couldn't seem to get close enough. He must have felt the same way. His arms encircled me as he lifted me onto the bed, one hand sliding along my hip and down my thigh. The full contact of his body had every nerve in me lighting up, and I swear it felt as if I was glowing.

Tread carefully, Charlotte.

His tongue circled with mine.

Screw caution.

I wanted this.

I wanted him.

Now.

My hands slipped under his shirt, tugging the material up his chest. Within seconds, he was shirtless, and I was able to continue my lingering exploration. Dear God. He had wide shoulders and abs I could sink my teeth into.

This was crazy. I'd never been so bold with a guy before, or so anxious to do something I'd never done. Regardless of my reputation in high school, everyone had it wrong about me. This was one cheerleader who'd never had her pom-poms ruffled.

His lips pressed against the spot under my ear, giving me a moment to catch my breath. It wasn't helping. There was something wicked about the little kisses he dropped all over my throat. He kissed in a way I'd never been kissed. Of course, I didn't have a lot of experience to compare it to, but Dash's kisses could be felt all the way to my core. Under the sweat, blood, and tears, there was passion. Explosive passion. Within minutes, I was dissolving into a white-hot flood of sensation.

I don't remember how or why, but I was no longer wearing my tank, and Dash's fingers were strumming over my stomach, evoking heat of epic levels.

My skin felt like silk under his touch, making my body come alive with electric currents. Dash was a different kind of danger than what lived outside these walls—an exciting, thrilling danger—and my body was ready to take the plunge. My heart was telling me to put on the brakes.

I could have gone on kissing him forever, gone on pretending there was no one else in the world but us. My body arched into his, and a moan escaped.

Had that come from me?

He stared down at my face. Time stretched, and the depth of his gaze did something funny inside me. If I could bottle the way he made me feel with just a look, I didn't think I would be sad another day in my life. He created a light inside me that countered the darkness inside him. "Tell me to stop." His voice was rough and raw.

"I don't want you to," I whispered and reached up, rubbing my cheek against his stubbly one.

But he pulled back, and our eyes locked. A wealth of emotion shone in his eyes. "Shit," he muttered, taking a ragged breath.

Not the response I'd been expecting. Not when my body was starved for contact, starved for him.

Chapter Twenty-two

———————— ❧❦❧ ————————

We were twisted up in each other, and my skin was flushed. "What's wrong?"

His eyes, shimmery silver, burned into mine. "There is nothing I want more right now than you. Nothing."

He had no idea what it meant to me to hear him admit his feelings. I could barely swallow. Dash had a way about him that made me feel loved, cherished, and crazy beautiful. Since I didn't have the words to tell him what was going on within me, I reached up to seal my lips with his.

"Wait. Just hold on a second," he murmured against my mouth.

What could possibly be wrong? Then it dawned on me. "Let me guess. There are no condoms in the new world." I might never have done the deed, but the last thing I needed was to risk getting pregnant in this world. Thank God one of us had sense to remember.

He let a nervous chuckle. "There are other ways."

"Good." I assumed we would go back to kissing, but he only stared at me. Why did I feel like there was a big fat *but* coming?

"But. ..."

And here it came. My arms dropped away from his neck as I waited for him to tell me what was bothering him. The haze slowly began to wear away, and I noticed the lines of unease wrinkling his forehead. I brushed away a strand of dark hair that had fallen over his forehead. "What is it? You can tell me anything."

"I never expected to feel like this. No matter how much I want this—and trust me, I want you—we can't do this."

I lay there shocked, stunned, and stupefied. "I don't understand."

"It's complicated."

"I get that sex is complicated, but I'm not asking you to marry me."

"It's not that," he replied.

"Then what?" I pressed.

He exhaled right before he dropped the bomb. "There was someone else before the mist."

I was rendered motionless. And then it hit me all at once, what he was telling me. "You have a girlfriend," I accused.

He closed his eyes and nodded. "I don't know why I didn't say anything before. It's no excuse. I should have told you, but I stupidly thought I could resist you, resist this pull I can't seem to control that draws me to you."

The life was sucked from the room, a piercing ache stabbing my heart. I shoved at his chest, throwing his body off me. "Why are you just now telling me this?" Pain lanced within me, making my voice crack. Being smacked would have felt better.

Lying back on the bed, he raked his fingers through his disheveled hair. Tousled by me, I might add. "Because I'm a jerk. I didn't know things between us were going to get. ..."

He didn't need to finish. I'd heard enough. "You're looking for her."

"Yeah," he admitted.

I tried to rein in the anger suddenly assailing me as it accompanied my great disappointment. "But you found me instead."

"I never intended for things to go this far." His voice was soft and flooded with regret.

He had warned me, and maybe I should have listened, but it's not like he had made it easy on me: kissing me, flirting with me, touching me. He hadn't acted like a guy who was in love with someone else. "It's a little too late." If he apologized, I was going to lose it. I didn't want to hear he was sorry he'd kissed me, sorry he'd touched me, sorry he'd developed feelings for me.

I rolled over, pissed off and cursing Dash Darhk to seven different kinds of hell. I bit my lip, refusing to let the tears that threatened to spill, even though my chest ached so badly.

"Freckles—"

I flinched and shook my head, and a flash of lightning cracked outside. That was Dash's cue that I didn't want to talk anymore tonight. And if he'd tried to touch me again, I would have singed all the hair from his body.

Silence ticked away the minutes. Eventually, he sighed and rolled over. Back to back, I inched as close as I could to the edge of the bed, putting space between us. With my nose kissing the wall, my comfort mattered very little. It wasn't as if I was going to sleep at all.

We might be safe here for a night, but I wasn't comforted. I'd never felt more alone in my life. And it wasn't until I heard the gentle inhales of Dash sleeping that I gave in, allowing the tears to flow freely and purging myself of my internal emotional mess.

Tonight I let myself be a girl. I let myself hurt.

Tomorrow was another battle.

I'd never woken up with such a strong urge to kick someone off the bed. The only problem: when I rolled over, he wasn't there. I was alone on the squeaky, old mattress. Blinking away the sticky residue of sleep and tears, I searched the room.

If the two-timing scum had left me here, tucking his tail between his legs and running, so help me, I'd track him down and do more than squeeze his balls. I'd—

Wow. I sounded like one of those psychotic girlfriends who slashed their boyfriends' tires and stalked their Facebook. And I was definitely not one of those girls. Or hadn't been, prior to meeting Dash.

What was he doing to me? I'd never threatened a guy's manhood in so many ways in my other life. I wasn't convinced Dash was the best influence on me, but it didn't stop the hurt of being rejected or my heart from wanting him.

In a span of less than thirty seconds, I managed to get myself worked up, and it was all for nothing as my eyes settled on Dash. The morning light cast fluttering shadows over his face as he sat, brooding, out the ivy-covered window, and my heart stabled to a reasonable pace.

Why did he have to be so damn good looking? Why couldn't he be fat and short, instead of the perfect specimen of male? Why did I have to fall for someone who was honorable and unavailable? My chest squeezed.

To my great disappointment, he had tugged his shirt back on, but the same could not be said for me.

Crap.

I was more or less naked.

Trying to make as little movement as possible, I scanned the bed and the floor for my shirt while, at the same time, keeping the blanket wrapped around me. It wasn't precisely an easy task.

"You're awake." Dash's voice filled the quiet room.

My eyes snapped up, and I tried to remove any lingering dewiness from my expression.

He strolled over the rickety wooden floor and scooped my shirt off the floor, my eyes trailing his every movement. "You looking for this?"

Heat traveled up my spine, and awkwardness descended. Here I was, sitting in the bed, shirtless, and the guy I should spurn was making my heart gallop.

He tossed me my tank. "You thought I left you," he said, reading the range of emotion still on my face.

I angled my head, giving him a challenging glare. "Can you blame me?" I channeled my embarrassment into anger, but more than anything, I was hurt. I refused to let it show, so anger it was.

Sitting on the edge of the mattress, he took a deep breath. "I should have told you from the get-go."

I snatched the tank off the bed. "Yeah, you should have," I said, whipping the material over my head, irritation shedding any propriety I might have felt.

"I can say sorry until I'm blue in the face, but it won't change the past. It was never my intention to hurt you. I've done nothing but try to protect you, as hard as that is," he added, muttering.

I cut him a sharp look. Now was not the time to joke. I didn't feel like laughing. Scooting around him to the end of the bed, I looked for my boots. I couldn't stay in this little house another second. I needed air.

"Okay, bad joke. But seriously, you can't stay mad at me forever."

That was what he thought.

But he was probably right. My feelings for him got in the way, making it impossible to stay angry for long, though he deserved it ... and more. "Just until hell freezes over."

"I think it already has."

He had a point.

I laced my boots, and without a backward glance, I trekked down the stairs, snagging my bag on the way out. I'd miss this little house, and before last night, I'd thought it had been the answer to my prayers—a little slice of life prior to the mist untouched and preserved.

Dash had tainted that dream.

Throwing my hair up into a messy bun using some twigs, I worked my way through the tangle of vines. This was more effort than it was worth.

Dash was waiting for me, leaning against a tree when I finally broke free. I didn't bother to ask him how he was suddenly outside.

There was something different about him. Guilt. Remorse. I couldn't put my finger on it and chalked it up to what had happened between us last night. Of course, things were going to be different. No matter how much I wished it could be otherwise, things had changed between us.

And it saddened me.

Nothing was going to be the same. There was this weird vibe—neither of us sure how to act around the other—and I had almost no one in this world. I couldn't afford to lose the one who had been there for me since the beginning. There were bigger things than my disappointed heart. I still needed to find my parents, and I couldn't leave my sister in the power of the Institute.

Everything was so messed up.

How did my life become a tangled web?

I had no idea how I was going to find my parents or save my sister, but I had to. And that was where Dash came in. I needed him. Without him, I was a lamb in the lion's den—bottom of the food chain.

Trees lined a stony path as we began our journey toward Somber Mountain—and somber it was. We couldn't afford to stay in the same place for more than a night or two, the perks of life on the run.

The air seemed to be saturated in a perpetual mist, but as I squinted, looking in the distance, something caught my eye through the fog—the peak of a tower above the rolling vapor. There was only one place in this vicinity that had a fortress that could reach the sky.

Diamond Towers.

My even footsteps wavered. We were headed in the wrong direction, not away from the white city, but right toward its front gates. I stopped. "I thought we were going to Somber Mountain." My sense of direction might not always have been on point, but it was hard to mistake the gleaming city.

What is Dash up to?

"So does this mean you're talking to me?"

I risked a glance at his face. Wrong move.

It was almost impossible to stay mad at him when he used his dimples, and I hated him for it. My defenses dissolved, making room for sympathy. "It does if you tell me why we're headed to Diamond Towers." I was probably being paranoid and there was a rational explanation, but it didn't stop the curdling of sour in my stomach.

"Change of plans," he informed me.

I didn't like the sound of that.

"I've had some time to think, and—"

Well, so had I. And I'd come up with a few of my own ideas. "I want to go after Monroe," I interrupted. "I want to save her." Whether it had been accidental or pure luck, Dash had done what we had set out to do: find my family. Well, part of my family, but I couldn't abandon her now. Monroe needed me, more than I needed Dash to love me.

He shoved his hands into his back pockets. "I knew you were going to say that. Twenty-four hours ago, I would have told you the idea was insane. I would have done everything possible to change your mind, maybe even kidnapped you, but ... I understand."

"You do?" I was all prepared to give him this long-winded speech about how I couldn't abandon Monroe/Ember.

"I still think it's a crazy idea," he grumbled.

"The Institute kidnapped my sister."

His brows slammed together. "Trust me, I get it. If it was my brother, nothing would stop me, which is why we're going to Diamond Towers, not Somber Mountain. I'm a step ahead of you."

I crossed my arms. "Then why the gloom and doom face?" He was hiding something. It was in his eyes.

His scowl deepened. "So, I might have an ulterior motive. I've been trying to figure out how to tell you."

Ugh. I knew it. There was more. There was always more. I folded my arms and shifted my weight to one foot. "Just tell me. If you know something. …"

He didn't say anything for a long moment, and I thought I was going to have to threaten him. "The moment I realized Ember was your sister, it fell into place."

"What did?"

Dash looked at me. "Charlotte, I know where your parents are."

"What do you mean? How could you possibly know?" The tense lines on his forehead and the dismal silver eyes made me uneasy. He was going to tell me something I didn't want to hear, like my parents were dead.

"They're in Diamond Towers."

My mouth dropped. I wasn't expecting that bomb.

"At the Institute, to be specific," he clarified, making matters worse. "Your parents are one of the founding trustees. They run the Institute."

He was lying. He had to be. I honestly didn't know what to say. "You can't be serious. My parents? No way."

He sighed, rubbing his palm along his jaw. "I wish I was wrong."

Time stopped, and the balance of the universe shifted. I didn't want to believe what he was trying to tell me. I'd only known Dash for a few weeks. My parents had been there for me my entire life. "You're serious."

He nodded. "Afraid so."

My throat felt like steel wool as I swallowed, and my shoulders slumped in the finality of his words. "I-I don't understand." Everything he'd ever told me about the Institute portrayed them to be monsters, but my parents weren't. They were loving, kind, and smart.

"Neither do I," he said. "At the Institute, Ember was one of the younger recruits. She was already there when I woke, and it didn't take long to figure out her rank in the Institute. It was because of who her parents were that gave Ember the cocky, borderline bitchy, attitude."

I narrowed my eyes. This was my sister he was talking about, but after seeing her the other day, I had to agree. She had been a bitch. It was hard to hear the things he was saying about my family. Everything I'd heard about the Institute had been bad. "I need to talk to them. I need to see them"—with my own eyes. How could my parents be mixed up with something as corrupt as the Institute?

He nodded. "I knew you would say that, which is why you're not going to Somber Mountain."

"But Diamond Towers? Isn't that risky?" My voice was flat.

"Everything with the Institute is a risk." Eyes tapered, Dash looked at me. "I'm convinced you're trying to get me killed."

I held up my wrists, lips twisting. "Guilty. That's been my plan the whole time. I'm a secret agent."

"I knew it." He smiled, but it was forced.

I bristled, reading the expression that settled across his face. I didn't need to be a mind reader to know what was coming next. "You're not coming with me," I guessed. In the back of my mind, I'd always known we eventually would part ways, but now that it was here, I wasn't ready to say good-bye.

Dash cleared his throat, avoiding my gaze. "I can't. You know I can't. The Institute will just put me back in the dungeon or worse. And I still need to find my mom and brother."

My heart stuttered. "Find her." I hated the jealousy in my tone, but there was nothing I could do to prevent it. The idea of him with some other girl ate away at me, filling me with bitterness.

He lifted my chin. "I promised her I would."

"Right." I rolled my eyes, squelching a burst of disappointment.

His gaze veered toward the towers as he went back to that day when devastation hit in the form of a toxic vapor. "Before the mist rolled in, we'd been together," he began.

I wasn't sure I wanted to hear this. Kicking a rock, I told myself to hear him out, because I could see it was important to him that I understood.

"I picked her up from school when the emergency warnings started going off, followed by the public announcement. Chaos hit: people running everywhere, cars jamming together on the roads trying to escape the bustle of the city. I don't know how, but together we made it to one of the safe zones, and it was there we got separated. We were ushered down different halls, and before she disappeared, I told her I would find her."

And he was the type of guy to keep a promise ... or die trying. That didn't mean I had to like her, because I didn't. Right now, as shallow as it might have been, I wished he would never find her. Then maybe he would see what was right in front of him—what we had together ... what we could have together.

It made perfect sense to me, like the universe was telling us something. I didn't think Dash just happened to find me in that holding pod, or that I conveniently woke up when his lips touched mine. There was something between us I couldn't explain, but I felt it deep within my bones. Call it fate, but no matter what name you slapped on it, there was no denying the natural connection. For me, it was crystal clear.

I could wait.

Or so I told myself, but faced with the knowledge this might be the last time I saw him, caused my heart to lodge itself in my throat, and for a moment, I couldn't catch my breath.

Lightning cut through the sky behind him, casting his features in a ghostly glow. My emotions were getting the best of me, causing me to lose my grip on reality. I didn't know what to do. I didn't know what was right from wrong—what was good or bad.

Dash dropped his hands to his sides, careful not to touch me. Wise move. My body was humming with the current in the air. "Don't be mad. I'm going to make sure you're safe."

"And how do you plan to do that?" I asked.

"I don't want to fight with you, Freckles. You have a choice. I won't force you to go. I have no loyalty to the Institute."

I didn't want to part at all, as unrealistic as that was. "What does it matter?"

The lines around his eyes softened, and he caught my chin between his thumb and finger, tilting my face up. "I don't know. It just does."

There were so many emotions pouring through me, but I couldn't voice them. He needed to leave. I wanted him to stay. I wanted to stay with him. But our paths had come to a fork, each of us with a different path before us. There were things we needed to take care of, but afterwards. ...

"So how do I get to them?" I asked, accepting my choice. "Am I supposed to just walk through the front gate and announce who I am?"

"You could, but I wouldn't suggest it." His eyes shifted toward the city before he sighed. "Okay, this is going to make you mad."

I kicked him in the shin. Not hard, but enough to have him frowning.

Dash raised a brow. "What the hell?"

My eyes flared. "That was for whatever you're going to say to piss me off."

He shook his head. "You're impossible."

"So I've been told. Now what were you going to tell me?"

"Look, I know you're scared, and I don't blame you. You're going into the enemy's territory, but if you at any time change your mind, I won't be far away. Ember promised me you wouldn't be harmed. I told her I would deliver you to the gates of Diamond Towers but she had to give me time to explain about your parents."

"You talked to Ember?" I racked my brain. When had that happened?

He nodded. "Yeah, when you passed out, we struck a deal."

"A deal? Since when are you in the market of making deals with the Institute?"

"I didn't have a choice. There was no way I was going to outrun them carrying you."

Right. I should have just been grateful he hadn't handed my unconscious body over or left me behind. Instead, he had made a deal with Ember and given us the chance to say good-bye. "And you trust her?" I asked, thinking maybe this was a trap and the Institute was going to double-cross him somehow.

His lips formed a straight line. "No. I don't, which is why we are going to do this my way."

"You don't have to do this. I'm sure I can get to the city on my own. I don't want to be the reason you get caught." He had done enough for me. If my parents were really there, I needed answers.

"That's out of the question." He snapped his mouth shut. "And if you try anything funny, I'll drag you into the mountains."

"Okay, smart guy. How do you plan to get me there without getting caught?" I knew enough about Dash's character to know he would make sure I was safe before taking off.

He smirked. "I have a plan."

"And that's what frightens me."

Chapter Twenty-Three

The clouds had darkened as we approached the edge of Diamond Towers. I was close to tears, mainly because I couldn't bear the idea of being separated from Dash, and I was scared of what waited for me inside the walls of the white city.

Diamond Towers was situated smack dab in the heart of the four quadrants. Depending on what zone you were in, the landscape surrounding the city was different, moving from snow to desert to woods to mountains. We crept up to the threshold of the wild hedges that grew just beyond the stone wall constructed around the gleaming towers. There was an archway, leading to what I assumed was a courtyard. My eyes weren't sharp enough to see past the entrance.

We'd come as close as Dash could without the risk of him being seen. I searched his face. He was tense; being nearby the place that had terrorized him was taking a toll. If I would have gotten my way, he would be making his way deep into the mountains, instead of hanging out in the bushes with me.

Not that I wasn't glad he was here … because I was. Honestly, I didn't think I could have walked across the field and through the gate without knowing he was there.

Dash touched the curve of my back, bringing my mind to the here and now. I was stalling. Shadows fell over the side of his face, and I blinked furiously. "I don't know if I can do this."

Meeting my gaze, he took one step forward, and I launched myself at him, wrapping my arms around his neck like a demented octopus. "This is what you wanted," he murmured, running his fingers through my hair, "to find your family."

It was, but now I wasn't so sure. I wasn't sure of anything, except my feelings for Dash. And right now, I didn't want to go to Diamond Towers without him. It was frightening and foreign. "I know. I just thought it would feel … different." I buried my face into the side of his neck, inhaling the scent of him and storing it in my memory. I wanted to remember the way he smelled.

"You're incredibly brave, Freckles. You're also strong and courageous. Don't let them change you."

It was time to say good-bye, and trepidation propelled through me. "What if I've changed my mind?"

He set me down on my feet, but it was difficult to make my arms let go of him. Sorrow dampened his silver eyes, his lips pinched with desolation. "You're going to get hurt if you stay with me. I won't allow it. I can't have your blood on my hands. And you need to see your family. I can't ask you to give them up, not for me. It would always hang over our heads. I'll be in the area for the next couple of days to make sure you're safe. If you need me, if you find yourself in trouble, all you need to do is light up the sky, and I'll find a way to get to you."

His words tugged on my heartstrings. "Dash," I pleaded. I didn't know what I was asking from him, I just knew this feeling inside me was pestering me. I wanted to tell him I would talk to my father and clear this whole mess up. Or maybe I could show him, instead. If Dash was going to hang around, it gave me time. Once my father heard what Dash had done to protect me, to bring me home, I could get him to lift the warrant on Dash's head.

"This isn't up for debate." Lines of remorse crinkled around his eyes as he brushed a strand of hair off my face.

I didn't want to leave him. I didn't want to lose him, but everything in my heart told me this was good-bye. My insides felt torn in half. I wouldn't see Dash again once I walked through the gates of Diamond Towers. "I hope you find what you're looking for," I whispered. Tears welled in my eyes as I pressed my lips to his in one last kiss. At first he stood firm, hands fisted at his sides, and then he was kissing me as if he needed my lips to breathe. The desperation we both felt reached me in my core. I threw my arms around his neck, pouring every ounce of love I had into the kiss.

I realized in that moment that I had fallen in love with him. It was an elating feeling, overshadowed by the possibility that I might never get the chance to tell him how I felt. And with his warm lips covering mine, I never wanted to let go and wouldn't have, if Dash hadn't peeled my arms off him. I stared up at his face and opened my mouth, but the words I wanted to say were clogged up in my throat by raw emotion.

I loved him. Oh God, I loved him more than I loved shopping and chocolate croissants. I loved him more than cheerleading. And that was some serious, hardcore love. But I couldn't utter the words. If I told him how I felt, he wouldn't let me go. I wouldn't let him go. I wouldn't get to see my parents and ask them about Monroe. I had to do something—save her, get her out from under the Institute's control—but to do any of that, I had to go into the walls of Diamond Towers and leave Dash.

If I didn't, Dash wouldn't find his mom or brother or the girl he left behind. I didn't want that guilt between us. It would always be there—the what-ifs.

"Good-bye, Freckles."

My eyes burned as he backed away, keeping his gaze steady on mine. Messy, hot, sticky tears rolled down my cheeks. I wanted to scream his name, beg him not to leave, to stay with me. What was I going to do without him?

My knees shook as I stood there, tears waterfalling down my flushed face, pressure crushing my chest. It felt like I was never going to see him again. My eyes clung desperately to his ridiculously, book-cover-handsome face, searing each feature to memory. I didn't want to forget anything.

I was actually going to miss the nickname "Freckles." Who would have thought?

I would find him again, I vowed, as soon as we got Monroe back. I would comb the boundaries of all four quadrants until I found him. I swore it, for my heart would never be complete without him, even if he wasn't ready to admit the connection between us.

I was even willing to help him find the girl he still thought he was in love with, because I knew in my heart, once he saw her again, he would realize it was me he loved. But until then. ...

Dash turned and gave me a sad smirk right before he disappeared into the woods. My whole body slumped, knees wobbling, barely keeping me upright.

The walk toward the gate was the longest of my life. No matter how many steps I took, the span between the white city and me never seemed to close. Maybe I was dragging my feet. Maybe there was some sort of spell to prevent unwanted visitors. And just as I was about to check if I'd fallen down a rabbit hole and entered Wonderland, a distinguishable voice sounded.

"Charlotte."

After one long wistful look at the spot where Dash vanished, I turned around. My father looked just as I remembered, dignified with a touch of dork. His temples were peppered with gray, and his green eyes filled with warmth.

"Charlotte, I thought we'd lost you." He held open his arms.

I started to make my way across the field, my feet picking up speed as happiness bloomed inside me. A soft breeze swept over my face, tossing my loose curls and carrying a light scent of honeydew. Tears I couldn't contain collected in my eyes. I hadn't ever been sure I would see him again.

Movement behind my father caught my eye, and a great sense of foreboding took root and spread rapidly, breaking my stride. Something felt wrong about this joyous reunion. Why were there so many people? The crowd gathering along the wall turned out to be guards, their blue uniforms coming into focus. I came to a halt just short of reaching my father. "What is all this?" I asked.

The smile on his face faltered. "A safety precaution. You understand, don't you, dear? The world isn't a safe place anymore."

Now that I could really see him, there was something off about him. I couldn't pinpoint what it was, but a shiver rippled through my muscles. This man might look like my father, but his mannerisms were different. The way he held his head. The lack of twinkle in his eyes. My father had been a brilliant man. This man before me had a devious ambiance. I glanced over his shoulder at the gleaming white city sparkling in the distance. Its fortress walls and iron gate didn't appear welcoming. It felt like a prison.

What waited for me inside those walls didn't feel like home. A chill skirted down my neck. It didn't feel safe, and I had so many questions for him. What was he doing inside Diamond Towers? Didn't he know what the Institute was doing? How could he be a part of something like that? What about Monroe? How could he have let Monroe, now Ember, become a lunatic with a fire complex?

"Where's mom?" I asked, noticing her absence.

"She is waiting for us inside. Come, Charlotte. Let's go home." He put an arm over my shoulders, and I let him start to lead me toward the gate. "I've waited a long time for us to all be united again—to be a family."

"Monroe. ..." I started to say, but the sound of stomping feet roared over the ground as a truckload of guards poured out of the entrance, and I halted.

There were so many of them, all wearing the same blue uniform with the white star, but that was where the similarities ended. The phrase, *the freaks come out at night*, instantly came to mind as more than twenty good little soldiers shuffled onto the field, including my sister.

I blinked. Panic seized my gut as what felt like a wave of death swept past me. *No. No. No.* This wasn't a welcome home party, it was a trap.

They were after Dash, and my father had used me as bait.

I whipped my head toward the man I used to idolize as a little girl, accusation glaring in my eyes. "You used me," I hissed.

He put on his I-know-what-is-best-for-you face. "I know you think you know him, but Charlotte, he is dangerous. He must be apprehended."

"You don't know him. He saved me."

"That may be, but it doesn't erase his past crimes."

"Please," I begged. "Let him go. He just wants to find his family." This was going wrong—horribly wrong.

He remained stiff.

I looked at my father's face and realized it was a winless battle. Nothing I could say was going to change his mind. This man was only a shell of the father I remembered, and it was a hard pill to swallow. I backed up, deciding to take matters into my own hands.

Spinning around, Dash's name fell from my lips, and I whipped toward the woods, taking off. "Dash!" I screamed. "Dash! Run!"

I didn't get very far. A hand wrapped around my arm, abruptly bringing me to a halt. "You shouldn't have done that. I was hoping to avoid a scene," my father said, his voice flat.

A scene? If he wanted a scene, I'd give him a sight to behold.

Static gathered in my veins, humming to the surface of my skin so the hairs on my arms stood straight up. If he wasn't willing to listen to me, then I was going to make him listen. I was feeling so betrayed, I didn't think about what I was doing.

His fingers immediately released me, eyes sharpening. "So it's true. You're gifted."

I couldn't believe I had actually shocked my father, but he was acting like a madman. "I'm radiating with untapped talent," I scoffed.

"You must come with me. We can help you, Charlotte, to learn to control the power inside you."

"I've done just fine on my own," I said.

"It's okay. Everything is going to be okay," he said, stalking toward me.

How could he say that? Nothing was going to be right again. "Don't touch me," I croaked. It dawned on me that I'd just shown the Institute a glimpse at what I was capable of.

I froze as the guards rushed forward. Never had I seen anything like this before.

Instinct finally kicked in, and I secretly thanked my father for insisting I take fencing lessons. They were going to pay off today.

I didn't have a plan, only to get away from the guards and make sure Dash wasn't harmed. The fly by the seat of your pants worked for Dash; here's to hoping it worked for me.

I whirled around, prepared to unleash a fury like the Institute had never seen, but his dark form appeared at the shadowy edge of the woods, eyes glowing like silver glass and his bow drawn.

What was he doing?

I shook my head, silently telling him to get the heck out of Dodge. There might not be hope for me, but he could still get away. If they got their hands on him. ... He had said countless times that he was never going to go back. Why would he reveal himself now? Damn him. He was protecting me, even now. I showed the Institute what I was capable of, and they would undoubtedly try to use me as a weapon. But for what purpose?

Our eyes locked, and a wealth of emotion shone on his face, but I wouldn't ever forget the terror or the look of helplessness.

I shook my head. *No. No. No.*

I wasn't going to let him surrender himself for me. Maybe he knew we were outnumbered, that there was no way I would be able to get away. Maybe he thought he could save me ... but not this time. He was probably stupid enough to try though.

He held up his bow in the air as he walked out from the shadows in surrender, and I couldn't believe what I was seeing. Dash never gave up, so that made me think he was up to something. I carefully slid my fingers down my thigh, hovering over the tip of my blade.

Everyone was on pins and needles as they waited to see what the slayer's next move would be. Dash didn't let them down. When he reached the edge of the clearing, it became open season.

He slid over the ground, releasing arrows as he went.

Holy crap. What was he doing? He was going to get killed.

Arrows rained down on the guards, taking out three before the line of guards reacted. I should have known Dash wouldn't run from a fight but run straight toward it. He let a howl of anger as he sent another arrow in the air.

Darkness like I'd never seen licked over the ground, smoky tendrils curling and spreading. A female guard was controlling the darkness as it danced toward Dash. It was time I got my hands dirty.

Two could play this game.

Flinging out my wrist, a bolt of white light shot across the field, striking her in the back. The impact knocked her down to her knees, causing the tendrils of darkness to dissipate, and the guard met a similar fate. The shimmery white light that had hit her spread, encompassing her entire body in a glow that eventually exploded and her along with it.

For a second, the flash of white light blinded me.

"Charlotte!" Dash shouted.

Holy shit.

I just blew up a guard.

I swallowed the nausea that started to rise up the back of my throat. Killing didn't sit well in my stomach. My gaze flew to Dash. I caught sight of him as he engaged two guards who had tag-teamed him. Dash whirled, slamming his boot into the chest of one and then ducking as the other took a swipe at him with a blade.

Bright orange balls of fire formed on Ember's hands. Dash shot out of the way at the last second, giving me a heart attack. The balls of fire slammed into a tree behind him before fizzling out.

Things were getting hectic.

"Charlotte, run!" Dash bellowed.

Ember wasn't about to let that happen. The world turned tawny and gold as she unleashed a maelstrom of flames.

I took off, my feet flying over the ground.

Heat blew at my back, but I didn't stop.

Dash was firing off arrows, incapacitating the guards standing between him and me. I ran, faster than I'd ever run in my life.

I didn't know how he managed to dodge the rain of fire at the same time he fought with a guard. For each hit the guard landed, Dash struck back harder. Fingers humming with electricity, I was just about to fling a multitude of light at the guards rushing Dash when the flash of a knife glinted. My wild eyes found his, but even as I was ready to release a flash of lightning, it was too late. I'd never make it in time.

"No!" I screamed, letting the lightning burst from my fingers. Heat flew across the courtyard, but it was a wasted effort.

Dash's eyes went wide as the blade pierced his heart. He made a silent gasp of shock as he staggered backward, the dagger still in his chest and blood leaking out of the wound, soaking his shirt. "I'm sorry," he wheezed, right before he collapsed.

A scream rang in my ears, and I only faintly realized it was coming from me.

I blinked, and the horror around me vanished.

My father stood before me, staring at me with unrecognizable eyes. Dash was poised on the cusp of the woods, bow in hand. It had all been a glimpse of what could happen. If I didn't go with my father, go to the Institute, Dash would die.

I wasn't going to let that happen.

With a heavy sigh, I glanced over my shoulder and prepared myself to go into the heart of Diamond Towers, a place feared by many.

I needed to go peacefully to avoid the mayhem—to avoid Dash's death. Now that I'd seen my father and what he was capable of, the very last thing I wanted to do was go into Diamond Towers. But there was no other choice.

I would be brave.

I would be strong.

And I would be smart.

But most of all, Dash would be alive.

My knees shook as I stood there, my eyes clinging desperately to Dash's face. A tear rolled down my cheek, pressure crushing my chest. "I love you," I mouthed, finally admitting my feelings. I needed him to know, for I wasn't certain I'd ever see him again.

"Don't, Charlotte!" Dash cried. "I was wrong. Don't go."

Hearing his desperate plea, my whole body slumped, and my wobbly knees weren't going to hold me upright for long. He had no idea how incredibly hard it was to turn my back on him, and as much as my heart was bleeding, I wanted him alive.

I tipped my chin, meeting my father's stern gaze. "If you let him go, I'll come with you, but you must promise me no harm will come to him." Dash would sacrifice himself before he let the Institute take me, but it didn't mean I had to sit back and do nothing. "Please," I begged. "Don't let them do this. I wouldn't be here if it wasn't for Dash. Let him go. He hasn't done anything wrong." No matter how hard I pleaded, it was like talking to a brick wall. Through blurry eyes, the man standing before me was a stranger.

"I'm sorry, Charlotte. It has to be this way."

Oh, God. What had I done?

A prick pierced the side of my neck, followed by a chill filling my veins, spreading throughout my body. I gasped, staring up at the man I'd thought would always protect me. How could I have been so wrong?

My father had injected me with a serum, but of what I didn't know. It would make itself known soon enough. The effects of the drug were working their way through my system.

Tears rolled down my cheeks as I stole one last peek at Dash. "Oh, God," I whispered.

A burst of cold encompassed every cell in my body, rendering me immobile. I couldn't move. I could barely breathe. I couldn't hear. I screamed, but nothing came out; there was no sound, except for the cry for help inside my head no one heard.

Dash went ballistic, fighting the guards, doing everything in his power to reach me. His mouth opened and screamed my name, fear lacing every inch of his face—fear for me.

But it no longer mattered. I was drowning in darkness.

Epilogue

Dash

Hands bound behind my back, I was guided to the not-so-nice part of the city. One of the guards gave me an unnecessary shove down the concrete steps. My feet stumbled, but I managed to keep upright, blood pumping as I thought about how sweet it would feel to exact my revenge on these assholes.

It was no surprise where they were taking me; Diamond Towers' underground jail was a place I knew well. I'd had the unpleasant experience of being there before. It wasn't like the ones from the twenty-first century; modifications had to be made for the alterations to the state of the world.

The silver metal cut into my skin, burning from the acidic oxides reacting to the change in the atmosphere. The farther underground we went, the worse it got. The entire place was made of the stuff to keep the prisoners in and the nasties out.

I was roughly maneuvered down a narrow hallway dimly lit by lanterns. It didn't occur to me to fight, not when Charlotte was somewhere within the walls of the city. I couldn't leave her, and if I was going to find her, I needed to be in a position to gather information.

What better way than in the dungeons?

You'd be surprised what knowledge comes and goes through the tunnels under the towers.

The chains at my wrists dangled as we moved past the occupied cells. "You're not such a tough guy, now, are you?" the guard behind me sneered, feeling like a top shit now that they had me cuffed.

"When I get out of here, I'll kill you," I promised, and it was one I meant to keep.

The guard took a shot at me, hitting me squarely on the left side of my jaw. "You're never getting out of here, Darhk. Get used to your homey quarters." The fool laughed, as if it was the funniest thing he'd ever said. Then he shoved me in.

The door slammed closed with a clack, followed by the clicking of locks. I spit blood onto the floor and glanced up. "We'll see about that."

They had taken my weapons, but the rage I was feeling was as dangerous as any blade. They would never take away my will to save Charlotte and get the hell out of this craphole. I rested my head against the iron bars, berating myself for my error in judgment. I never should have let her within a mile of the Institute. Why did I possibly think her family would protect her? This was entirely my fault, and it was driving me fucking crazy not knowing where she was or what they were doing to her.

My hands gripped the cold, metal bars. "Charlotte!" I screamed.

The guard who'd brought me down smirked. "You can scream until your lungs bleed, but that sweet little piece of ass? You'll never see her again."

My silver eyes burned with hate. He was a dead man.

I moved so fast, I startled the guard. My hands shot through the bars, grabbing the front of his starched Institute uniform. To think I'd once been proud to wear it. "Do you honestly think you'll be able to keep me in here?" I hissed.

"We can try," he replied, losing a bit of his cocksureness.

I laughed, shoving the guard before I choked him with my bare hands. "That's your plan? You better have a backup."

He straightened up, daggers shooting from his eyes. "The commissioner is going to want to pay you a visit. Of all the people you picked to hijack, you choose his daughter. Classic."

That wasn't quite how it went down, but the less the Institute knew about my relationship with Charlotte, the safer she'd be. "If you let me go, I'll spare your life, otherwise. ..." I cracked my knuckles, my dark eyes slitting.

A shiver rolled through the guard. "Either way, I'm dead. I'll take my chances this cell will hold you."

Hold me? Please. "Suit yourself. It's your deathbed."

"Get comfortable, Darhk. You're in here for the long haul."

That was what he thought. I sunk down in the corner of the cell, dropping my head back against the wall. Above, on the ceiling, several marks had been carved into the cement from the previous occupant. I didn't want to know how they'd managed to reach such heights or why they were no longer occupying this particular cell. Unconsciously, I rubbed the spot on my chest where my old scar was—a trophy of what happens when you cross the Institute.

The depth of being underground, with the combination of the acidic oxides and alloys, neutralized most abilities, but not all. There was a special hell for those who couldn't be contained deeper in the ground.

She was here, somewhere in the city. I could feel it in my bones—sense her fear, her sadness, and her desire for freedom. I would give her that, I vowed, or die trying.

"Freckles, I'm coming," I whispered.

Charlotte and Dash's journey continues in book two:

ENTANGLED

Coming 2017

Sign up for J.L. Press and receive a bonus scene told from Zane's POV and a free copy of Saving Angel (Book One in the bestselling Divisa Series)

http://www.jlweil.com/vip-readers

Stalk with Me Online:

Website: http://www.jlweil.com
Twitter: @JLWeil
Facebook: http://www.facebook.com/#!/jenniferlweil

About the Author

About the Author

USA TODAY bestselling author J. L. Weil lives in Illinois where she writes teen & new Adult paranormal romances about spunky, smart-mouthed girls who always wind up in dire situations. For every sassy girl, there is an equally mouthwatering, overprotective guy. Of course, there is also lots of kissing. And stuff.
An admitted addict to Love Pink clothes, raspberry mochas from Starbucks, and Jensen Ackles, she loves gushing about books and *Supernatural* with her readers. She is the author of the international bestselling Raven & Divisa series.

Read More from J. L. Weil
http://tinyurl.com/zpnhlt6
www.jlweil.com/

Made in the USA
Lexington, KY
04 October 2017